RELUCTANT
IN UNIFORM

C J Harcourt

A CIP catalogue record for this book is available from
the British Library.

ISBN: 978-1-908720-81-8

Dedicated to all who have served.

'Dear Mother,
It's a bugger, sell the pig and buy me out.'

'Dear Son,
Pig gone, soldier on.'

1

Born, as he was with his nation in armed conflict Logan was a significant statistic with special title. He was a war baby. All of which puts an entirely different slant on the Second World War being only a German cock up and presents an entirely different meaning to the term war effort. That's how it is with the cosmos. Some are born insignificant, some achieve insignificance and others have insignificance hoisted upon them.

Conceived with his country in conflict it was perhaps only fitting that he should find himself in uniform later in life. Conception and the army have no known usual connection but with a birth certificate listing father as 'some soldier' it had in his case. Someone well meaning struck a thin red line through the entry and wrote Tommy. It was a nice thought.

Logan reached manhood with all the usual characteristics needed for comprehensive failure in life and was without any developed sense of direction other than an extreme aversion to work and a love of leisure. All of this must have pleased the cosmos no end planning as it was for him to join the army. It was having a bit of struggle, not the least of which was the ending of national service the year before and the growing of national hair. Not discounting this and the general lack of international hostilities in the early sixties other than the cold war thing there was also Logan's inherent aversion to authority and short hair which went out when the Beatles came in and Cliff Richard went down with a dose of slant jaw.

Mindless of all this empyrean stuff Logan was in the pub spending what was left of his dole and casually misspending his youth without a care in the world. Harold Wilson was on the radio telling his party they were a moral crusade or nothing in an age when nothing really meant something.

'It was not long ago when we were never having it so good from the other Harold' said John the landlord reaching for the off switch.

'What, Steptoe?' said Logan.

'Macmillan' said the landlord easing the cat along the bar.

He was getting an earful from a couple of L S Lowry matchstick men look-alikes droning on about the cost of their necessaries and the price of clogs. It was one of those toothless 'I remembers' guaranteed to piss everyone off over four foot ten without rickets and a cloth cap. Logan had heard enough and was draining his beer to leave when he caught sight of Bernice's two big brothers. Not only was it a time to leave, it was a time to leave quickly...oh yes.

It wasn't that Logan didn't like Bernice who at times during his puberty had a lot going for her including availability but simply put there was no way of ever really knowing who the father was short of a blood test of course, and what kind of a man would put a girl through all that he asked himself. The girl was as nymphomaniac as a ship's cat and with a loving generous nature pregnancy for Bernice was as inevitable as the sun rising in the east and being offered salt and vinegar in a fish and chip shop. On his long circuitous route home Logan passed the army recruitment centre and on the sudden thought that the army would protect its own from would be castrators he went in.

In the days following his signing up Logan remained ever vigilant and cautious. Coming out only at night, wearing a big hat and keeping well clear of his usual haunts he stayed safe but with just one day left before reporting to Catterick Camp Logan chanced a last Saturday evening beer at the local. The door opened to a crowded room and something of a celebration as Logan peered gingerly in through the smoke. Bernice's eyes hit on him in an instant.

Frantic to avoid even the slightest hint of recognition Logan scanned the room with an invented blank face before turning quickly away. He was through the door and off like a hare from the gun racing on up the road and heading for a personal best well before the first corner. Fast though he was with the best part of a firkin of bitter in him Logan was always going to lose the race and when Bernice took off her heels there was no contest. As the sound of stiletto heels turned to a pounding of laddered nylon it was all over but for the fat lady. Desperate to escape Logan's eyes hit on the light of a pub and ran in looking for sanctuary. What he found was the two brothers.

'Well hello' said Logan as the click of a closing latch sounded behind him like the portentous turn of a jailer's key.

'Here you are' said Bernice seconds later bursting through the door and hopping on one foot to slip her heels back on.

'Me and my little brother here have been looking for you...' said one of the brothers as the door opened again behind Logan and another runner arrived.

'We've been looking everywhere' said little brother peering down at Logan from six four up as his frame momentarily took the light...a shadow fell over him.

'Really?'

'Where've you been you silly boy' said Bernice throwing her arms around Logan's neck and pecking a cheek, 'we have been looking everywhere for you haven't we Billy darling?'

Billy darling? Who the bloody hell was Billy darling? said Logan to himself as he turned to see Billy Drinkwater the teacher's sneak and old school wimp.

'Hello Logan' said Billy darling pulling Bernice's arms away from Logan's neck, 'hardly recognize you in that big hat and the dark glasses.'

'Well if you can't fight wear a big hat is what they say Billy...don't they?'

Logan was utterly disgusted to learn of Bernice's blatant two timing of him and the others and more than disgusted to learn he was being thrown aside for Billy The Wimp. There was absolutely no way Billy Drinkwater could be the father felt Logan. Look at him, the man could never be up to the job. Nonetheless, there it was and to cap it all off Logan was to be best man, which was the reason for all the searching and chasing. He breathed a real sigh of relief to learn the matter was all over and dusted apart from the wedding which wasn't going to be a big do, although not being for some months yet Bernice would likely be by then of course.

At the last pub on the pre nuptial celebration pub crawl they finished their beer scraped The Wimp from the floor and left the best of friends laughing and joking out into the night. What a family of head bangers they really are Logan said out loud as he collapsed into bed without a care in the world. What a day he said and was asleep that instant. It was the sleep of salvation and the drunken dead both and mercifully mid Sunday morning before he was awake to the world.

Eyes opened to the new day and the smug self-contented relief of the escape from Bernice with all his bits. As vision returned with the cold light of day Logan's eyes suddenly focused on a partly packed suitcase. Logan sat up with a start as a full and terrifying realisation hit him. He had only just signed up for twenty-two years bloody army service...he was a soldier for God's sake!

2

The journey to the station was largely uneventful apart from a seagull incident, which the taxi man said was lucky. It wasn't for him when he looked for a tip that's for sure. Catterick Camp, Logan's posting, was advised to him by the army recruitment sergeant as being somewhere on the Yorkshire moors. He was missing the words deep, abandoned and forsaken from all reports Logan had been given from those ex servicemen in the know. Logan exchanged his rail warrant for a ticket and received a one-way third class single. It was a sign.

At each station en route more and more troops joined the train seemingly bound for Catterick in a confusion of peak cap and beret with every conceivable badge and rank that converged into the one collective khaki brown masse. Everyone struggled with either kit bag or a compressed cardboard green suitcase or both. Looking for all the world like disturbed ants carrying eggs they could be picked out on every station and by Darlington they packed into every carriage, jammed corridors, the buffet bar and everywhere including the guard's van.

They arrived en masse at Darlington to be funnelled by chalked blackboard onto a deserted side platform marked by another board reading in large letters 'Troop Train Catterick Camp – Special.' Logan knew special this was no special. As the train slowly chugged away from the station a general feeling of gloom descended on the carriages.

'Next stop's Catterick Camp Centre' announced the guard hopefully as he made his way down the train climbing over and through an entangled khaki mess of kitbag, case and sprawled squaddie.

For the last five miles to camp the train was taken by an eerie silence of the forlorn as the train announced their approach with a pitiful whistle and a half hearted rush of steam before screeching to a slow and reluctant stop. The train just didn't want to be there. Even as the special slowed doors were banged open and a spontaneous surge of bodies poured through the corridor to exit the carriages meeting the short platform. First out least trampled...last out no transport shouted a voice throwing his holdall ahead and jumping early for the platform to land just seconds after his string vest and the two pairs of Y fronts.

'This here's Catterick...Catterick Camp Centre...all change!' called a nervously sounding guard with a green flag bravely staying at his post as carriage doors began slamming along the platform to announce the impending charge. Ahead of the brown swell the guard bravely held his ground until the very last moment before stepping niftily back into his ticket hut just seconds ahead of the rush. The man was a veteran of many specials and an example to the youth of British Rail.

Thoughts of a taxi to the training camp went faster than the taxis but a line of three ton Bedford trucks waited with their own blackboards marked for each of the many camps. Standard transport for the army over any terrain, theatre of operation and in any weather the three ton Bedford was the army equivalent of the covered wagon said a Scottish voice in battle dress and Glengarry at Logan's side.

'You're sitting in a wind tunnel; sit near the open front in winter and you freeze your nuts off, sit near the open back and you choke on the sucked in fumes. The only things the army changes from desert to Arctic is the colour of the paint and the driver' explained the man as they climbed into the back pulling themselves up by a knotted rope left dangling for the job.

Their truck had not gone more than a hundred feet before Logan checked his nuts, the man was right about the wind tunnel.

'Recruit training!' shouted the driver to the back as Logan clambered out over the dropdown tailgate just seconds before the Bedford sped away in a haze of blue exhaust.

Bending under the red and white pole barrier he was suddenly alone outside his first guardroom. It was a pivotal moment of his life as he passed from civilian to soldier and he paused to take it all in.

The guardroom was an ageing latticed timber building painted matt black with a veranda running along its entire length that housed a variety of what must be statutory objects felt Logan. A fire point painted white with stirrup pump placed central to a line of four red buckets stood to the left of an open door below a well-polished large brass bell. At the other side a full-length mirror looking for all the world like those that distort you fat or thin at fairgrounds had a sign above that spuriously posed the question 'are you a credit to your regiment?' Logan looked at his dishevelled self with open spread dangling jacket and dark hair windswept over his face from the freezing truck ride. No he thought to himself pulling his coat straight and moving his hair from face when his eyes lighted on the brass bell. Thinking to knock rather than just walk in he presumed the shiny brass bell was there to announce arrival.

A rapidly approaching set of hobnail boots came at him from behind, the sound mixing with the fading ring of the fire bell. He turned to find a man with three stripes and a red sash approaching at speed from the area of the parade ground.

'That man there!' bellowed the man, which defensively turned every head within half a mile. Logan looked behind and pointed finger to chest as the voice surely was raised to attract attention of someone some distance away.

'You!' shouted the orderly sergeant. 'The one saying who fucking me!'

Suddenly startled Logan must have part made to run as the move was spotted. 'Stand bloody still when I am about to bollock you!' shouted the sergeant as he slithered to a halt pointing his pace stick now not two inches from Logan's nose.

'Corporal hoff the guard!' bellowed the sergeant at the guardroom.

His voice shook the windows and rattled the line of fire buckets rippling the water.

'Sarrhh!' came a voice from inside the guardroom followed by the sound of more rapidly approaching boots.

'Place this men ere hunder arrest corporal of the guard...nick him up.'

'Sarrhh!' said the corporal now calling out the guard who, as luck would have it for Logan began arriving on the scene in half dress.

There was a frantic and rapid fastening of tunics and placing of beret on heads as the guard arrived to spot the red sash of the orderly sergeant. It was too late. He was on them like a wild boar, ripping into them with an amazing fury. First one and then the other was taken to pieces but the poor bastard who arrived eating a pork pie was the one Logan felt sorry for until the last man arrived still clutching a toilet roll.

Whether it was the guard being the worse of the two evils or the sergeant had worn himself out on the man with the trailing toilet roll but by the time he got back to Logan he seemed to have forgotten why he was there. Seeing that Logan hadn't actually reported in to the guardroom at point of first bollocking he was let off with a warning and a lesson in army use of the word arsehole. He had sampled his first experience of a feeling that stayed with him for the whole of basic training...fear.

For seven days he saw no real uniformed personnel other than those at the stores who issued the basics of life such as knife fork spoon and a one pint brown enamel mug with an HMP arrow on the base. Uniform was two sets of light green denim fatigues, two shirts, a pair of boots and one pair of socks. Basics they termed them at the stores and basics they were. An early arrival recruit acted as liaison between them and the real army and Logan and the other recruits increasing by the day followed him sheep like until they began to know their way around and drifted off.

Training would begin on Monday they were told by the man who seemed to be everywhere the army was not. Apart from the absence of bells, canes and bike sheds the place had a first day at school feel Logan thought and it was some time before he began to find his way around enough to get lost. Barracks was a small room at the end of a corridor in one of a line of blocks each a quarter of a mile long and called a Sandhurst block by someone who obviously liked a joke. It had shiny red floors slippery as hell and a central concrete staircase rising three storeys up. The place was in perpetual panic and echoed with the bustle and yells of varied activity and the sound of studded boots on the painted red raddled corridor floors was everywhere.

Allocated his room, bed and a tall metal green locker by the recruit Logan took possession of his regulation six foot of bed space. It was a good deal if you were four foot six which was probably the average height when the regulation was first made he thought as he settled himself down on the bed to survey the room. Someone had polished everything and the room gleamed with effort. Everywhere was the smell of fresh lavender polish.

'I'll take it' he said to the recruit but he was long gone.

Furnished just by two lines of beds alongside the lockers and small wooden bedside tables, the room sat somewhere between Spartan and minimalist until Logan found a luxury three foot by two horsehair bedside mat in his locker. A framed photograph screwed to the back of the door showed a regulation locker layout for every item of kit yet to be issued. The army it seemed had a place for everything in the locker but the man thought Logan looking into the one foot metal draw reserved for his personal effects and suddenly taken with the realization of what he had signed up to before the door opened and the room filled to a crush with recruit.

The next days were spent in the company of like lost souls recounting misspent pasts and contemplating a collective and largely unknown future in a raw mix of uncooked regional and national dialect. This they did sat in circles on the barrack room floor bulling a second pair of boots drawn from the stores early to get a head start on their best parade boots. Head start for what thought Logan although one look at the shiny surfaces was giving something of a clue of what was about to come.

Exactly how to bull the boots was again given by demonstration through the early arrival recruit in a session showing how to burn down the small nipples in the leather using the back of a hot spoon heated by a lit candle. That the army supplied boots with such nipples on the leather only to then sanction the removal was received as something of a mystery by Logan and surpassed only by the knowledge that boot bulling was known to be detrimental to leather and thus the serviceability of the boot.

'It is officially illegal' said the early recruit 'and you can buy the banned candles at the NAAFI.'

'It's next to the Brasso, the blanco for your webbing, the dusters and boot polish' said a Scots voice at the edge of the circle clearly smarting from the cost of it all.

'Then' said the early recruit 'after you got your nipples off...rub polish in circular motion with a cloth and finger. Spit on cloth or boot, rub it in several tens of thousands of times and in four weeks you have a set of bulled boots, thereafter it's just a top up.'

After seven days Logan for one but not everyone ran out of enthusiasm, polish and spit and was actually looking forward to the start of basic training. At least they were until the day it began. They for Logan were a mixed bag of the nation's youth that seemed to cover every regional identity that metamorphosed to a transmuted stereotype as soon as their lights went on. It was the development of the group and survival of the fittest and a barrack room in formation and without wish, desire or intention their room produced them.

Within a day they had a comic, a tough guy, a smart arse, three dopes and a big mouth and the one keeping himself to himself. It was Logan.

Mixed within the developing variables of personality disorders, inclination towards such and genuine weirdo with latent intent came a rich blend of national types along with the regions of north and south, east and west and the bits in the middle that didn't fit anywhere but

13

in between. Add to this already complex soup a size variable of tall, short and neither, to shapes from fat to thin combined with body muscle type, athlete to sloth and way on down to slug and what you had was typical of every room in the block. One genuinely mixed up collective of rookie, ripe and ready for the army pot. Within weeks they would turn army without even knowing it and sat in circles burning nipples off their boots for fun it was already happening.

The rooms Jock was a man called Sinclair from Kircuddie, which they found out some days in was Kirkcaldy in the Kingdom of Fife. Jock had been in the T.A. for years and was an affable source of how not to do·things. Compton two beds along seemed to have his head constantly in a book and his nose in a hankie could have been from anywhere, as he never spoke much that first week. Brum was a man nice enough but with a bit of a chip and Scouse, as they could all hear came from Liverpool.

'Grew up in the Cavern Club me and our kid. We were there every week like. Know all the groups like...Gerry and the Mars Bars. They were called that before they changed their name right enough and The Beats of course...we knew em all at the Cavern.'

'Yeah, yeah, yeah' said Brum walking away.

They must have named the place after his mouth was the general consensus of the room by the end of the first week. It was then that Logan discovered new recruits had a seven day cooling off period and could have left on free discharge any time during that first week or so Chalkie White said. Of them all Logan took to

Chalkie once he began to speak some English and went with him on the second night for a beer at the NAAFI.

'I'm over for a beer and a snout is tha larking art t'nite?' said Chalkie clearly expecting his tyke to be understood.

This translated down as 'was Logan going out for a drink and a cigarette' but needed Logan to read the man's sign language for smoke although the word beer got through easily enough.

'Right with you' said Logan searching his locker for money.

'Thar's all rite I've got enough for a sneck lifter.'

'Oh right then' said Logan leaving the room before finding out it meant the man had only enough money for the one drink but not before it came to his round.

Coming from Yorkshire it was his own sneck lifter Chalkie had the money for. The man had a view on most things and was a natural to become the room mouthpiece. Wanted or not you were going to get it anyway although he did seem to have an uncanny habit of hitting things bang on the head. Or stating the bleeding obvious as the Brum said.

'This free discharge you were on about...that's why they start the training a week late' said Compton sometime into the second week. He was a thinking man was Compton.

'That's handy to know then' said Taff who was from somewhere unpronounceable near Swansea. There wasn't much that lad missed thought Logan.

Rumour had the cost of a man buying himself out at two hundred pounds which on Logan's wage of three pounds four and six a week he put to the back of his mind in the box marked perm any eight from ten. He knew deep down it was a waste of time but he did open a savings account along with many others.

3

The day training for war broke out the intake of forty split into troops seven and eight and paraded in three ranks outside the barracks where they met their troop corporal who was a Glaswegian called Jock. It's not everyday you meet God.

Corporal Jock had the mental age of a chimp and managed speech only by linking together obscure military phrases. These he delivered in a high pitched clipped voice through pursed lips with a head cocked back at an angle and a half closed squinty eye. It was as if he was trying to look at life through his top lip and the world was an unanswered question. This left anyone standing before him with one of those spot on face dilemmas where to look him in the eye you also appeared to be looking up his nose. There was nothing up there. The man should have been studied, certified or on a shelf in a strong solution of formaldehyde. Two days into training there was a queue for the job.

Addressing the squad that first day Jock outlined the weeks of basic training as he paced in and out of the three ranks he called a squad formation. During this time seven troop were in passage to pass from an undisciplined civilian pile of shit into the finest body of marching men ever to enlist. Logan looked around at his fellow recruits, not only was the poor man disillusioned but he was clearly myopic. Corporal Jock also introduced the squad that morning to parade ground speech where 'don't speak to me when I am giving you a talking to' has real meaning. His little talk over, Jock reverted to his clipboard and took a roll call before going for a quick body count as the sound of studded feet came at them from behind.

'Stand still at the back...face the front!' ordered Jock as the noise of crunching boots came closer.

Heads continued to turn as the crunch of boot came to a sudden and sliding stop.

'Stand bloody still on parade...yeou man!' boomed a voice Logan seemed to know from the way it rattled the windows.

'Face the front!' blared Jock again.

'Do you a feel something soldier?' said the voice quietly into someone's ear in the rear rank. Eyes flashed nervously left and right at the prospect of what might be just behind them.

'No sir' replied a squeaky little voice in the back row.

'Well you should...cos I am a standing on your fucking hair!...aircut and you and you and you!' screamed the voice walking along and through the squad tapping shoulders as it went.

'Aircut, aircut' echoed Corporal Jock writing onto his clipboard as the ranting continued through the ranks.

'Corporal Dimmelwick your troop is a bleeding disgrace to this ere man's fucking army. There's more air ere than on a line of chanting indu bloody Swamis!'

'More air than on a line of Hindu Swami...Sarrhh!' agreed Corporal Jock suddenly dashing forward and pointing a little baton stick with a brass knob at someone in the line. 'Stand still yeou and face the front...don't you do bendy rubber neck with me sunshine...stand bloody still when the sergeant is about to bollock you.'

The squint didn't help again; he could have been in deep communication with anyone in the front row.

'Face the front...you!...yes, you! The one with a swivel neck who's about to feel my stick up his arse.' called the voice somewhere further along the line.

'Pay attention at the troop sergeant' said Jock, as the voice now appeared to menace the front of the squad. 'Seven troop present and correct Sarrhh!'

'Thenk yeou Corporal Dimmelwick.' said the sergeant pacing up and down the line and eying the squad like a strike poised sidewinder.

For someone with such an incredibly loud mouth he was a slight jerky little man with pointy waxed black moustache and seemingly no other hair on his head as nothing showed from beneath his peaked cap. Dressed in a tailored battledress with razor-sharp creases the result of years shaving and pressing the cloth and boots that glinted in the early morning light the man was immaculate. He was the very epitome of a sergeant drill instructor and his swagger showed every inch of it.

'Listen in seven troop' said Corporal Jock backing up the sergeant's every move and following behind him like a shadow.

'My name for yeou to remember from nowanuntil the rest of your miserable an pathetic little lives...is ead.

Sergeant ead...got it?'

'Sergeant ead...got it' echoed Corporal Jock from behind.

'I am what is known in the harmy of the Queen...God bless er...'

'God bless er' came the echo again from Jock.

'As an troop sergeant. Furthermore an to whit I am your fucking troop sergeant...which is what these is ere' he said pointing to his upper arms. 'Not where I ave ad a quick wipe of me running fucking nose...not bleeding mars bars but chevrons and to whit three of same. Stripes is what these is and what you ave not got...heny of you...but what I ave.

'What he has and yous as not...got' said Jock.

'What are they...yeou!' said ead rounding on some poor sod to Logan's right.

'Mars bars' said the poor sod blurting out the first thought that came into his head.

'Stripes you dipstick!' roared the sergeant 'what is you thick or somethink?'

'Stripes' said the poor sod with a bit of a quaver on his voice and someone else in the rank behind him just in case he meant it for him as well.

Corporal Jock jumped forward at the man as if he had offered him out.

'Stripes? Bloody stripes? Say sir when you is addressing the sergeant!!' screamed in Jock. 'Answer properly as sir or sergeant when you is taking a bollocking or addressing an superior

NCO. You will be saying bollocks to the Queen next, God bless her'

'Stripes sir!' shouted the man at the top of his voice.

'Stripes is correct...' said Sergeant Head continuing to pace up and down along the front of the squad.

'Stripes is correct!' supported Corporal Jock.

'Yeou piss me around and I will piss you around and I ave more piss than any of you and don't any of you forget it...'

'Don't piss him around' said Jock after a long pause and still supporting from the back.

'You ave to be one hell of a big dog to piss up my leg...yeou what's my name?'

'Ed sir!' shouted the voice, which got Head thinking for a moment in case the man was taking the piss until with a look of recognition and a raising of his chin he spotted Logan.

'Oh shit' said Logan wishing the ground would open up as the man approached to look him full in the eye.

'I know you...you're Quasimodo the fucking bell ringer and in my troop is you?' he said remembering back to the guardroom.

'Yes sergeant sir' answered Logan.

'Watch this man what you ave got ere Corporal Dimmelwick' said Sergeant Head gesturing with his stick at Logan's face without looking before snapping his face sideways to look him full in the eye again. 'He's a degenerate, an earwig, what is he?'

Head darted his head away to eyeball the next man as the recruit physically jumped at the approach.

'A degenerate earwig sergeant' said the man, which seemed to satisfy Head's sense of achievement and moved him on along the line to eyeball some other poor devil.

'Correct!...' he said moving away and weaving between the squad as he spotted something else amiss 'an earwig is correct and you...the one with sticky out ears, your mother do that to you son? Pity, stand still...straighten your tie, buck yourself up for fuck's sake, button undone, do it up man, do it up...move yourself, move yourself. You have to dress yourself this morning did you. Hard was it?'

'No sir.'

'Don't answer me back when I'm giving you a talking to, haircut along with the other ladies and you...stay still when I'm about to bollock you...what the bloody hell...fuzz on my parade is it? Stand closer to the razor tomorrow or you're for it.'

'It's dermatitis sir.'

'I don't care what your fucking name is soldier shave closer when you come on my parade.'

'Its spots sergeant.'

'Don't you come spotty with me sunshine. I'll not have spots in my troop Corporal Dimmelwick see to it.'

'Sarrhh! No spots.'

'They are misfits Corporal Dimmelwick...misfits, earwigs and mistakes of bloody mother nature...if the country's enemies see this lot they'll piss themselves...I know I am. Grade one jumped up turned around never come down bloody misfits' ranted Sergeant Head as he walked from the squad to the warmth of the troop office.

Logan liked him better the first time he met him.

Corporal Jock marched his degenerates away to the store to be kitted out which was a bit of trial as apart from Jock Sinclair and one or two boy scouts nobody knew how to march. After much shouting the troop came to a ragged halt before the QM store and formed a long snaking queue inside looking like a line of sheep for the dip. The place reeked of dead moths and new woolly jumper. At the far door men emerged as a walking kit pile with an issue of everything including what the Quartermaster Sergeant was calling kit deficiencies. This came down the line as signing for something they were not going to get and by the time it got to Logan the logic of it had been lost along with the right to object. The army wanted a signature for everything even if it wasn't going to give it to him.

Signature one was for certain items that went out theoretical issue and were received back the same way without ever leaving the store. These items were termed unnecessary and superfluous to requirement although still on issue.

'Which is why you will not be getting them' said the store man behind the counter.

A lance corporal stood by the door bellowing out the rules of issue like a continuous recording as the troop entered the store. Inside a long line of issue kit had been placed in neat piles three feet apart along a wide shiny counter. Behind each pile stood a store man shouting for neck sock and boot sizes for those who had yet to draw boots.

'Move along the line stand behind a pile of issue, check your name in the pay book, sign on the dotted line...stand behind a pile of kit, sign your own name, best joined up writing on the dots at the bottom...move along the line...hold your breath, it will fit if you hold your breath...awkward bastard. Superfluous to needs kit is down as none issued issue kit on the back page of the pay book' said the tape continuing in monotone. 'Sign at the back to show you have not been issued it.'

It seemed fair enough for the man ahead of Logan so it was fair enough for him especially as Head, tea break over now arrived to check things were going well.

'So why are we signing for something we are not going to get?' said a voice out loud looking for logic.

'Why do policemen wear big cone shaped hats if they don't have cone shaped heads?' answered the store man as if that gave an answer until somebody further in the store ventured the question again.

'Sign again for the shortage issue, that is a piece of issue kit that you are issued with that you will get...but not today...because we are short, in short a shortage. Do not confuse this with kit that you have not been issued with and which you don't get. Get it now?' said the store corporal.

'No corporal' said the voice speaking for the whole squad but signing anyway.

No doubt the answer to it all lay somewhere in antiquity and veiled in some sort of allegoric rite thought Logan. It was little more than a blind act of faith as he signed along with the others for that which he would not get.

'I haven't got any netting on my tin hat corporal' said a protesting voice. It was Jock Sinclair who being ex TA was in the know of what he should have down to the last hole in his sock.

'There's no nets, cover type camouflage for this hat, tin one number Quartermaster Sergeant.' called the corporal talking technical store speak to the back of the stores.

'You what!' shouted the staff sergeant nearly dropping his bag of long lasting extra strength mothballs.

'There's no Ena Sharples on his tin lid Quartermaster Sergeant' shouted the tape reverting to something close to English.

'Issue it as a none issue withdrawn item then' bellowed the QMS from somewhere deep between the rows and sounding very much a man alone. 'Must I think of everything?'

'I need my Ena Sharples' said Sinclair sticking with it and holding up the bald tin lid. 'Where do I stick my bits of twig and leaves to make me look like a wee bush in a field?'

'Bush in a field? Oh you don't want to do that' said the tape shaking his head as if he should know about these things. 'Now what would be your reaction do you suppose when, looking over a hill with your rifle there in the middle of a field you see a little bush suddenly stand up and run fifty yards before sitting back down again...exactly. Bang, bang, bloody bang...and no more bloody bush.'

'It's alright for you but I'm the one who will get shot at.'

'Well stand behind one of your mates then.' said the lance corporal losing patience.

'What's the problem ere' charged in Sergeant Head hearing the disturbance and arriving from the bottom of the stores.

'He hasn't got a net for his tin lid Sergeant Head. Says he can't make himself look like a wee bush.'

'Share with him' said Head pointing to the next man and putting an end to it.

The trek back to barrack room was a struggling line akin to the migration of the wildebeest across the Serengeti. It was a route strewn with abandoned kit and everywhere predators prowled to pick off the weak and infirm as it was impossible not to arrive without having dropped at least something. Some items dropped that day would never be seen again and would remain signed for but lost on issue throughout a man's entire army service.

Back in barracks room three spent the rest of the day cleaning and placing their kit into the locker in copy layout of the photograph pinned to the room door. It was the beginning of an ever escalating series of inspections from layout to cleaned and bulled items from boots to room and down even to the daily folding of bed blankets into a rectangular three by two foot hamburger of sheets and folded blanket wrapped and placed to the head of the bed. Logan made his pack a dozen times that first day finally getting it right and just thirty minutes before he broke it up to go to bed.

Kit issue thought to be over for the day they were surprised to be called at ten in the evening to an issue of Corporal Jocks. This was a one gallon tin of soft pink polish and a twenty pound lump of cast metal with a bristle base and a hinged brush stave handle. Described by Jock as a floor bumper and pushed brush fashion forwards and back it was possible to achieve a shine on lino similar in reflectivity levels of that required by the Inspectorate of Her Majesty's Lighthouses.

It seemed to Logan and many of them that these daily kit and room inspections were getting in the way of training until he realized that this was the training. In brief the army was instilling discipline, control and authority all at the end of a brush. They were being taught not to fear the order but fear having to do whatever it was over again at the whim of whoever was in charge. The power to make this happen hung over their heads like a dangling giant tin of lavender smelling floor polish.

The sheer mind control held by the destroyer of a misaligned bed pack or dragger of kit layout from locker turned men to cowering wimps in a matter of hours. Havoc was being wreaked on the intake of number seven troop and all at the flick of a pace stick. By the end of the first day the army had everyone in the palm of its hand and without putting boot to neck, took absolute and total control. Even the Scouse shut up.

To add to their already growing pain Corporal Jock now produced a cleaning roster which he ordered pinned at the top of the troop notice board by Shorty Hardcastle from the next room down who wasn't up to the job. Eventually the task fell to a recruit called Miller who had arms down to his knees. Fortunately for Hardcastle he had read the thing before he passed it on otherwise he would never have known it was up there. It gave yet more cleaning duties this time for the barracks area with items such as sweep and bumper the main corridor, brush the coconut mat entrance or clean the ablutions and the ever needed removal of the dead spider from fire buckets and fag ends from the sand. The roster allocated the work in rotation under an inspecting NCO and was signed at the bottom by order of the inspecting troop officer who the intake had yet to meet but then it was very cold in the mornings before the sun got up as Chalkie said.

Reflecting on the roster Logan decided it defined the only three categories of work to be found in the military, that of worker, supervisor and inspector. In short other ranks did the work, the NCO supervised and the officer turned up to have a look.

'Two thirds of the army officially do nutten' said the Scouse doing a second reading of the list for Shorty Hardcastle and making a fair point for once.

The issue of the barrack room cleaning roster seemed to provide a spur for some turning them into *one of them* and sent those who were not one of them into total despair. Not the least of this despair for Logan was the announcement in daily orders of the start of drill practice. After the experience of the first few days marching he was praying it had something to do with dentists. Er no.

The parade ground is where a drill pig comes into his own and where the army begins the process towards total domination of the right hand side of the brain. Some even give up the left side too but in Logan's case they got nothing, a battle though at times this was. It's hard to describe the sheer excitement of the first few tentative steps onto the parade ground. The first two minutes were exuberant excitement and the third as boring as fly spotting. It was like learning to swim, one moment splashing around in anticipated excitement and the next treading water.

Parade grounds are devised by the army as a place where grown men can do silly things with themselves without getting locked up or attracting the attention of the Courts of Human Rights. To Corporal Jock however, the parade ground was where it all came together for him and was a hallowed place where he could do no wrong. It was a bit like The Inquisition without the Grand Inquisitor and the inner personal contentment of knowing you were being overall purified as he torched your fagots. With the parade ground there was only ever pain.

The sheer futility of marching over a flat piece of ground one way only to turn about at the opposite edge and march back to where you had just come from struck Logan three minutes in. The grand old Duke of York did it with his ten thousand men but at least they had a view at the top and exhaustion to contain the mind on the way up. What seven troop got was Corporal Dimmelwick and short, sharp, shocks of Sergeant Head.

Jock showed the intake the army way of drill contained in the drill manual. In fact there is only one way they discovered, enshrined in the manual and followed verbatim by every drill pig that ever put mouth to squad.

'Squad...squad hettenshun stand at ease, stend heasy...keep quiet and pay attention and look this way...and that means you at the back...who I have got me little beady eye on. (optional) This morning we is going to instruct you in the right turn which enables yeou to turn at an hengle of ninety degrees to the right, and in a smart and soldierly fashion...watch this way and I will show you hinstructorhonly...wait for it...right tarn! whantwothreewhan. (breath optional) You who have been watching closely will have noticed that I have now moved my body ninety degrees and am in fact facing to the right and that I remain in the position of hettenshun...I will now break down this move into numbers to make it heasy for you who are thick bastards to follow, hinstructorhonly...wait for it...left tarn! Hinstructorhonly right tarn by numbers whan. You will notice those that have been paying attention that on the command right turn whan. I moved my body swiftly to the right in an angle of ninety degrees by pivoting on me eel of my right boot and sole of my left boot while retaining the position of my arms down the seams of my tunic trousers keeping my thumbs pressed tight in and pointing to the floor and pushing straight with my left leg which you will notice is stiff and you will also notice that I do not wobble or pick me nose (optional) and that the top half of my body hasremained perfectly straight and rigid with my chin tucked into my chest and my shoulders pushed well back. On the word of command two I will snap my left leg forward until my thigh and boot is parallel with the ground before bringing my left foot sharply in to join my right foot at the position of attention with toes slightly apart and at an angle of forty five degrees...because unlike some of you misfits and mistakesof mother bleeding nature I'm not afraid of losing me bollocks (optional)while my eels are correctly positioned together... hinstructorhonly two...are there any questions?' (breath mandatory)

'Can we have a fag break corporal?'

It was when Logan fully understood that this really was how the army gets men to turn to the right and left that a genuine feeling of had he made the right career choice came over him. For the next two hours the intake practised until one of them got it right and for the next two days until everyone got it right at least once and then on for long weeks until the squad got it right together. After three days of morning and afternoon practice the majority of the troop could come to attention, stand at ease and turn left, right and about turn albeit for some with a bit of a wobble. An aide de troop was introduced on the first day with the introduction of a communally shouted timing to every order. It allowed most boots to hit ground together as one coordinated stomp but remained a challenge for many but particularly Wee Jock, Shorty Hardcastle and Lofty Miller where the distance of parallel thigh to ground differed by something approaching a parallel foot. Consequently the order right turn now became right turn one, two three, one. Or as Jock put it, right turn one...fucking two three...one.

This shout out of timing signified to the entire camp just where each intake was at with regards to training before the troop moved on to turning right without the two three but still with the aid of another appointed aide de troop, that of a piss man. He alone would sound a loud psst at the correct timing. A silent turn to the eye but with a psst for those close to or in the know it worked well but took days to weed out the voices still shouting two three.

'Thick bastards!'

How this loss of two three could foster troop spirit and increase morale was as mysterious as the pride they all felt when allowed to insert cap badges into berets or parade in peaked caps to wear them in. Something was happening to the intake felt Logan and when he found himself cleaning the brass on the padlock he had bought for his locker he knew whatever it was it was not healthy although the lock came up beautifully. So when room three was awarded best room of the week and a feeling of pride came to him he knew something was going seriously wrong in his head. To a man they were turning army. Some had gone over to the dark side completely and would never return and others strayed there for some of the time but like it or not they were all now some parts khaki, even himself Logan thought turning to speak to Chalkie, two three.

'Any of this bullshit worry you Chalkie?'

'Not now I got a good shine on my parade boots toecaps' said Chalkie holding his boot up and giving the toe a huh before a final rub with cotton wool 'what do you think?'

'How do you do it' said Logan and why he thought to himself smiling over.

'It's time to move the squad on' said Jock closing both eyes and wincing as he addressed the men in three ranks.

With stationary drill yet remaining a challenge for some the troop now advanced to drill on the move, an altogether entirely different animal best described by Chalkie as a bitch. Hard enough for some at close quarters drilling at distance when on the move became a nightmare. The simple right and left turn when on the move required ear, arm, leg, foot, leg arm and eye to combine in the one split second of the shouted order. The move is little less than a 'me and my dog' choreographic nightmare. Sheep were better controlled and certainly better led.

Juxtapose any of the six coordinated requirements into a different word of command and the result was what the intake got – an absolute and utter shambles. Add to this seemingly insignificant order of movement, a forward momentum of around four miles per hour, throw in additional complications such as rain, ice, uneven ground, shale and surface variation factors such as the coefficients of slip, trip and wind rush, sore throats, ear wax, airborne pollutants such as band noise, bad guts, car backfires, other shouted orders, twenty one gun salutes, thunder, honking fucking geese, aircraft, various acts of God, things only Arthur C Clark had explanation for and a general lack of interest and what had they? Massive and complete grand scale cock-up of epic magnitude.

'And none of it is our fault' said Chalkie.

'We are slowly being drilled senseless' complained Logan during a communal kit bulling session.

Compton had a theory about it all where he felt the actual stamping of feet sent a shock wave up the spinal column to enter the brain and disturb rational thought. Was he right thought Logan? If so they were being drilled stupid.

'Somewhere in Whitehall there must be a file giving the drill rates per unit loose brain in percentage terms' said Compton expanding the theory. 'In short, the resultant effect per drill hour to effect stupefaction to a level required to get people to do this stuff.'

'Eh?' said Brum.

Logan listened with increasing interest before moving on to apply more polish to his second toecap and watching with an incredulous fascination at someone polishing the sole of his boot. There had to be a reason for this he was thinking as Compton paused to take a drag of his fag before going on.

'The looser the screws the more aggressive the behaviour which explains both the formidable successes of the British army over recent centuries and their image of being the best drilled soldiers in the world.'

Every head began to nod in unison as the sole polishing was taken up by the rest of the room but for the one who had already done it.

'This is where your Jock Regiments come in as fighting men. They join up with something already loose.'

The last bit got him a half hearted thump on the ear from Sinclair who until then was nodding along with the rest of the room. If he had understood him he would have kicked the shit out of him there and then. Suddenly there was movement. Scouse who talked a good fight and was always looking for opportunities to show he was tough jumped to the defence of Compton and immediately squared up to threaten the much smaller Sinclair with a bloody good hiding. Nobody moved, they had seen it before. It was a weekly occurrence with the Scouse squaring up on someone for one reason or another. Last week it was Shorty Hardcastle and this week it was Wee Jock.

'Come on then tough guy, do you want some, come on then' called the Scouse fisting up to the smaller man as the two of them pushed and shuffled around a bed. 'Come on then...come on then' he was still saying as Jock hit him bang in the mouth.

Scouse picked himself from between the beds, wiped blood from his lip and pointed threateningly as Jock beckoned him to come on for a bit more of it.

'Just don't push it Jock' said Scouse pointing his finger and swaggering out of the room with what was left of his fading tough guy image.

'I wanted to do that' said Chalkie to Logan but then they all did.

'Me too' said everybody watching him go.

The afternoon returned them to the drill sheds with more Corporal Jock and more bollockings. At least with Logan it was for the want of trying. With some they were just physically not in charge of either body or mind. How anyone can march with left arm and left leg both going forward together was beyond Logan. There had to be nobody in there. So alien to mankind was this walk they used it on Dr Who as the walk of the Cybermen.

Harder to believe than double pin walking for Logan was the frequency at which some would persist at turning to face the left when the order was to turn to the right or to end up facing to the rear when the rest of the troop were facing the front – and not to realise.

'You would expect some sort of doubt to creep in when you end up looking eye to eye with the man in front wouldn't you think?'

Brum was a regular offender on this one and would remain statue still in the hope he would be missed. A lone beret back of head in a sea of smirking faces. Corporal Jock slowly approached his ear.

'Can all the others be wrong on this one Brummie? Might we venture a wee guess here...fucking dipstick!'

Compton also seemed at times to be directionally dyslexic unless it was a problem with his ear wax. More than once he was left standing alone as the rest of the squad turned and left in another direction. Some managed it daily and some like Compton managed it hourly and bright though he appeared to be in so many other ways telling left from right for him was a bit of a mystery. At length Jock decided to weed them out and dismissing the squad from the parade ground reformed them in the drill shed.

'Squad stand easy, no talking in the ranks you...now then, on the word of command hands raised, I want all yous right hands to go up. Squad...hands raised.' Jock walked along the ranks checking the arms before returning to the front of the squad nodding away to himself.

'Hands down and now left hands...squad hands raised.' All hands went up again.

After several attempts Jock paused obviously in some sort of turmoil that turned out to be some hands going up late.

'Some of you bastards are copying' he said at length before manhandling the front rank into an outwardly facing circle.

Ordering the rest of the squad to face the rear of the drill shed Jock issued the same hand raised order progressively to each rank until, with smug assuredness, he had it down to three poor bastards that he called to stand at the front of the squad. The order to right hand and left hand raise sure enough provided a split decision much to the amusement of the rest of the squad. Jock dispelled the laughter with a threat of an extra hour's drill before producing from his pocket pieces of blue ribbon, which were tied to the right boot of each defaulter. Returning them to the squad the troop were drilled with 'right blue ribbon and left no ribbon turns.' In less than an hour the ribbons were removed as having done that which life and education had not managed to over many years.

For sure it made the rest of the squad listen in but then maybe that's what it was all about in the first place thought Logan. Days later a series of eight or so unconnected digits given out as an army number were being recalled instantly by men who would look up if you shouted there's a dead bird.

'If only our schools could apply the techniques used by the army to get men to remember an eight digit army number for the rest of their lives the benefits to the nation would be incalculable' pronounced Compton from his bed before closing his book and using his little blue ribbon as a bookmark.

4

It had been a miserable week and most of the intake was desperate to escape the camp. Rumour had it that room two had a tunnel going. Home leave was not allowed in the first months presumably for fear some would not return so most recruits slept through the weekend rising only for food the ablutions or to bull their boots.

'It's a little known but absolutely recorded fact that there were over fifty mutinies for Britain's military in the first half of the twentieth century' stated Compton suddenly.

'There must have been more than that' said Logan thinking it through.

Catterick Camp at the weekend he felt was a hole above ground and about as exciting as pole perching but when it's all you have you get on with it. Even Chalkie didn't like it and he came from Yorkshire. Reports were circulating about what there was in Catterick Camp for anyone looking for a good fight or a night out. Early recruit had the low down on a NAAFI club called the Harewood but nothing else unless you travelled well away from camp centre which sounded to Logan like the roundabout was ground zero with no life forms until you were well out of the drop zone. Desperate men however, will try anything and things were desperate enough for a one-man recce. Being a native speaker Chalkie was despatched to camp centre and returned less than an hour later.

'If you want saving and like brass bands and collection tins there's the Salvation Army or if you're happy and you know it there's TOC H down the road but a bit of a way out if weather's raining.

'Why should that worry us?' asked Taff being well used to rain in the valleys.

'And if you're hungry there's a fish and chip shop further up.'

'That it then?'

'And there's Johnnies at the side of the roundabout.'

'Disgusting habit that is' said Brum.

'Johnnies' said Chalkie, 'it's a coffee bar.'

'That's cool. I had twenty-three frothy coffees at one sitting once' said Scouse 'huge coffee machine this club had. A Gaggia triple it was, top of the range.'

Scouse stood to make a show, pulling down with his hand like pulling a pint and sucking air through his teeth for showy effect.

'Sounds like a Wimpy bar does that' said Brum wanking his own hand down behind Scouse's back.

'Twenty-three coffees, were you alright?' asked Compton intrigued more than interested in his health.

'Yeah fine, couldn't sleep that night though, and the next.'

'A frothy coffee bar that's something new then' said Taff 'they got them in Swansea, full of Beatniks and cool chicks with black eyes and ribbons in their hair. That's me for tonight then boys.'

'Not for me' said Chalkie.

'No?' said Taff.

'Don't like camp coffee.'

Oh that kind of coffee bar' said Logan, 'coffee with a Scotsman on the label.'

Only Jock looked up from his bed before returning back to his paper.

'But the place has Bovril' said Chalkie giving a thumbs up 'and sauce from a red plastic squeezy tomato.'

'I like them I do, they make noises' said Brum 'anything else?'

'Loads, salt and pepper, plastic stand up menus, dead bluebottles and a juke box.'

'Well that's something then' said Taff 'music brings the girls out, anything good on it.'

'Gerry and the Pacemakers when I passed.'

'Our Gerry?' said Scouse like he knew him.

'Always reminds me of the collective noun for a man of the Rhineland does Gerry' said Compton.

'A what?' said Brum pulling a face as Scouse began to sing behind him.

'How do you do what you do to me...I wish I knew?' sang the Scouse as Logan for one winced.

'And if I knew what you're doing to me I'd do it to you...but I haven't a clue! Priceless line that' said Compton 'someone got paid good money to write that.'

'And there's also Peculiar Clarke and Cliff Richards' said Chalkie so he must have gone in for something thought Logan, probably a Bovril.

'I like Cliff I does' said Brum.

'Is there anything naff you don't like Brum?' asked Logan.

'The Villa' said Brum after thinking about it.

'And there's a club called the Harewood some bloke said in Johnnies...it has dances on Saturday nights.'

'Dancers?' said Taff mishearing and going off the frothy coffee idea.

Compton now said he had heard about the Harewood from someone in the last intake which would have saved Chalkie the walk in.

'Why didn't you say?'

'The bloke said the place was like an institution in Catterick with bars, table tennis and billiards, thought it sounded like Broadmoor.'

So it was with great expectation that Logan produced his ID card at the door and ventured into the Harewood Club. Saturday night and the place was heaving and with the Women's Royal Army Corps camp close by and a line of local girls standing at the door asking to be signed in they entered throwing caution to lust. Downstairs and near the entrance the place was mostly bowling alley set next to a cafe but further in they found a bar called the Long Bar and alongside a dancehall complete with a stage and revolving mirror ball.

'The only thing missing are Ted's in drainpipes, drape jackets and brothel creepers' said Chalkie looking in and expecting to have to duck.

'And ducks arse haircuts' said Logan completing the image.

Dated dancehall apart the Harewood for the most part was a place of ping-pong and recreational activity for service personnel but on Saturday it was not ping-pong and snooker that packed them in or the bowling alley. On Saturday it was the fairer sex.

'And for fairer sex I just mean sex' said Logan as they moved down into the club like God's gift to women to check out the prospects.

Chalkie looked agog around the bar at what was on offer; as if he would be so lucky. What he saw was mostly female army on the pull and what they saw from the haircut was a rookie. He hadn't one chance in hell.

The official collective noun for the Women's Royal Army Corps is a contingency they discovered some time later.

'A herd would be nearer the mark' felt Chalkie coming straight out with it.

'Bit harsh that Chalkie' said Logan pulling a face but mostly at the McKewen's Heavy as clearly the man had a fair point.

In very loose terms a WRAC can be described as a female soldier or one on't loose as Chalkie said. Logan for one had never met a woman in uniform other than at the dentist and at hospital although he had fond memories of Bernice in the bike sheds. Expecting something akin to the Israeli army lovelies seen on Panorama or in Newsweek the actuality strayed to something altogether shorter, fatter and generally not as nice looking. This of course was true of their male counterparts not to mention the majority of mankind but what both lacked in looks was evidently more than made up for in musk and lusty intent.

'It's nature's way' said Chalkie 'we can't all be good lookers.'

'Yes Chalkie, I think you are on firm ground there' said Logan leaving himself out of the supposition, if Chalkie had why not me he told himself.

After weeks away from females other than big Elsie behind the pies in the NAAFI and a well thumbed naturist magazine stuffed behind the cistern in bog number two these lady soldiers took on a status entirely disproportionate to their physical attributes by a factor approaching light years. Even ones with average looks were pulling blokes that on a good night might have turned down stars of the big screen and even Brigitte Bardot had she turned up in the NAAFI queue minus her knickers thought Logan before remembering something about French women and commandoes that he kept to himself.

Nothing it would seem brings on myopia more than time away from sex, home and four pints of McKewen's on top of a well shook packet of salt and vinegar crisps. Certainly it made for sorry and desperate men and Logan for one had to admit he was both.

Life for the average WRAC in Catterick was therefore, on the whole glorious and with men outnumbering them twenty-eight to one give or take a battalion or two it was unashamedly the single reason most of them joined and with such disproportionate numbers beauty went unmeasured. Whatever they had was certainly at a premium in Catterick and ones with even the slightest hint of good looks could get the choice of an entire intake of recruits although no self respecting WRAC would involve herself with one. Sad though it was, a recruit in Catterick was seen as the lowest form of life beneath which nothing crawls. In short and in terms of pulling power their chances of pulling anything that Saturday night were less than a minus nil.

'And a nil minus is about as low as it gets' said Chalkie being optimistic for once.

In spite of this not inconsiderable handicap it was with a great personal loss of pride that after not even starting at the top or even near the top Logan had over the course of one and a half hours descended to be sat in the Long Bar next to a female Corporal Jock. Lovely natured though the girl undoubtedly was in a count out of ten she was a two 'and you got a one just for being there' Chalkie kept pointing out.

'Women around here don't grow on trees Chalkie' said Logan whispering from the side of his mouth.

'They swing from them' said Chalkie although having to admit there wasn't a real three in there discounting 'a seven at the door when we came in, that one in black uniform, the one with the tin...she was something else she was.'

'The Salvation Army girl? That's an unchristian and unclean thought that Chalkie and disgraceful as well...and disgusting. Give one to a bonneted Sallybash? That's only one down from shagging a nun' said Logan 'and I bet you never put anything in her tin.'

Logan turned his back on his disgusting mate although he was right about the seven and returned to the bird in hand that was little more than a one in the bush.

'I didn't say she was a goer, I was only giving it a rating' said Chalkie disgusted at the thought before leaving to get the round in 'put something in the bloody tin? I don't think so.'

Even this small success for Logan was by no means an inevitability as twenty others waited their chance should his patter fail or his money run out or should he foolishly leave his seat to splash his boots. Fascination, chemistry, drink, the white kinky boots or just the plain intrigue of it Logan was in there and was not leaving.

It is generally given and rightly that physical beauty isn't everything but Sharon, for that was her name, had a most unappealing personality to go with the looks and one or two very nasty personal habits that captivated all sat at the table.

'I just heard at the bar that she threw her family cat out of an upstairs window once' whispered Chalkie on his return 'don't you just hate women who throw their pussy around?'

'I'm not moving Chalkie so you can push off' said Logan ignoring the man, although he agreed with him that she was the kind of girl that would smoke in church at her wedding or be cruel to animals, but he was not to be put off as the pursuit of Sharon became the focus of the evening.

Yet more recruits were entering the bar joining a mix of trained soldier unlucky enough to have Catterick as a posting and others returned there under extended training. This mixture of old sweat, young blood and something neither one thing nor the other made for a heady volatile mix. By nine o'clock the bar was heaving full and the queue to be served stood twenty wide and four bodies thick.

Fortunately Sharon was going for her own pints, as Logan could never crush through to the bar like she could without being offered outside. Logan had stopped drinking at the point Sharon went onto Irish whisky chasers and began her post adolescence life history which ended with a brief career as a ballet dancer before joining up in Belfast. His mind raced at the thought before finally stopping short at an image of the Sugarplum Fairy. More your nutcracker judging from the shape of her he thought. For sure she was no sugarplum and several pounds and a hell of a long way from being a fairy. More a goblin he said quietly looking at her closely as she paused mid dirty joke to down what remained of her pint. It was a full hour before Logan finally got into her Northern Irish brogue as his mind wandered back to thoughts of the corps de ballet.

'Ah!' said Logan at length having a eureka moment 'you said belly dancer!'

It was during one of Sharon's refuel trips to the bar that her empty seat was spotted by an exceptionally large Para. Thoughts to stop the seat disappearing swiftly moved to discretion with the arrival of the ranger's four mates. Averting his eyes from the seat Logan missed Sharon's return to the table. She arrived precisely at the moment the Para sat himself down or would have done had the seat still been there.

For such a big man the Para was very quick to get off the floor and for such a dopey looking one he was also quick to realize his seat was now comfortably under the lady from Belfast.

'Scuse me' said the Para raising himself up to full strop height and making a big expansive play, slowly pushing sleeve to elbow before finally placing both hands on hips.

He was about to issue a threat of death to the table when Sharon without the slightest glance to locate direction or distance elbowed him square in the balls. The Para's legs and eyes crossed in unison and down he went like a dropped chimneystack. A simultaneous and mighty intake of sucked breath silenced the bar as forty sets of eyes watered swiftly followed by a loud and synchronized gasp of male sympathy arriving just ahead of the smirks and smiles compulsory for anyone catching one in the nuts.

With the exception of the Para and his four mates all about him thought the scene hilarious until the Para got back up again and laughing ceased. All that was with the exception of a lone Scotsman. The fight started between Para and the Jock and suddenly widened into an inter regimental match with the entire bar pitching in with strange and newfound alliances. Epicentre to the mayhem was Sharon thumping and head butting herself some space to swing a chair.

Those not able to get at the fray proper now joined in from all sides with whatever came to hand as the room darkened to a shower of flying beer glass, bottle and the odd stool. From all around came the crash and shattering sounds of breaking glass and the cries and screams of the fallen wounded now underfoot in the melee as the shutters slammed down along the bar in well practiced routine protecting staff and stock alike. More men appeared at the doors arriving as reinforcements to a battle instinctively knowing which side to thump in on. Everywhere were the shouted offers 'do you want some' that many seemed unable to refuse as Logan ducked and dived and followed Chalkie to the door to cries of 'the MPs are coming' as from outside came the sound of a far off whistle.

By the time the first MPs arrived Logan and Chalkie were outside the bar and in the growing crowd watching the action with a keen eye to miss the odd flying ashtray. It was Chalkie who offered sensible advice, suggesting that they might be positioned to more strategic advantage if they were to surreptitiously distance themselves from the ever-expanding fray.

'Leg it' he said as they turned and ran up the approach narrowly escaping through the expanding cordon of freshly arriving red cap land rovers.

At the top of the approach the sound of broken glass and Sharon's swearing could still be heard in the far distance as they made their way back to barracks via the chippy. Come Monday morning Logan still had a growing bruise to his ribs where Sharon had pushed him away to drop one on the Para and coupled with the hangover from the hair of the dog of the night before that always gets you more pissed he decided that going sick was the only way he could face the morning. He found Compton there and in deep conversation with half a dozen of the other malingering regulars.

Going sick with Compton had become something of a regular event as the man had been far from well from week one. Whatever anyone had Compton had also he would say only worse, or would likely be getting it shortly. Other people's ailments seemed only to kindle an inner need in the man to be suffering worse than they were and stimulated an inner need to be continually and progressively sick.

'What you got?' Compton asked appearing to show genuine interest but really only building an ailment bank for his own malingering use.

'Badly bruised ribs' said Logan doing his best wince to show just how bad they were 'and a banging head.'

'Bruised ribs and a banging head, two aspirin fit for duties' pronounced his little group in unison with a knowing shake of heads.

No doubt ribs had been tried earlier by some of them as Logan's turn arrived and he limped his way in. The MO took less than two minutes to confirm the group prognosis, diagnosis and treatment and he rejoined the troop ready for weapons training clutching his two aspirin and his bruised ribs. It was to be a morning spent rolling around on bare floorboards and did wonders for his ribs and even less for his bad all round attitude. He could hardly wait for bayonet practice as he queued for the first time to draw his rifle.

5

Drawing of weapons that day was an exciting thought for most of the intake as getting out your weapon was something not many people get to do without being arrested or worse still getting followed down the road. For many it was a scary thought and something of a rite of passage where it announced them as would be soldiers. What excitement they would have felt on the Somme thought Logan as he signed out his personal rifle at the armoury. It was the equivalent of being given a bow without arrows, as it would be some time before they would actually get to fire at something. Before then came weeks of weapons training and the all important weapon handling and the fun of how to drill with them courtesy of Corporal Jock. Only when all this was accomplished would they get to shoot the damn things.

The holding of weights at arm's length to strengthen the bow arm was standard practice in the fourteenth and fifteenth century and had unquestionable merit for the English army when it had the long bow. Why it was still done with a rifle was a bit of mystery to the intake but a source of delight for the weapons' instructor sadist that he was. Weapons' training was in a bare room in an old wooden hut that must have fallen on hard times in the years after the first world war but had been given a new lease of life along with a felt roof and a bucket for the drip. Set back some way from the rear of the accommodation blocks it was a throwback to earlier times and had served the nation well against England's natural enemy the French said Compton before acknowledging this was not always so for Wee Jock until Napoleonic times that is.

'Probably where they found the long bow training manual is this place' said Chalkie 'it's in a time warp.'

'It's in a mess' said Logan moving away from the drip.

The instructor who was a qualified armourer had attended the 'make it hurt' school of instructional technique that placed elbows and knees on hard wooden floors that did little to concentrate the mind on the lesson but then neither did the pool of water.

'Quiet, never mind the leaks, pay attention and look in...today we are going to do the naming of parts. This here is a 7.62 SLR Self Loading Rifle with gas operating recocking mechanism with the following named external parts; cocking handle, sliding cover, weapon break catch, safety catch, bayonet catch, anti muzzle flash, magazine holding twenty rounds, plus one up the spout if you want it but never keep a magazine too full or you will strain the spring, magazine release catch, the stock, the butt, the barrel, foresight, back or rear site, lower sling swivel and upper sling swivel which in your case you haven't got...any questions?'

Why did it have to be the upper sling swivel and not the bit where the sling hooked onto thought Logan and anyway they didn't have any slings but he kept his mouth shut as the instructor stripped and reassembled the weapon with a practiced matchless speed that dropped jaws to the point of an open mouthed drool.

One moment it was rifle and the next a pile of other named parts and then a rifle again. The man could even do it behind his back with a blindfold and balancing on one leg although the reason why escaped all of them fascinating though it was. Watching the man's every move Logan noted that more than one of the parts had the capacity to be inserted back into the assembled weapon with a degree of radial and lateral error. In brief upside down, wrong way round or both. Give such variables and parts to ten idiots per training group and you were asking for something to go dramatically wrong and so it did. Life was easier with a bow, an arrow and a length of string kept dry in your hat noted Compton finding a part left over 'this bit your's?'

'Agincourt' he said to Logan, 'bowmen kept their draw strings dry under their hats...it was heavy rain before the battle...1415?'

'I knew that' said Chalkie overhearing at the back 'still pissing it down at 1445 as well.'

In mathematical terms some parts had less than a one in eight chance of going back in wrongly inserted and at times not at all having gone missing on the training room floor. Done at speed against a stopwatch some never made it and was a common occurrence in Logan's group or the misfits as the instructor began to call them. With the chances of correct assembly far from good some pieces just never stood a chance until well into week three was how Compton saw it.

Proof of a correct reassembly was the climax of every lesson and accomplished by the firing of the empty weapon. Once cocked and if assembled correctly the weapon would give a distinctive click as the trigger released the fining pin. Held back for dramatic effect the order to fire was given to each man in turn as clicks came down the line like an approaching idiot cap awaiting the silence or clunk of an incorrect assembly. Dexterously challenged as he was Compton struggled with the mechanics of weapon training as much as he did marching. With release to a NAAFI break depending on a one hundred percent correct group assembly he had delayed more than one but not this morning as they were saved by the early arrival of Corporal Jock.

Formed up outside to their dismay they were marched not to the NAAFI but to the rear of the guardroom to await the arrival of one of the camp's regimental policemen who was to give them fire drill training said Jock. Chalkie knew the RP from an early close encounter and delivered a potted history of the man given in whispers from the back of the squad beginning with him being a right twat.

Unlike the military police that join a corps and are professionally trained to be disliked regimental police are generally selected from the itinerant unloved dross of a regiment whose foremost job is to run the guardroom and raise up the red and white painted pole barrier said Chalkie or something to the like. Secondary to this is their other job of touring the camp area at intervals to stamp some sort of authority by intimidation. It was the army equivalent of a motorway patrol car driving at sixty-nine miles per hour.

'Serves only to speed everybody up once they leave the motorway to make up for the delay?'

Clearly Chalkie didn't like the man and all in the rear rank at least were getting the message.

'Right' said Logan searching for the transferred logic but getting the general picture.

'Other than that they sit around the guardroom doing nothing, and get called Staff even as a one stripe lance corporal' said Chalkie continuing with his brief.

'Not a fan then Chalkie?' asked Logan as Chalkie went on with the story of a run in with this one when he walked over some grass in the first week of training.

'Local rank, one striper, unpaid and unwanted' he said rounding off as they waited for the nice man to tell them to 'settle down' before rushing back into the guardroom to return with a forgotten training aid.

'Listen in yous lot. Now, fire fighting vital equipment apparatuses and their uses' said the RP holding up a bucket and pointing with the other hand.

By the time he finished with the bucket the NAAFI break was long gone. Resolved to the loss the squad settled down and made like they were listening as with a quick check of his notes the RP hooked the bucket to the rear of a hand drawn green fire tender. With his red upper armband with RP in big black letters and wearing a white thinned down version of an officer's Sam Brown belt and white gaiters the man looked the part whatever the part was.

'At least you can see them coming' said Logan but what stood out for him was the doctored peaked cap the front of which lay flat down to the man's forehead. He looked to Logan like he was wearing a Norman helmet or had been hit in the face with a shovel.

'They slash the edges of the peak and shove it up into the cap band at the corners, it drops the peak flat' said Chalkie.

'Same as the guards do' said Wee Jock squashing his nose flat with his palm.

'The twat's missing only the stubby little moustache the boots and an Iron Cross second class' whispered Chalkie.

'Keep the noise down yous at the back' said the RP 'my name is Hhhough...haich – ho – u – g – haitch...uff.'

'Fairy nuff' said Chalkie who really didn't like the man.

'And you lot address me as Staff Hough because I am a regimental policeman as it says ere on my armband, Horr P. Right you lot form a circle around me at the front so you can see what I am doing...close in those at the back...move yourselves, move yourselves...'

'Yes, that's the arsehole' said Chalkie shuffling to the rear of the squad.

The intake now assembled in a rough semicircle before an army hand drawn green box on large red wheels with red spokes. A unified moan went up as the RP lifted the lid and produced a fire hose and nozzle before turning to face the troop.

'Hand drawn green fire wagon, standard mark three issue fire tender...with dangling bucket...fire putting out for the use of. Fire wagon, fire bucket, standard issue andle an wheels.' He said pointing to the bits.

'Circa 1843' whispered Logan.

'Are we alright to smoke' asked a voice to laughter.

'No...right you lot listen in' began the RP pausing for greater effect as he scanned the circle of men to his front before clearing his throat with a purposeful cough.

Included with the pause was a deliberate shrug of shoulders and a thrusting of both arms to his front. This sequenced shrug and thrust of arms was used whenever he ended either speech or movement and seemed to be his way of presenting a full stop to a word or any action.

'Pay attention all of yous...shrug thrust...listen in at the back...shrug thrust...this ere is an fire ose and coupler in this hand and this ere is an fire ose nozzle in this hand.'

Seven troop nodded to a man as the RP scanned the ranks before giving a shrug and thrust.

'Ose and coupler here' he said raising one hand.

'Wait for it' whispered Logan.

'An ozzle!' said the RP raising the other.

'Can't fault you' said Chalkie.

'Male and female' he said sticking his tongue out with a leer.

Once again the troop nodded more in sympathy than understanding as the man now deadly serious continued with the lesson.

'You at the front,' pointed the RP 'what do I ave in my and ere?'

'An ozzle?' Logan answered hesitantly taking the piss, then maybe he had missed something?

'Well done that man...that is correct' said the RP 'now the nozzle goes here on the end of the hose, see? And screws on like this, see?'

The RP screwed the ozzle to the end of the hose coupling as the troop watched on mystified and struck silent to a man by oversimplification.

'Once the nozzle is on and in the correct position at this end of the ose and with the other end fixed to the tap over there.'

Seven troop followed the RP's moving head from nozzle to end of the hose and back again like a primary school intake.

'The water comes down the ose and out this end here...now is there any questions before we move on to the tap end?'

There was an incredulous pause as the RP scanned the line of astonished blank faces looking for signs of life.

'There's life there but not as we know it' whispered Chalkie at the back as the troop stayed transfixed to a man before Logan broke the long silence.

'The nozzle,' Logan asked innocently 'does it always go on this end of the ose?'

There was a general snort of restrained laughter about him.

'Quiet' said the RP 'this is important...er yes recruit it does.'

'You couldn't go through it again could you please staff' said the voice of Chalkie coming from the back starting an outburst of laughter, which filtered out when the RP went through it a second and then a third time. At length and convinced they now knew the wet end of a fire hose from the dry end he released the squad back to the returning Corporal Jock.

'That seven troop' said the RP back in the guardroom and speaking to the RP Sergeant as he watched the squad march away to a missed NAAFI break.

'Oh yes?' said the sergeant only half listening as he flipped through a Playboy left by the last night's guard.

'There's some right thick bastards in that troop' said the RP doing a final shrug thrust before sitting himself down.

'We can only do our best with what we've got Staff Hough. Bloody hell look at the size of them beauties, you don't get many of them in a pound...you don't get many in a bucket either, eh?' said the sergeant turning the page around.

'Oh shit' said the RP suddenly reminded 'I forgot to give them the bit on use of the fire bucket!'

'They'll pick it up soon enough if there's a fire Houghy' said the sergeant before pausing to think 'ha! pick it up...get it?'

'Get what serge?'

6

Major Rory Calhoun sat in the squadron office sipping his morning coffee. Today was to be a very special day in the life of the Calhoun family. After years of piracy, sheep stealing and countless thousands spent putting the half-wit Rory through a succession of crams to get him the three GCE passes needed for Sandhurst would all have been worth it. Rory was to take a pass out parade attended by a royal and one still married to boot. Brushing shoulders with an HRH rated as high as a night with old matron wearing her rubber gloves for the major or a Jean Shrimpton in a gymslip for the other ranks.

The visit was the consequence of a series of events beginning with a misrouted message. Marked FLASH the highest priority in the army the message was sent down the lines at the speed of light before they gave it to a man on a bike. Brigadier General the Hon. Diarrmiud (Paddy) de Dildao D'Arcy mistakenly received the signal in North Eastern Command with an original addressee and routing for Southern Command. D'Arcy who was extremely well connected on his brother's mother's first husband's step mother's side completely ignored the addressee and claimed the HRH by right of possession for Catterick Garrison.

It was the sort of thing his ancestors had perfected centuries before when they claimed huge chunks of Scotland and entire segments of England by royal grace and favour. This favouring was something the D'Arcy ancestors were particularly good at down the centuries, even managing on one occasion to serve both King and Queen at the same time due to a forbear with a fortunate genetic indifference who was also well connected with a prominent bishop of the time. Richard (Ever Ready) Dick D'Arcy went down in history and was a much revered ancestor who was given a knighthood for his services to the King albeit a lower class one for all the good work he allegedly did with his bishop.

The family of the GOC North Eastern Command apart; a swift check around the training depots eventually provided a timely parade required to give some point however slim to the occasion. Colonel Samuel Cholmondeley was beside himself with excitement to the point of peeing down his leg.

'Ever met the man Adj?' he said casually flicking a cuff and desperately trying to appear nonchalant about the entire event.

This was difficult when you are being fitted for a new uniform and your hair is having a second trim in as many hours.

'Sandhurst passing out Sammy' said the adjutant moving the colonel's ear with the comb to get the scissors in. 'I can't have been more than a half a mile from him, nearer actually.'

'Really' said the half colonel well impressed at the short distance.

He had never got over the disappointment of attending a garden party at the palace and finding himself one of 3472 others plus those bloody dogs. The day had been spent queuing at the Portaloo with an Olympic twenty kilometre walker from Huddersfield and a postman called Pat as HM the Q would not let him inside buck house for a pee but he still had fond memories of the event although he never got near the cucumber sandwiches.

'For some damn Senegalese dancing troop with turbans and a fecking short arsed jockey from Wetherby...scoffed the bloody lot between them, greedy sods.'

Another half a mile away and alone in the squadron office Major Calhoun was practising future casual name-dropping in a mirror. It would be the single event in an entirely undistinguished career that would be introduced into every social conversation he would ever have for the rest of his life and he was keen to get it to perfection.

'Calhoun, how de do, yah...met the Duke have we?' It was sounding better by the gin.

'Haven't you?...oh really?...one has...ectually.'

To troops five and six the unfortunate troops centre to the event all was extra drill, bull and a pain in the arse. For the rest of the camp and seven troop all was extra cleaning, bullshit and also a pain in the arse. To Logan's mind it was bad enough having to be inspected by those in charge of training never mind someone not even in the army proper and he said so but at least he wasn't having to line up for inspection.

'There's something not quite right about being inspected by someone who didn't dress himself this morning' Logan said receiving agreement from Chalkie for one, 'and anyway at best the bloke's an ex bloody sailor.'

For the Duke it was a couple of free gins yet again and a pee break on his way to a stag do. Actually an end of stag do if the Duke and his mates could find one slow enough not to outrun the hounds this time. For their part in the affair seven troop were set to sweeping loose parade ground shale into uniform straight lines. Corporal Jock had devised an army drill for this which had them brushing at an angle of forty-five degrees and in broad sweeps of the parade ground and parallel to the drill sheds. The reason for this was in order not to give a straight line comparison to the eye from the saluting podium as the troops marched past in open order line. This was fair play Logan felt as the alternative would have them brushing the shale into bendy banana lines which was how troops five and six usually marched past in open order. It was either that or a complex series of random interchanging and juxtaposed variables on the letter S that would give risk of bringing on the colonel's migraine that decided it as the order came down from Colonel Sam via the Adjutant to Major Calhoun through the still missing troop officer and via Sergeant Head and Corporal Jock to arrive at the brushes of seven troop.

'Chain of command' said Logan with a shake of his head as they marched off with brushes to port.

As a group the intake were growing more republican by the minute and turned into a group of card carrying anarchists when they missed their NAAFI break.

'What the hell' said Chalkie 'this visit has already lost us our weekend off and two days military training for the entire camp.'

The event had also cost the tax payer a fortune in white paint, Brasso, car polish, illicit telephone calls to relatives, numerous signals to Whitehall and had disrupted Yorkshire Constabulary in a two hundred mile radius of the camp. It had re-routed fourteen aircraft, two trains, three fire engines, rescheduled the diaries of two brigadier generals, one major general, six colonels, and an assortment of mid ranking and junior officers, several thousand other ranks and Corporal Paddy The Irish Wolfhound OBE of the Irish Fusiliers not forgetting the Mayor of Richmond, his missus, a handful of councillors, hangers on and the deputy head and dinner lady supervisor at Richmond Tech who did the sandwiches.

'What was seven troop's NAAFI break worth in light of all that' asked Chalkie to the silence of the room.

It was the morning of the passing out parade and seven troop were approaching the fifth sweep of the parade ground when Logan lost one of his fly buttons. The opportunity to pick it up on the next sweep past was denied him as with parade time rapidly approaching and to the sound of the band warming their umpa up Corporal Jock marched them off brushes at the slope to be hidden away in the barracks. The red helicopter of the Queen's flight roared overhead as seven troop squashed nose to window to catch a glimpse of the awkward bastard.

Compton who knew a lot about royals said he always pilots his own fixed wing aircraft as it's free and keeps his hours up for his licence but there is always another pilot in there in case he wants to go for a leak, adding knowingly that they always make a point of going before they land to save him asking where the gents is whenever they visit anywhere or even worse having to queue up at the urinal.

Only a recruit in a room further down the corridor called Ojuku stayed away from the windows as he was on nodding terms with a half dozen kings out in Nigeria never mind princes and anyway he was a prince himself. Chalkie said they wouldn't give nowt for a prince where Ojuku comes from. After the events of this visit there was a lot of them leaning to the same way of thinking felt Logan.

The band struck up some obscure march known only to the bandsmen and some egotistical military composer as troops five and six marched onto the square led in front by the sword carrying Rory Calhoun.

To his right Clan Calhoun were massed more than at Culloden in 1746, completely taking over the one official stand made up of stacked gym benches on a platform of boarded scaffolding. There were Calhoun aunts and uncles there that even his mother hadn't met. Alongside them the invited families of the passing out troops had been stuffed unceremoniously into the back of the drill shed. Their view of events was as guaranteed as a Wimbledon centre court seat by queuing to get in. Theoretically it was possible.

Besides all this and to the front of the raised gym stand stood a much enlarged white podium. It took a full half hour saluting to get the brass on the stand and after much shuffling they got on Paddy the Wolfhound, the Duke himself, Brigadier General the Hon. Diarrmiud (Paddy) de Dildao D'Arcy, Colonel Cholmondeley and his long suffering cholmon the Adj. and every bit of spare military brass north of Watford gap and the greater Catterick Garrison area.

'If the enemies of the state threw a grenade at that podium they could wipe out the army's entire Northern Command' said Chalkie doubtlessly wishing he had one.

'I reckon there must be a fair percentage of the army's medals, pips, crowns and cross swords standing on that platform...it's amazing that the podium stands up' said Compton standing on his bed to get a better look.

'Bullshit doesn't weigh heavy' said Chalkie 'all this fuss, you'd think the Queen was coming.'

The parade was into the fourth march past in column of route and the two troops were beginning to get into the swing of things and a bit of swagger was coming in due to the band. Calhoun had taken to discreet waving to relatives with his free hand along with a supercilious leer to whoever came into eye contact. One more march past the podium with an eyes right salute, a turn or two at the corners of the square and a halt of the parade before the podium. 'Parade...parade...halt...right turn' came the shouted order.

'Psst' went the piss man as boots hit the ground in a crunch to face the podium.

The band knocks off with a double hit on the big drum to an eerie silence but for the sound of a lone crow in the distance and the lesser girly crunch of an officer shoe on shale as Major Rory Calhoun officer commanding troops five and six now marches to centre stage. He approaches the podium, halts before the Duke and salutes with a slow expansive wave of his Wilkinson sword.

'Permission to dismiss the parade and march orf sir?'

Maximum flash of cameras and whirl of Super Eight, slight pause for good effect and it was all over but for the last triumphant march past the podium. With the end in sight a sudden surge of adrenalin ran through the squad filling it with a collective new found exuberance. They feared nothing. Fear of mistake now gone the pace began to quicken as the front rank lost syncopation with the big base drum. Crunch of boot on shale went mid beat and the squad lost the step.

'Fuck' said the bandmaster trying to help by slowing down the beat.

A frantic ripple of corrective double shuffle stepping ran through the ranks like the quickening wheels of a steam locomotive on an incline. Fearful too that his shouted order would not be heard by the men to his rear Calhoun raised his voice to the absolute maximum an officer can go to without losing his accent. The 'eyes right' snapped into the ranks of the leading troop who as a man moved their heads and eyes in the direction of the podium.

Calhoun's sword hand moved out and forward and would have completed the expansive manoeuvre of a full salute on the march had not his heel come down at that very moment on a small circular piece of abandoned metal. It was Logan's lost fly button.

'Fuck' said Calhoun in a language most unbecoming of an officer and gentleman.

The movement of right foot forward, back, to the left and then forward again is an amazing action to follow but when completed without the second foot being in contact with parade ground it had all the signs of being entirely dangerous. A resultant stumble might have been checked had not the sword's scabbard, now discarded by controlling hand in an attempt to keep balance, fallen between the major's splaying legs.

Calhoun went full arse over tit and would have done so entirely on his own had not the front rank caught up with him. Eyes still to the right as they were they marched on and into the pirouetting major to fall in a combined and ugly heap of officer and other rank before the podium. The second rank now caught up and arrived, tripped and went to shale quickly followed by the third and fourth ranks. With eyes right and oblivious of the mayhem at the front the troop marched ever onwards. They went down to a man.

It was a pile still growing when the Duke assumed command as senior officer on parade and called a halt to it. Thankfully the man had left his side by side Purdey in the red chopper or he might have been tempted to answer

Calhoun's pitiful cry from the epicentre of the mayhem.

'Shoot me please...somebody...shoot me.'

'I'd have done it' Chalkie said but I think they all would.

7

After a morning of drill followed by cleaning the block until it shone well enough for the evil eye of Corporal Jock they were released to the weekend. The intake was glad to see the back of him reflect off the corridor floor and down the steps to the corporal's mess for his pint of heavy and a wee dram. It was Saturday and with nothing to do for a whole day and a half until first works parade Monday the feeling was glorious.

With the once a week only option for a lie in on Sunday first thoughts immediately went to the Saturday night out and how best to get pissed. With only the Harewood or the NAAFI on camp the how best to was quickly settled as second first thoughts went to the dance and the chances of pulling something that had over the weeks fallen from something to frankly anything. Inevitably they would fail yet again Logan felt although Chalkie this week was sounding more optimistic as he proudly announced to the room that he was on first name terms with two girls from the WRAC camp.

'You two don't have a cat's chance at the Harewood' said Scouse as he watched the preparations move into full over splash of Old Spice, 'even I haven't pulled in there yet.'

'Don't bet on it' said Logan wishing he hadn't.

'A bet?' said Scouse sensing easy money.

Logan and Chalkie set out for the Harewood with a mission convinced this was their lucky night. A similar feeling makes people fill out football pools and buy raffle tickets. Deep down they know they can't possibly win or in the case of the Harewood pull.

As the evening progressed and beer took hold of common sense both felt they were still in with a chance. That this was a feeling likely held by two or three hundred others seemed not to dampen spirits. Saturday night the Harewood took on a smell all of its own and reeked of Old Spice and Max Factor well into Monday before turning to Dettol. Amazing faith in miracles is what this is thought Logan but with Chalkie on first name terms a quid bet with Scouse was well on thought Logan becoming more optimistic as the drink took greater hold. He was ready to try anything and would need to.

The girls in question on first name terms with Chalkie were known by the collective names of the cousins. It was a convenient title that suited both of their mothers who not surprisingly were known collectively as the sisters. Somehow the cousins had contrived to join up at approximately the same time for little more than the good time they were clearly enjoying from where Logan was watching the queue. In truth the girls were a couple of crackers or as Chalkie said well worth one.

'For a man living in the 1960s that really is an unacceptable and Chauvinistic term Chalkie, if you don't mind my saying so mate' said Logan making him apologize although he had it spot on for the shorter one of the two.

In a pelmet mini skirt looking like a belt and knee length brown suede boots she had the pulling power of an industrial magnet and the looks of a two armed Venus de Milo.

'Never was so much offered to so many by those two lovelies' said Logan and acknowledging that it was true of the girls also.

Clearly money would have to change hands to pull either girl for Chalkie and some of it clearly was in the form of exotic drinks from all sat within lecherous range of the two WRAC lovelies. Even with Chalkie on first name terms it was a mission impossible and especially when the Chalkie first name terms relationship dissolved into only knowing their names; something just slightly up from knowing that they both had names in Logan's view. Both men sulked away to the far side of the bar to wallow in self-pity reflective of a mission impossible.

The earlier time spent in the dance had been a disastrous failure as Logan for one couldn't jive and Chalkie had twisted his back trying to do a flash drop to the ground move during a Chubby Checker twist up which did his back in he said. This left only the slow ones where everyone then paired up with their regular gropers.

'You're not helping by asking if they want to sheck their pelts frankly Chalkie if I'm really being honest even if it works in Leeds.'

'Classic failure of the dance hall for pulling is this' said Chalkie.

'What is?' said Logan trying to keep up. He was only half listening as his eyes scanned the room for strays.

'Going dancing if you can't dance...you have no chance at the ones that are easy to do as everyone is up and you can't do the ones that are hard to do when no one's up. Rest of the time the girls form a ring around their bags and dance together. It's a Brownie toadstool thing...a communal grouping around a pot to pound the maize thing don't you think?'

'Right' said Logan making a conversation of it although it went way over his head. After several visits split between bar and the dance floor and a line of black stamps rising high up their arms they decided to give up, stay in the bar and get pissed. The night would be an ogle at what was in there already matched up or about to be lined up for the end of the evening stagger home.

'Fish and chips on't way back then?' said Chalkie looking to end the night on a high note and getting Logan's vote as they entered the bar 'for a last couple of drinks on your mate Chalkie.'

'It's your bloody round anyway Chalkie.'

'Is it?' asked Chalkie at the bar.

'So go on then what are their names?' asked Logan looking to at least take something from the evening other than the sore head he was sure of when one of the girls approached unseen behind him and heading for a powdered nose.

'Roxanne' whispered Chalkie as she passed.

'Roxanne!' said Logan somewhat over loudly even for the noisy bar as he turned to look back only to come face to face with the very girl in question. Eyes met at the precise moment of Logan repeating her name.

'Yes?' she said momentarily pausing before moving away from the dumbstruck Logan and the raised warning eyebrows and shake of head of Chalkie that arrived too late.

'And the other one with the big knockers is called...just look at them, like two puppies under a blanket' he said moving his eyes back to the table just in time to catch a wiggle wobble from the girl remaining at the table.

Pretty well it was all just too painful to watch and when Roxanne returned they decided not to. Leaving their glasses at the side of the bar they headed off for a last scout around the dance floor before an early cod and chips ahead of the rush. With just ten minutes left before the dance closed the room had packed full with similar lost souls having the same last ditch strolls looking for and certain to get inevitable disappointment. What was now on the floor had turned into a tangled mess of arms and necks and had paired and what was off the floor was incomparable. A move back to the bar was the only sensible option where the rush there had left last orders called early. Shutters were already starting to come down as they entered and they were lucky to retrieve their drinks.

MP's now appeared to intimidate the bar encouraging all to drink up early and head off including the cousins and their entourage of amorous would be suitors. Each hanging on in there maximizing their investment to the point of harassment and eager to be the chosen one. From the look of it neither girl had interest in any of them felt Logan.

'Take your pick for the walk up the road, bet it's that loud mouthed one pulls the one with the big pair of...' said Chalkie talking to himself as Logan suddenly up and left him to approach the table.

Bending slowly to be within earshot of only Roxanne Logan whispered quietly to her ear as the table went into an astonished hush. The girl now nodded silently as Logan backed away to return to the equally astonished Chalkie. Finishing his drink Logan placed it next to the line of growing empties before turning back.

'Roxanne' he said looking over to the table.

'Yes Logan' said the girl quietly her eyes fluttering sweetly.

'Ready?'

Both girls stood and walked submissively to him before taking an arm each and leaving the room. Behind them an astonished bar watched in silent disbelief as they made their way out of the Harewood and on up the road towards the WRAC camp.

'Come on you lot, let's be having you' said the voice of a red cap MP looking to clear the bar of the dregs.

Away at the WRAC camp Logan and the girls arrived at the group gathered before the gates saying last goodnights as others left the cover of the well trampled bushes opposite with a final adjustment of dress and hair before reporting in. Both girls paused at the gates, gave a peck to each of Logan's cheeks and entered without looking back.

Logan made his lonely way back down the road and onto his own camp where the guardroom groupings were of an entirely different kind with someone having a kit check carrots and all and a group emerging from the bushes with a final adjustment of dress having been caught short at the gate. He entered the barrack room with Chalkie still expanding on a story growing by the telling and was in bed and well asleep before the man had finished giving it to the late arriving Scouse.

'Pulled just like that he did...the bastard' Chalkie kept saying bastard like he had just witnessed a miracle.

'Just like that' said Brum joining in 'the bastard!'

'Two words in her ear and she stands like a woman in a trance...yes Logan she says all submissive...and then the other one, the one with the huge...' Chalkie's hands outlined the shape of a good sized melon.

'Oh I know them, I likes her I does' said the Brum shaking his head with envious disgust at Logan's fortune as the words jammy and bastard echoed around the room like a lecher's chorus from those still awake.

Logan slept soundly through it all with a smile to his face that lasted until well into the next day.

'Roxanne, you and your mate here are going to have a hell of a job getting out alive past this lot. My name's Logan and if you want out I will take you to camp and leave you at the gates. Nod if you think it a good idea and I will say Roxanne ready.'

'Yes Logan' purred the girl in his dreams.

'Jammy bastard' said the Scouse as he paid up the next day.

'So what happened?' asked Chalkie for the tenth time since breakfast.

'Nothing, I just walked them to the camp and left them at the gates like I said last night.'

'Oh yeh...go on then. So what really happened, come on Logan?'

'Nothing honestly, nothing happened.'

'Oh yeah...oh yeah, go on then what happened.'

Chalkie was still going on with his nudge, nudge wink, winks as Logan began to get ready to go out later that day. Sunday evening was usually broke night but with money in his pocket from the Scouse why not he was thinking and anyway it served to add even more mystery to the event and his increasingly growing reputation.

'Which one are you meeting up with tonight then or are you giving them both one...again?' asked Chalkie snatching back his Old Spice bottle and shaking it for content before locking it safely away in his locker. 'Cost money does that stuff, you're splashing it on like it was free.'

Chalkie thought about that one for a moment before returning to the interrogation of Logan convinced as they all were he was off on the razz.

'I'm meeting nobody' said Logan to the room telling the truth of it with the sincerity of face that belies a lie before smoothing down his eyebrows checking his teeth in the mirror and wishing the room one and all 'a very good evening' ending with 'and don't wait up' that deserved the howls and near miss of the flying shoe as he left the room.

Oh how we laughed he said to himself as the howls behind him echoed down the corridor and out into the night. He was heading for the Harewood and on Sunday and with Scouse's cash in his pocket and didn't he love it.

The Harewood on Sunday took on an entirely different feel. It was almost empty for one as it turned into more the sports and leisure club that was the original charitable intention of Lord Harewood who knew nothing about Catterick and randy soldiers. Only this, the dance and the myth of the traditional British Saturday night out turned the Harewood into the Sodom and Gomorrah of Catterick. Likely one day it would receive the attention of Yahweh but not so on Sunday where the pong of stale beer was taken over by the ping of the returning ball to bat coming from the halls upstairs.

Taken by the quiet of the place for one and the emptiness of a closed Long Bar for another Logan ventured upstairs following the noise and shrieks of distant female voices. To his amazement he walked into a knock out game of table tennis keenly attended by several girls from the camp and looking entirely different dressed as they were for a different kind of sport. Not unnaturally Logan decided to hang around to watch as he was always a keen fan of sport and girls in shorts and as his eyes grew used to the dim light surrounding the lighted tables a voice came to him from his side.

'Hello Logan' said the voice of Roxanne.

The interest in the game of table tennis was never greater than at that moment and it stayed with Logan well into the final game of the evening where the urge to join in with the mixed doubles was still on his mind as they entered the

WRAC camp. Somewhere in Logan's mind the camp was a forbidden fortress, a place of female mystery where man does not get to go. A bit of a mix between Nirvana and a Shangri-La he thought but the NAAFI was packed with an invited lucky few there by kind invitation of love struck ladies.

Deposited at the canteen door Roxanne left with the other girls to shower and change promising to return leaving Logan with a coffee and a biscuit sitting alone and feeling very much like a spare at a wedding. Watching couples holding hands over a cruet set just didn't do it for Logan and when the door to the television room opened to his side he escaped to await Roxanne in the anonymity of a darkened room. It had been a long day and a busy weekend and Logan stifled a yawn as the news bored on into the empty dark of the room.

The sound of the television end of transmission tone woke him with a jolt as the tone disappeared with the returning voice of the announcer.

'And you won't forget to turn your television off will you' said the voice before the annoying tone resumed. Turning to leave the room the duty sergeant, a woman of some noticeable charm in the half light from the door clicked the switch and was suddenly aware of the waking Logan alone in the room. She was at him in a second.

'I had no chance' said Logan relating the story to Chalkie, 'bloody woman was all over me, I was powerless to refuse I was, anyway she outranked me'

'That's crap Logan, you could have called out.'

'I did...well I did the second time' said Logan with the sincerity of face that belies a lie.

8

This morning Logan awoke to the strangest of floating sensations and it was when his head bounced for the second time that he fully realised his awakening had been in a position somewhat equidistant between ceiling and floor. Only when the mattress dropped down over him that he realised fully where he was.

The screams and protestations of the occupant first bed from the door was a guaranteed alarm call for the whole barrack room. Once dumped, the occupant was surely awake and immediately let everyone in the room know about it. Bells, buzzers, bugles and bombs had all down the ages been known to fail but the foul-mouthed utterings from beneath an upturned bed could awake a eunuch's sex drive.

It saved Corporal Smedley from having to go back into the room in the sure knowledge that at least one person was incredibly awake if not minus some strategic part of their anatomy. Deciding that he really couldn't get used to the man's cunningly clever waking device every morning Logan swapped bed spaces with Chalkie who was an early riser. Smedley or Shitehead Smedley as he became quickly known to the troop was a late arrival to the training cadre having been posted in from Hades. From the first day there was not one doubting mind as to where Smedley had come from and by the second day everyone knew they would like to see him go to. That one man could produce so much ill content and so quickly was due in part to his late arrival where all had grown used to Jock's rantings and Head's little aberrations once it was established that both were just a sad couple of army daft psychotics or daft army twats as Chalkie had it.

Smedley however, was something extra, he was weird with it. Some like Taff thought him to be an alien and said so to the room.

'You mean he is alien Taff not an alien' corrected Compton.

'Correct' said Chalkie.

'No' said Taff sounding like he had thought it through 'I mean he is an alien, not of our world, see. A visitor.'

'I think from his accent you'll find he's from Smethwick' said Brum dissecting the strangulated vowel of a Birmingham accent with a precision of a few hundred yards as only the Brummagem ear can.

Maybe Taff's right thought Logan having never been to Smethwick but had heard about it as they all had other than Taff who must have thought it a planet as he continued with the theme.

'It's something to do with the pointy ears or his droopy lobes or those sneaky eyes darting left and right then down and then up, that stare at you through his eyebrows.'

'Oh that' said Brum like it was nothing unusual.

'Or the nervous tic and jerky upward twitch of shoulders and the body twitches like the man was waiting for his cogs to catch up with his windings?' said Compton also now taken with the concept. 'It's like watching an automaton twitch before springing to life.'

'A life of sod all use to nowt but army' said Chalkie.

'Add that invented clipped falsetto yelp of a voice and the annoying deliberate swagger to his walk and you have the man' put in Logan.

'Or the bits you can see on't surface...goes deep down does weirdo.'

'Add in an IQ of a wooden plank and oversized ego, throw in smarmy and nasty then put him in charge of a squad of recruits...and what have you got?' asked Compton.

'A right bastard' Logan said.

'Don't you like him then?' said Brum getting the general feeling from Logan that he was still hurting from being dumped out of bed the week before, 'I don't think he's from Smethwick now I get me ear on him he's more Wolverhampton and black country...a bloody yamyam if you ask us.

'I had a cousin from the black country' said Taff 'never knew they were called that, the family never called him that.'

'So what did you call him then?' asked Logan.

'Eric' said Taff as the room went deathly silent but for the sound of the groan.

Flying mattresses apart the first indications that Smedley was strange came early with his insistence of a change to the established timing of the marching pace. Ingrained over the weeks of repetition and now into their psyche it was at the very core of their drill and some were even brushing teeth to it.

'And masticating too' put in Compton.

'Really?' asked Brum having a think about it.

'For no other reason than to get his own way' said Compton to the nodding heads.

It was a game of them and him and an egocentric power thing that had the correct and faster pace given by Jock at the rear at times catching the feet of the slower marching men to the pace called by Smedley. With the rear ranks at odds with the front and the front ranks at odds with the rear naturally those in the middle wavered and being neither right nor wrong were left stranded somewhere between the two. Terrible as this was when working as a pair, working alone without his controller Corporal Smedley was a dog unleashed. Seven troop were in the control of a man out of control felt Logan.

Smedley liked being a bastard, he was good at it and would deliberately put the squad wrong just to enjoy the bollocking was how most saw it. Calling the wrong timing on the march or throwing the squad out of step by slowing the pace were two of his favourites alongside delaying the second part of a right or left turn. This immediately split the squad into an infant ballet class, half poised stalk like with one leg raised and on a wobble as the remainder balanced toe and heel and rocking like a line of weebles.

'It's just another power thing' said Logan falling over.

Some days in to the arrival of Smedley the troop were marched to the square for their regular morning drill. Barely dawn and cold enough to freeze nuts the overnight wind had formed the shale into frozen lumps that crunched underfoot as boot hit icy parade ground. As the wind picked up with the coming light the wind chill sent the temperature down through the pain threshold to somewhere sub numb. Freezing was just too warm a word for this morning as the squad approached the square in a rising mist of frozen breath and early morning smoker's cough. Late to arrive due to a miscount at roll call that twice missed Shorty Hardcastle in the dark the parade ground was already full to the sound of shouted orders and rising steam of men on the bash.

As the troop arrived they found Smedley sheltering from the bitter wind in the rear of the drill shed, it was not a day to be hanging around. Nipping his fag for later as they approached the man beamed as Jock handed the squad over before leaving for the troop office on some urgent business to attend to by the radiator with a hot pint of tea and two sugars.

Squads were already deserting the square and heading for cover and alternative duties as Smedley addressed the ranks. On cold early starts it was the practice to keep the squad moving and seven troop had arrived at the double. Slightly sweated and now at attention Smedley immediately placed them at ease but not easy as they were to a man in desperate need of movement. For once even Logan wanted to start marching.

Soon to spot the distress he was causing Smedley decided he would inspect his charge and moved slowly through the ranks with a meticulously picky eye. No button left unturned, no tie off centre, no epaulette over collar and no one left in doubt; the man was a grade one bastard. Wind ripped through and into them howling in from across the open square as slowly at first the men began to shiver. Protesting voices began to sound from the squad and growing louder by the second. Before long an involuntary shivering took over the entire body of men.

'Stand bloody still' blared Smedley as chattering of teeth and a communal shiver ran down the ranks like an infecting rash.

Taking the body's natural defence against the cold as an unacceptable insubordination of an order Corporal Smedley began to rant and scream at men and nature both as he moved down the lines repeating the order to stand still. Too dumb to realize the cause of the shiver was that which he was ordering them to do Smedley continued to rave as the shivering continued. He was losing control of the squad as men went into open dissent of the order, rubbing arms and stamping their feet to keep warm. To a man they were on the point of mutiny. Shouts of anger came from about the squad before Smedley backed down and marched them from the square to extra barracks cleaning.

'The man clearly has to go' said Logan.

'If only the bastard would' said Brum currying favour in the room and taking it in the neck for Smedley being a man of the midlands even if he was a yamyam.

With Smedley disowned by his near neighbours if not his kith and kin and still recovering well into the afternoon from the chills of the morning Logan, Brum and Chalkie decided on a warming Newcastle Brown that turned into several until they ran out of money, Chalkie first.

A staggered return to the barracks lay as a right angle around the square and with the wind howling and the sudden drop in temperature plus the darkness of the evening Logan for one decided he was for a more direct route. It was a brave move brought on by the best of Newcastle as they hurried across the square spurred on by the howling call of the wind, when another side of nature called. Never one to refuse the call of nature Logan turned back to wind to the relief of himself and the others up wind who now joined in with the joke with much noisy laughter until there came a searching beam from a single light.

'Pervert!' shouted Logan as the light of the guard on stag duty approached for a closer look.

First to slip away and button up Logan made off at speed to barracks arriving well ahead of the others and was straining to see out from an open first floor window as Brum and Chalkie approached below. Behind them in full pursuit but not gaining was the man on guard slowed only by the blowing of his whistle and the dropping of a pickaxe handle. Making straight for the stairs and going at quite a pace for drunks Chalkie and Brum were soon alongside Logan.

Now at the entrance the guard paused beneath the light to look up and return the abuse raining down from the window. After much crude and ignoble gesturing from all three safe as they were within the confines of barracks, suddenly the jeering stopped and the silhouettes disappeared inside only to return within seconds. There in clear silhouette shone the hairy shape of a well rounded Brummie arse.

Moving closer to hear or nearer to have a better look would never be known for sure but approach the man did spurred in no small way by the sound and sight of an approaching red sash and the noise of a very loud fart. Attracted by the whistle and the jeers from above the duty guard commander now came on the scene largely ignorant of events overhead. He arrived at the precise moment the water from three fire buckets hit the general vicinity to be immediately followed by the empty buckets for full and good measure.

Off and away before the buckets even landed and well ahead of the scream the three raced on up to the next floor and the sanctuary of their room. They were in bed feigning sleep long before the guard picked up the unfortunate duty corporal who largely ignorant of events was recovering with a pain in the head to match the pain in the arse he was to all who knew him. For it was none other than the evil Smedley.

'On the night of the fourteenth, did you Corporal Smedley get a good eyeball at any of them what was the cause of the affray before you were hit by this ere exhibit A. Namely and to whit the bucket?' said the RP sergeant looking to solve the crime of the year and playing up before the members of the enquiry sat behind a bench.

It was a no brainer or actually it was a brainer explained the RP adding that the guard on stag was clueless as to who or what had 'it em' and remained in deep shock 'at what he had seen that night' even now. The RP sergeant paced the room before turning to the bench.

'No sir' said Smedley as he turned.

'No sir, he did not! As the light of the window shone out and behind the perpetrators of this diabolic occurrence on the evening of the day before yesterday' said the RP sergeant turning to Colonel Sam and answering his own daft question before grasping the lapels of his battle dress.

'No' said the pathetic and feeble voice of a smarting Smedley behind him as he adjusted his head bandage to miss his lump.

'Just a bit of the bucket before it all went black and it was all too dark...there was no moon.'

'Ah, I thought you said one of them, how do I say... displayed himself Corporal Smedley?' said Major Calhoun finding the business of it all rather distasteful but going through the motions as he was taking notes for the colonel.'

'Not that kind of moon sir' said the RP 'it was hovercast and blowing han ooley.'

'So do you remember anything at all then Corporal Smedley?' asked the colonel sympathetically.

'Just the hairy arse sir I will remember that arse to my dying day I will. It was horrible sir.'

'Would you recognise it in a line up' asked the RP somewhat over crudely and raising a look of shock with just the hint of expectation on the faces of both officers that suggested something of an earlier memory.

The colonel quickly dismissed the spectacle as likely to bring back too many unsavoury memories for Smedley and likely you too thought Calhoun to himself recalling he was just two terms after the colonel at school but said nothing.

'Could you describe it again Corporal Smedley?' said the colonel pressing the issue.

'Big and round sir.'

'No not the moon, the incident leading up to it man.'

That the moon was shining or not mattered little to the outcome of the enquiry and that the wet footprints led up the stairs to the second floor before drying out mid corridor clinched the enquiry outcome for both the colonel and Calhoun. An unprovoked attack with a far flung bucket by person or persons unknown that caused damage to military property.

'Namely, the said corporal...' said Calhoun writing in the report.

'Namely the said bucket' corrected the colonel somewhat unsympathetic to Smedley's wound. 'Moreover and not withstanding the effrontery to piss on my parade ground...disgraceful. Only the white horse at RMC Sandhurst gets to piss on an army parade ground, and the adjutants Labrador of course.'

In the days that followed the suspect rooms beyond the footprints were questioned by the

RP's who received only blank looks to add to the deaf ears. It established that nobody heard a thing in the entire length of the corridor and that room three were all soundly asleep thirty minutes before lights out. Clearly they were lying through their arses but short of having a bend over bum inspection line up to find a hairy one there was no proof. The case against room three ground to a halt or so it was thought until returning from the cookhouse two days later Logan entered the room ahead of the others. The reflection of a lurking RP hiding behind the end locker could be seen in the window and as clear as a mirror. Logan turned to the others pointing frantically to the locker as they entered.

'You know all my friends, here in room three...what gets me in all this...is that the entire camp knows, do they not that it was those that is in the next block what done it for the poor drill corporal' he said nodding wildly towards the locker and winking like he had a nervous tic as Chalkie now took it on.

'Straight up...cor lummy how very right you are there my good friend. Appen, that is also what I have been led to believe from hearing two of them...from that other block...talking in the NAAFI bogs when I was in there when caught short t'other day.

'Ah, you must have heard the same rumour what I have also overheard...oh look room three...it is time to leave for parade...and we do not want to be late for parade for our corporal do we fellows.'

'Nooh...' said everyone in unison.

With that they left early for parade and when all went quiet in the corridor outside the RP slid out from behind the locker clutching his pad and pencil. He made his way hot foot to the guardroom.

'That seven troop serge. You know I said they were some right thick bastards in that troop the other week after fire ose training?'

'Oh yeah...'

'Well they are all in room three serge, but I got an important lead by going under cover' said the RP corporal reading down his notes, 'it was those what is in the next block what done it for the poor drill corporal.'

Calhoun received the information with some relief as blame passed over to an adjacent block not of his direct responsibility. The case went immediately cold leaving Smedley with a posting to eight troop and still smarting at the injustice of it all that changed the man from being a right bastard to being just a bastard. Never after discussed it was an outcome to be proud of although everyone knew which arse was big and hairy in seven troop including Corporal Jock who had the truth of it snitched by a toady sometime after the event. He didn't like Smedley either as the man messed with the pace of his squad and so kept quiet but he did keep a wary eye on the fire buckets until well after seven troop passed out later the following month.

9

Corporal Jock assembled the troop into three ranks and set off for yet another mystery tour of the camp. Although it was there on orders Logan hadn't looked and Shorty had not been lifted so it was a mystery to both of them when the squad halted alongside a green board marked A E D. Appearing as they did in Jock's typed orders the evening before they had many guessing. You could have got evens on a spelling mistake and 100 to 8 that it was Jock's word for head.

Clearly everyone with brain to think had the A as army and the intellectuals amongst the troop got the D as department. This left a long list for the letter E that produced everything from effluent to execution. Not until they were dismissed to enter the building and take a desk that they found it was the Army Education Department.

'You wouldn't have thought the army would have one would you?' said Logan sounding genuinely surprised.

The words education and army did not easily sit side by side to Logan's mind.

'It's like putting chalk with cheese or officer with gentleman' said Chalkie to someone at the back.

'They are probably the clearest definition that can be given of an oxymoron' said Compton to a line of blank faces...'It's an oxymoron...' he continued to explain before giving up and sitting down at a free desk.

'Call me one of those again and you're looking for a smack in the gob alright mate' said one of the Londoners.

'Sit to attention' shouted Corporal Jock at the back as a door opened to the education officer and two of his little monitor helpers.

'Sit at ease seven troop' said the captain bending his officer cane before placing it across a lectern in a practised way that got everyone's attention. Bums began to squirm around the room as memories of school returned and there was even a discernible ooh from someone at the front. I've wondered about him from day one Logan whispered to Chalkie. All eyes now watched as his helpers began to hand out sets of papers print face down. From the silence it was an ominous sign for many as a 'don't turn your papers over until I tell you' feeling fell about the room.

'Don't turn your paper over until I tell you' shouted out the captain sticking to form and in that practised authoritative tone that defines the teacher.

'Knew it...a test' said Chalkie moving his hand away from the paper.

'Supercilious bastard' said Logan nudging his paper up the desk.

'Don't!' said one of the little helpers as someone tried a sneak peek.

'You have all done one of these before at the recruitment office' said the officer as men shuffled nervously in their seats. 'They are aptitude tests...aptitude, a good word.'

The captain went to the board and taking a chalk wrote in capitals the word APTITUDE before turning to face the room.

'Aptitude. A good word...meaning? Natural ability,' he said at length brushing his chalky palms and answering himself in that annoyingly condescending way some develop from a life spent cloaked in chalk dust. Like everyone didn't know that.

'I didn't know that' said Taff quietly to Brum.

'Dumb shit' said Brum, 'I knew that.'

Returning to the board the captain took up the chalk to write another heading PSYCHOMETRIC TESTING.

'Now then' he said turning back to the room and clearing his throat. 'Now, who here can tell me what that is?'

'Don't you know sir?' asked Logan to the amusement of the class and annoyance of the officer.

'Name' said the captain.

Five minutes later and Logan's name in the naughty book the papers were turned over and the testing began. It was the first of a series of similar written examinations set over the weeks in order to classify for the army what it had ended up with and what best to do with it. Nothing would be thrown away although some of it had been dumped, missed or given up on by the nation years before. Raising the level of all by ten percent was of more use to the army than ten percent raised to a level of a university degree said Compton at his side.

'Five hundred words discuss' said Logan as Brum set to with a fury thumping away with his little metaphorical hammer forcing triangles into squares and leaving the circles for after the milk break.

In part the papers took the form of the usual multiple answer questions and matching dominoes or little stick men with black and white flags into sets before developing down the paper into combinations so obscure they had to have been produced by a sick mind or someone having a laugh as Chalkie said.

After a series of these and having a natural hatred of teachers Logan set to in a concentrated effort and even managed a stab at a few on the last page. Towards the end he was working on the logic that a one in three chance of a right answer isn't that bad odds and that any correct answers for the hard ones must really cock the system up. Teach you to put me in the naughty book he thought to himself as he handed his papers in before leaving for play time.

Included within the new classification was the army's own IQ bandings called Standard Gradings the officer explained. These were required for certain levels of training. An SG5 was the minimum needed for digging a hole as the captain explained at Logan's post test interview, whereas an SG1 was needed for certain technical training. Like telling them where to dig thought Logan but remained silent.

'In brief it tells us at a stroke what the man is capable of taking in and if he would pass the training...we can't all spend our time sat behind desks now can we?' said the captain teacher sitting behind a desk.

'Them that can, do...sir' said Logan annoying the captain who concluded the interview with an under the glasses leer at his paper and twitch of index finger that said run along now.

'Send the next man in' said the captain dismissively and not even looking up as Logan saluted the top of his head.

His fate decided according to the Education Officer Logan left the room and closed the door. 'Just hang around, he will come out for you in five minutes' he said to the next man as he left for the barracks. 'He's busy pickling one of his heads.'

Back in his room Logan discovered from Compton who seemed to be in the know about these things, that an SG2 was needed to become an officer. This to Logan's eyes explained a lot of what he was beginning to suspect about the army and it raised some disturbing questions. For one it stated that the intelligence needed to mend a radio was more than that required to tell someone to go mend it. Further, that the army officer corps was clearly realistic with the levels it laid down to recruit its own membership and that the idiot behind him shouting charge might not be qualified to wire a plug. But more than that for Logan was that the army actually knew all this. For Logan it was something of a moment of enlightenment. There's sod all we can do about it he said to Chalkie but then it's best to know as Chalkie said.

Choice of training for Logan had from the start been a radio operator on the assumption that radio meant HQ, which meant officers; three squares a day, roof over his head and some ways back from any action at the sharp end. Chalkie said it was always HQ that gets taken out by an air strike and in the films it was always the radio operator that gets it first.

'Shot full of holes with a burst from a machine gun just before he transmits the vital message' agreed Compton.

'Or a grenade through the window' put in Brum.

'Either that or he's sat at his radio happy as Larry tapping away on a Morse key, when a commando with a camouflage green stripe across his face and wearing a black bobble hat sneaks up behind and pulls out a fucking great big knife' said Chalkie.

'Or a home made piano wire cheese cutter' put in Compton.

Strangely Logan hadn't thought of it that way or that for every receiver at the blunt end there is a transmitter at the sharp end. His emergency application to become a clerk or a store man was rejected by the captain of education on the grounds that his SG1 was too high. You really would have thought they would try and keep the ones with intelligence, was how Logan put it to the captain feeling he must have added a few points on his score for making him get up from his desk.

Having realised too late that he had placed himself in what was now advised by Chalkie and the others as a potentially dangerous choice of occupation, Logan determined to protect himself by learning what he could in the remaining weeks. Weapon training for Logan now became a means of personal survival and he actually tried. When orders informed them they were off to the ranges he for one was ready although Brum was still harping back to the tests.

'I hates them IQ tests I do, did one once for an apprenticeship.

'Oh yes,' said Compton looking over from his bed, 'and?'

'I failed it...' said Brum.

10

Troop orders for the week had a surprise item for Friday that got everyone talking other than Shorty Hardcastle. After countless hours cleaning, stripping and putting it back together and what had been many weeks of marching with them they were finally going to fire their rifles. The week progressed with an intensity of weapons training until the day finally arrived and the troop loaded into a Bedford to head for the ranges. It was a first for most of the intake and knees were knocking in the back like a long line of Newton's cradles but not all due to the cold, as some were visibly fearful of firing their weapon.

There is something incredibly scary about loading up with live ammunition for the first time and it immediately occurred to Logan that the only safe gun on the range would be the one he would be holding. One minute he had in his hands a lump of wood and some machine tooled metal bits and the next a weapon. With every other weapon having the potential to point toward him simple maths made his a lone gun against all others. Logan was outgunned twenty muzzles to one and it just wasn't good odds.

Sergeant Head paraded the troop before the firing range, which was a flat plain grassed area set between raised banks two hundred yards apart and running the full length of the range towards a raised grass bank. Head referred to this rising bank as the butts, which he said was where the targets were. Compton said it was the name for the stump of a tree in Middle English times.

'The stump was where they stood the targets against' he said 'dates back to the time of the archer does the name butts.'

'Archery is correct' said Corporal Jock 'Where you got one in the butt if you were daft enough to stand close up.'

Either way it's up yonder was what Chalkie said putting an end to it for most of the intake who were more interested in watching the medics arrive with a mobile ambulance before being distracted by the arrival of the tea urn. Immediately behind the butts and rising into the morning mist was a much higher soil bank on top of which fluttered a red flag. Would this be the enemy thought Logan. Along the field and at measured intervals of one hundred yards were a series of ditches that turned out to be measured firing points.

There was Logan thought, an altogether silent eerie feel to the place made worst by the mist and cold of early morning. Head addressed the intake to explain the army's basic anti carnage rules standing alongside a man drinking something steaming from his own flask and wearing a bobble hat, ear muffs, gloves, a scarf and a sheepskin jacket. They had met their troop officer Lieutenant Snotty, as he became known from then on although it was a close run thing with Lieutenant Vick Vapour as the poor man reeked of the stuff.

'So he does exist' said Logan as Head asked and received permission to carry on followed by a chesty cough from Snotty.

'Now listen in you lot, we don't want anybody shot like last time' Head began before reading from a list of simple rules. First up was a gimme.

'Keep all bleeding rifles pointing down the bleeding range when they is bleeding loaded up.'

'And might one add also Sergeant Head, do instil on the men to exercise extreme caution and moreover, utmost care should be taken in the interests of range overall safety and range awareness so as not to direct their weapons in the vicinity of other attending personnel thereby increasing the inherent dangers associated with live range firing, Sergeant Head' interrupted the lieutenant.

'Sarrhh' said Head turning back to the intake, 'you heard the officer, don't point the fucking things at your mates or worst still shoot one of them...or one of us.'

Head deferred back to the officer for further comment before receiving a nod to carry on.

'And lastly don't look down the barrel if you get a bastard misfire like that twat did last month' said the sergeant before moving onto the orders for the butts.

Pretty much this was summed up with another gimme but timeless classic of never look over the top to check if the firing party are ready to fire. All simple enough stuff for anyone with a modicum of intelligence, which worried Logan for one as a sobering thought hit him as they lined up ready. Behind and around him were the barrels of his intake including that of the non-dexterous Compton.

Split into two groups of butts and firing point half their number were already making their way to the butts as Corporal Jock opened the ammunition and ordered each man to load two magazines. The intake moved forward with mixed emotions ranging from abject fear to eager excitement likely based on a genetic disposition to kill or be killed or so Compton would have it. Not altogether a happy thought felt Logan recalling that Compton would regularly drop his weapon in weapons training even on a good day. The man also held the troop 'leave off the safety catch' record and by the second week of training was unanimously voted 'the man most likely to kill a mate' in a straw poll taken by the armourer. By week three this had grown to three mates and the intake had yet to move onto machine-guns.

At the order for the troop to split into two groups nineteen men shuffled ten paces back leaving Compton alone on the firing point. Corporal Jock moved forward in annoyance and split the troop with his pace stick. Annoyingly for Logan his lot was to be with the Compton squad. Like it was standing next to a ticking bomb he was thinking.

Remembering the man's predilection towards hypochondria someone really should have checked the man out before letting him attend the ranges. A quick physical by the medics would have discovered his latest affliction was earache and, on discovery that he was to spend the day out on the ranges, Compton came suitably protected against the wind with olive oil soaked cotton wool rammed hard into both ears with a stick. The result of this protection was deafness to a level not far away from that laid down by the Royal Institute For The Deaf.

Naturally enough Compton completely missed certain elements of the brief on the safety rules of army ranges according to Sergeant Head. He would be playing this one by ear, or more accurately without them. This was further complicated by the distribution of the 'you what' rubber earplugs recently issued to all military training regiments by an army directive derived from a safety at work campaign that also forbade rusty bayonets under the Geneva Convention. Stuffing these to both ears would have a not unexpected effect on anyone but for Compton on top of cotton wadding it turned him absolutely and totally stony.

In isolation this would have been bad enough but everyone else now began stuffing their own issue plugs in ears. Seven troop instantly entered into a 'you what' phase where every sentence or word ended with the words 'I am speaking up you deaf bastard.' With all communication now returned by 'you what's?' Compton's own raised voice sounded natural enough to all within and without earshot.

Filling of magazines was accomplished well enough and the firing party gathered in a loose formation practising sign assisted speech and lip reading. A developing sense of survival came over Logan, which moved him progressively to the rear and away from where Compton now stood. The movement started a general exodus from the firing point when Corporal Jock called the squad to a halt and in the most unfair of decisions called forward the nearest and furthest away to fire first. Subsequently Logan found himself next to Compton on the firing point. On seeing the movement to his left Compton turned to give a deaf look.

'Army tradition on ranges is the firing of two rounds into the rising bank behind the butts and is an order to warm up the weapon.' Shouted Jock in explanation to the intake before ordering both men to make ready in the prone position.

'That is two warmers into the bank' said Head from behind the troop.

Compton following Logan's action as a shadow.

'Load!' ordered Corporal Jock in a full parade ground voice and scaring the shit out of everybody as is the army tradition to wake everyone up and advise those within earshot that weapons were loading at the firing point.

Both men now cocked their weapons and awaited the order to fire which again by tradition follows seconds later in muted voice, so as not to startle men with itchy fingers into a rushed shot or worse still letting off an un-aimed round.

'Two warming rounds into the bank, in your own time carry on' said the Jock adjusting his own ear defenders and sticking two fingers to ears in anticipation.

Compton, fully aware he was stony set on a plan of copying Logan's every move but a second or two behind. The scratching of his nose copy and rub of chin should have given Logan some warning and the itch of crotch must have been a dead give away to someone watching at the back but alongside and on the firing point all went unnoticed. They were as together as a couple of synchronised swimmers.

Logan removed his safety catch and fired his weapon to a resounding and entirely uneventful click of a round stuck in the breech malfunction.

'In your own time carry on' whispered the corporal for the second time.

'Malfunction' shouted Logan to the rear, as was his training.

'Unload' came the order back which he duly did taking magazine off to re-cock weapon to eject or clear the stuck round.

'Clear' shouted Logan as the malfunction was cleared from the weapon before standing up to await for inspection of the empty breach.

Compton, his complete shadow until then and oblivious to the click lost Logan on the magazine removal and saw no logic in removing the magazine from a perfectly fireable weapon. He was a man with a dilemma.

'In your own time carry on' said Jock agitated at the lack of loud bangs from the prone Compton. 'Carry on Compton. Fire when ready Compton...let one of the fuckers off Compton...for Pete's sake fire the bloody thing!'

Corporal Jock finally gave in to the frustration and moved forward to a point directly behind Compton's head.

'Fire!' shouted Jock in a shout that would have awakened dead.

Compton's head twitched straining on the air. He had heard something through the plugs and oiled wadding. Something was going on behind but what? Was it all over and why was Logan now standing alone alongside him? In desperation for clarity Compton raised himself up on one elbow and arching his back, turned from the firing point to shout for clarification of the position. The barrel of his loaded weapon followed his turning upper body.

There was a dramatic movement to ground as the entire troop ducked beneath the approaching barrel in an instinctive and spontaneous Mexican wave. Men fell down and rose in sequence as the mystified Compton sought clarification first to the left and then the right of the squad. With the entire troop now flat to the ground Compton's eyes finally stopped on Logan as the solitary person still standing.

'What's he say?' asked Compton.

'Fire' said Logan.

The round hit the firing point, ricocheted between the Jock's legs, went straight through the tea urn and came to rest in the spare tyre of the ambulance. Compton was overpowered at a rush and the weapon made safe. He was immediately charged by Jock with 'shooting a tea urn.'

At OC's orders the following day Major Calhoun, still bruising from the pass out parade read the charge sheet duly rewritten by the guiding hand of Sergeant Head.

'Indiscriminate discharge of an army weapon and damage to army property?' said the major.

'A standard issue ten gallon Royal Army Catering Corp tea urn' said the Sergeant Major.

'Full or empty?' asked Calhoun as if it mattered.

As a tea drinker Calhoun had the mind to give Compton several months nick when he heard the guardroom cells were full with AWOL from the last intake and so gave him extra duties and weapons training but only on the strict proviso that Compton promised never to do it again. With Compton under temporary disgrace cleaning the camp area and Calhoun's shoes and Sam Brown the troop got down to serious classification on the ranges. This transpired to be little more than the shooting of a modest number of holes into a cardboard target from varying distances observed the week before.

At five hundred yards a standard target is the width of a foresight but at fifty it's the size of a man. Having reasoned that it was a waste of time missing from five hundred or indeed from four, three and even two hundred yards Logan held onto his rounds until he had a reasonable chance of hitting something. Consequently he arrived at one hundred yards with virtually a full magazine and let rip.

At the count up out of a possible twenty hits he had managed twenty-seven and was given a maximum.

'That's not bad shooting even at one hundred yards' he said climbing up the grassy bank to look over the butts. He found Chalkie had been his opposite number raising the target and pasting over earlier hits with suitably cut pieces of coloured paper. Being the all round good egg that he was he had naturally assisted whoever was missing the target with the occasional pencil made hole. The action applied a natural justice to counter a nasty gusting wind on the day and put a whole new meaning to the phrase shot full of lead.

On the whole felt Logan the whole thing was luck of the draw thing with many combinations that could affect outcome. Clearly in the snap shoot the man shooting at Long Arms Miller's hand held target had more to shoot at than Wee Jock's and with Shorty Hardcastle it was just the top of a head complained Brum. And how about the target that just didn't come up? And what about number four coming up late?

'Number four never came up, number six is still coming up, number eight came up late at an angle, stuttered and went down again and nine fell over. What are you all down there in the butts, chicken?' said Jock speaking on the range telephone.

At the end of classification the troop had four marksmen, Logan and Chalkie by reciprocal arrangement and the two intakes firing either side of Cross-eyed Smith.

11

Corporal Jock this morning addressed the squad with a shake of his head and a surprising announcement for some. The intake were halfway through their training and some might even make it to the end. One of his little jokes thought Logan.

'This may come as surprise to those of yous who arrived here already half baked but you is half way through yous training. The easy first half.'

A stifled cheer went up from the back of the squad as Jock continued his piece. Things were going to get tougher now and training would be stepping up.

'And her majesty the Queen God bless her and the colonel who is above God have seen fit to issue yous lot a forty eight hour weekend pass...that is for them that wants it, ha!' Another of his little jokes felt Logan. 'Yes Hardcastle yous arm is up at the back I think, or is it Wee Jock?'

'How long's forty eight hours corporal' asked Shorty Hardcastle with an eye on the there and back again from Catterick to Mevagissy in Cornwall where his girlfriend lived.

'How long's a forty eight? A fucking long time for someone your size Hardcastle and a lot shorter for Miller and Lofty with his ead in the clouds at the end here right son? Now, for them that wants to go home to mummy and daddy and yous bastards what hasn't got any, or lost them or is unsure about it or was raised by their aunty Doris...or likes pasties we need your applications for rail warrant in the troop office by 1600 hours.'

Only Chalkie and the other Yorkies got a good deal as they were just about home anyway but Logan for one decided to go home just for the hell of it. The relief he felt on leaving Catterick Camp was something akin to the relief an Indian fakir must feel when the sword is pulled out and there is no blood spurt. Tightness gripped his stomach as the train slowed to enter the station. Before him spread the city lights of his youth, milling people and that heady early evening diesel and the rising smell of frying onions from the hot dog stand outside the station approach. He was back in civilisation.

Choice of what to do first was decided by flip of a coin. Heads it would be a pint of Boddingtons and tails he have two. On the fifth flip he realised he had yet to go home and savouring the last dregs of the beer of his adolescence he left the pub to the evening drunks and shouldering his bag hailed a taxi. The cab sped off away from the city and out into the mist of the night. Within twenty minutes they were pulling into the red brick rows of houses that had been Logan's entire world only weeks before.

He had been told that the first time back is a special time for every returning soldier and so it was for Logan as memories returned with the sights and places that he knew so well. Memories of childhood long gone and thought forgotten came flooding back...bitter sweet times of growing up and everywhere so much smaller than he remembered. Logan smiled, it is always like that he said to himself as he wiped clear the misted window of the taxi to peer out into the gloom of the night. Nothing was as he remembered, even after these few short weeks. A lamppost he had forgotten ever existed shone light into the murk of the evening and those lazy heady days of times past. Logan paid the driver and tipped handsomely before with eyes closed he turned to savour the moment of his first return. The bloody taxi had only dropped him in the wrong bloody avenue.

He arrived at the house to find it empty but for a note. The note explained the family absence.

Dear Son,

Aunt Florrie's eaten something that didn't agree with her again. Sorry to miss your first leave but I am away looking after her until late on Sunday. Please feed the cat. There's cat food in the kitchen and milk. Help yourself if you want something to eat.

Love,

Your mother.

PS Saw Bernice the other day, she's certainly put a lot of weight since you left.

Striking out for the pub washed and changed Logan left the cat food for the cat and was entering into the bright lights of his local within the hour. The landlord greeted him with a pint on the house and asked when he was going back.

'Sunday' said Logan smiling.

'Sunday? said the landlord nodding as if it meant something to him as the 'so soon' that followed did to Logan. 'Hardly worth it for the one night is it son?'

He's never been to Catterick thought Logan but said nothing as he moved away from the bar. Nothing had changed, neither place nor people but in some inexplicable way Logan knew he had. After a time and growing increasingly tired of the bum notes from Elsie on the piano and continually being asked when he was going back from bar to loo he left for a look around old haunts. On the way he passed the British Legion. It was a place he had passed many times before without giving it a second glance, as it was always never a place to go. Suddenly amused with the reality that he was now at least to some part military and it being an ex serviceman's club Logan felt drawn to enter.

A modest queue had stopped before a small signing in table and a book where a youth in an oversized dinner jacket was pointing to a members only sign. Before him stood a man of obvious war service years, who as Logan overheard, was attempting to enter a branch of which he was not a member. This, the youth explained with assured assertion bordering on rudeness was not possible.

'As although we are a registered service charity we are also a private club' said the youth waving others in and doing his best with the raffle ticket tin as they passed through.

At length the raised voices brought forth a duty committee member similarly attired who confirmed this as true fact.

'Apologies and all as a member of the legion and an ex serviceman but you are not a member of this club.'

Besides this continuing minor fracas members were passing through the swing door on a nod of recognition with the doorman who looked to Logan's eye to be as far removed from military as an Action Man he said quietly at the back. This sudden realization surprised Logan as he had always assumed the place an ex serviceman's club.

Not being in the best of moods at being held back at the door in the cold Logan waded in on the side of the uniform which it emerged from the argument had never been on the back of the committee member either. Somehow an ex serviceman not being allowed to enter an ex serviceman's club by two who have not served seemed to hit a chord of the ridiculous with Logan as he moved forward to support the older man.

Now inside the entrance Logan looked through into what was a rapidly filling concert hall as a door opened and the sound of an overloud microphone announced arrival of the pies.

'There's nothing closer to a uniform than the white coat of a drinks waiter in there' he said receiving the most amazing of dirty looks from the over officious committee member.

'So they also serve who stand and wait is true then?' questioned Logan to the now growing assembly at the door.

Matters had by this time gone too far to give in and with what looked like bouncers now arriving and with the man's membership card of another branch declined Logan searched his pocket and threw down his ID card. With the issue now moving into deep muddy waters for the committee member he backed off and signed both in as a guests of the youth but only to the back bar. The card got both in but not in the concert hall as it was 'a turns night' said the member, which was likely reason for both dinner jacket and the refused admission. To enter as a guest of the youth insulted both him and the older man Logan felt but enter they both did just for the bloody hell of it.

The place was in much need of decoration with bare smoke stained walls but for the mandatory solitary picture of the Queen set centrally above the bar. At the counter the old man bought them both a drink. Logan felt it an odd feeling to be standing at a bar with a stranger that he somehow felt he had some fellowship with and after the compulsory when are you going back was established both went strangely quiet as if knowing the other's thoughts. At length the older man spoke.

'They need you when they need you son' he said suddenly pensive 'until it's all over and then who needs a Bren gunner.'

With that he drained his glass and wishing Logan good luck in his career quietly left the bar. Logan watched him go raising his glass to the closing door before turning to place his still full beer on the bar and leaving himself. The voice of the committee member on his inspection rounds called behind as he walked to the door.

'Something wrong with the beer' said the man abruptly.

'It's got a nasty taste to it' said Logan throwing a Parthian shot as he left.

Once outside Logan made tracks for home stopping first for the daddy of all cures to a mother of crap evenings. Three popadoms and with diced onions and lime pickle as a starter and a chicken vindaloo with cold lager that down the years had always sorted him out one way or the other. Some things are timeless and never change he thought as he entered to the sound of the sitar and the world of dim lights and heavy red flock wallpaper. Three lagers later he was a changed man. He had been missed Ali said and was surprised to learn he had joined up.

'When are you going back?' he asked spoiling the moment when the door opened to the most welcome of unexpected surprises.

'I'm going to have to go' said Bernice slipping the front of her bra around and sliding them in. 'I'm a good girl now and it's getting very late Logan.'

'Yes' agreed Logan smiling to himself in the gloom.

Logan looked over at Bernice getting back into her clothes or the ones that had come off or been flung off or had got in the way. We shouldn't be doing this Logan she had said in a voice as sincere as Logan's was when he agreed with her. She hadn't put on much of a fight or weight for that matter Logan felt.

'I thought you were, you know?' said Logan looking at the flat innie and outy bits.

'Oh that' said Bernice 'silly dieting said the doctor it was me trying to look like Jean Shrimpton.'

Bernice straightened the dangling strands of hair at the wardrobe mirror with a mouth full of clips.

'Shtill tonight was naughty but it was ruverly' she said from the side of her mouth.

'Nothing rubbery about it' Logan said pulling his pants back on 'Billy Drinkwater's a very lucky man to be getting you.'

'Not tonight he isn't' said Bernice with a wickedly naughty smile that was about the truth of it.

'When are you going back' she had said as they left the Bombay Palace with the thought to share a taxi home although her two friends knew where both were really going and would cover for her as old friends do.

Nobody likes a school wimp and neither could see what Bernice saw in him other than him being boringly dependable.

'That and his family being loaded' said the one.

'I always thought, you know...' said Lil nodding her head towards Logan as he and Bernice left for the taxi.

'Ah therein lies a story' said the other girl.

'Tell then' said Lil shuffling nearer on the seat and cocking an ear for the low down even if it would only be half true.

'Well...'

So all in all the weekend wasn't a total loss but something of a memory. It certainly seemed it when Logan arrived back late on Sunday night, it seemed light years away but then so did normality as he checked daily orders on the troop board for the next day.

'Weapon training' said Chalkie passing on his way back from the ablutions 'on the Bren gun at long last would you believe, exciting aye?'

Chalkie's comment took Logan back to the British Legion. Not worth the hassle of getting into the place he was thinking as he followed Chalkie down the corridor to the barrack room. The most exciting thing in there was that picture of the bloody Queen...God bless her he said to himself quietly.

12

Back in barracks everyone but the recruits that had gone AWOL quickly settled as memories of home faded and the squad got back into the routine. They were nearing the end of training, another few weeks and the intake would be licensed to kill. It took James Bond three years Wee Jock recalled and he was a Scotsman ye ken? With a light now showing at the end of the tunnel an overall feeling of having survived it ran through the troop. That the light might be from the proverbial approaching train seemed to have been missed by many but not Logan who felt something like how a grouse must feel a few weeks before the glorious twelfth. One day part of the hunting fraternity's conservation effort and the next one of its targets. Very well named is the grouse felt Logan.

Orders that night showed a list of names for 'post recruit training' which sounded at first like they were all going to be given little red bikes and post bags. What it became was the training for those surviving basic. In Logan's case and a few of the others it was confirmed to be in telecommunications as an operator with a posting to a signals training regiment a mile or so up the road from the Harewood. Some view of the world this man's army was giving said Chalkie.

'Join the army and see Catterick' was how he had it adding 'why not Japan or Korea as they make all the radios.'

A brainless rumour went around that the radio operators were going to be trained by Radio Luxembourg which was a worry as there were some right weirdoes over there as everyone with a transistor radio knew. As it turned out it was just another rumour like the one about the Russian Parachutists attacking camp centre earlier in the year. Amazingly that rumour grew and grew eventually ending up on the desk of the Provost Marshall who sent a team of his best red caps in.

'Hello, yes it's me Grimshaw speaking to you on the telephone Provost Marshal...saluting you now sir.'

'Thank you Grimshaw, try and remember you have to press button A for answer when you use the telephone and B to get your money back if you don't get through, now get on with it will you or you will get the pips for more money.'

'Yes sir, sorry sir, there's no Russians here you know, me and Hoskins have looked...he's over there now still looking Provost Marshal, you what Provost Marshal? Right you are sir, hang on I'll put the phone down. Hoskins!...the Provost Marshal says have a good look in the flowerbeds.'

'Can't be true' said Brum listening to Compton tell the tale?'

'Oh yes,' Compton said 'one of the blokes from next block overheard from the next telephone box.'

It never ceased to amaze Logan how quickly the rumours spread or for that matter just what people would take in. The bigger the improbability the more likely the belief was the rule for rumours and the one about the exotic stripper in room three cleared the NAAFI and was almost a riot as men arrived demanding to know where they had her hidden. For most it was a bit of fun and turning up knowing there would be nobody there was all part of it, although some were outside for ages looking for the snake and her bongo drum. So when the rumour spread that the intake was to go under canvas on the Yorkshire moors in what was said to be the coldest winter since 1945 everyone including the dopes laughed it off. Few were laughing when it proved to be true.

'Camping, camping?' said Compton 'It's been snowing on and off since the beginning of autumn, are they mad?'

'I like camping me, I was a boy scout me, a patrol leader I was' said Brum to a look of absolute disinterest from all the room, 'until I got us lost.'

Corporal Jock tapped the thermometer in the troop office, it showed eighty-four degrees Fahrenheit but then it would sat on a radiator. Outside the snow was falling like foam from an airport fire tender and was deeper than three quarters of seven troop within two hours. Good King Wenceslas would have stuck two fingers up at yonder peasant and put another log on the fire. Sire he lives a good league hence did it for Logan in this weather and fuck him was what Chalkie said.

The troop camp or operation 'frozen nuts' as it became better known was scheduled for the next day. Four days on the Yorkshire moors in a tent was a chilling enough thought in high summer and in February 1962 it was promising to be positively dangerous. One man immediately went AWOL and when the event appeared in orders as 'Moors Week' many were hanging to the hope it would be a week in Broadmoor or even Dartmoor. Given the choice many would have chosen either one.

'A week in a cell with a serial killer as a cell mate offers better odds than yon moors' felt Chalkie going on about it.

'Cold is it?' asked Brum.

'Cold as a subway flasher's dick.'

'Oh that cold' said Brum having in depth knowledge of Birmingham subway systems 'that's really cold is that.'

Being as Yorkie as a chocolate bar Chalkie knew about yon moors right enough and let everyone know what to expect.

'Few races on earth can survive yon in winter, I'll say no more.'

'The Inuit?' said Compton.

'The what?'

'The indigenous North American Indian...the Esquimaux?'

'Safely tucked away in igloos lending their women out to folk the kinky bastards' was how Chalkie saw the Inuit.

As a native aboriginal himself he clearly had doubts they would survive a full week, for as he told the room, you don't get many seals in north Yorkshire these days and you don't have holes with fish in them either.

'The most you get out of a hole in Yorkshire is a lump of nutty slack' Chalkie advised everyone 'but it's the finest coal in world is Yorkshire coal, oh yes.'

'Next to Wales mind' said Taff quietly from his bed.

Officially the met office, who could tell it was snowing with the best of them, had it heading towards the coldest conditions of the century and the troop notice board had the official dress posted as combat dress. This included the same hairy army shirts and combat jackets as worn for summer but with the addition of a V-neck single ply cotton jumper and a scarf as optional. Not that the moors were cold although they were certainly that, it was just that the army and specifically this intake was not equipped to be out there.

'Arguably the coldest conditions of the century and we have been drilling in cotton fatigues in camp and are being sent for a week on the moors in shower proof cotton combat gear' said the Scouse looking to start a union day of action.

With fur hats and hot water bottles not down as official issue regardless of any conditions all that stood between them and death by freezing was the speed of march, smoke breaks in the back of the drill shed and a warm up at NAAFI breaks. On the moors all that would stand between them and death was a six-man tent and a suck on a Fisherman's Friend felt Logan. The whole idea was ludicrous even before the NAAFI sold out of lozenge and the candles went two weeks before the event.

On the day of departure men paraded wearing double everything and looking like a squad of Michelin men. Never having seen snow before Ojuku arrived even wearing two berets which gave him the look of a Rasta but without the dreadlocks. Snow was falling heavily and with only blue berets sticking above the snowline they looked like three lines of early spring snowdrops. Corporal Jock was furious that the roll call was a beret short and went through it six times before they found Shorty Hardcastle. As seven troop boarded their Bedford even the agnostics were praying and Moshe Bernstein from room two was already crossing himself said Compton before changing it to crossing himself already.

It took four hours to reach the camp arriving a little behind the snowploughs sometime early to mid afternoon to be met by a farmer with a tractor wearing a potato sack which he wouldn't sell but he did sell straw for the tents from his trailer at a fraction less than the price of the tractor. The man had a kindly blue face showing just a touch of early frostbite and had 'gone t' trouble of stamping down yon snow for us tents' as Chalkie said to a line of blank faces after speaking with the farmer and regressing back to dialect.

'Sheep shagga as gone t' trouble o' stampin daahn t'sna for wee' said Chalkie.

'Nice' said Logan getting not a word of it but picking up on the definite article reduction of the t' word.

'I do wish he wouldn't do that' said Compton 'I don't have a word of Yorkie.'

'He cor elp it can ee' said Brum explaining this was what you call Yorkshire hospitality until he stepped in something left by 'what ad done the stamping.'

Beneath the snow and steam of the late dropped pancake lay permafrost that defied pick axes. It certainly defied wooden tent pegs and as evening approached the troop had only managed to put one tent up. Logan for one was surprised at Corporal Jock's apparent lack of concern at the slow progress until he realised it was the commissioned officer and NCO tent that was going up first.

As night approached the fear of death produced four more and as darkness fell and with the tea urn and sandwiches finished there was a dash for tents and cover. Thirteen men packed into a six-man tent wearing every item of clothing they stood up in and they were still cold. By dawn the tent and even the straw had frozen solid and those who had removed boots found them like chipboard the next morning.

Melting knots with a lighter Logan finally crawled out through a hole in the tent flap hardly bigger than Scouse's head. Out in the field they found others had survived the night and were queuing for what the cook was inventively calling breakfast. To everyone else it was dry cornflakes and pieces of flame seared bread but the man had managed to brew tea and was melting lumps of iced milk in it as Logan arrived at the queue. Next to him was a brace of troop corporals, a sergeant and a gentleman officer in the shape of one Lieutenant Snotty. Since the ranges it was rare to see both out together as they had been over wintering in the troop office occasionally shouting abuse from the window at some minor transgression below or turning out for the Friday night weekly kit inspection.

Likely as part of the survival training the Army Catering Corps had provided the camp with both a short straw cook corporal and a Mark 3 army field cooker. More accurately described as a burner than a cooker was the Mark 3 but then so was the corporal cook or Rarebit as he was known back at the barracks.

'Welsh he is see Rarebit' explained Taff thinking to enlighten the tent. 'It's a Welsh delicacy is what it is.'

'Cheese on bloody toast is what it is. That's what we call it in Yorkshire.'

'Caws ar dost is what we call it in Wales you pwdn' said Taff having enough of him for the day.

'You what?'

The burner took two cans of petrol and a box of Swan Vestas before Rarebit got it to explode with a loud bang and some flying pieces of shrapnel. Unhappy but fearless the cook set up a second standby Mark 3 for another go.

'That Welsh cook's only having another go with a standby cooker' said Brum excitedly as he returned to the shelter of the tent. 'He nearly killed himself with the first one.'

'Fearless cooker the man is, he's Welsh see' said Taff.

'Careless fucker right enough as you say' said Chalkie finding a piece of the Mark 3 smouldering in the snow outside and turning everyone's heads to the cook tent to await the next explosion.

With such a pitiful breakfast the lunchtime menu was eagerly awaited as the sound of a roaring burner came from the cook tent echoed by a sardonic cheer.

'The menu's up' said Scouse arriving back at the tent with his pickaxe from the first attempt to dig a pit for the latrines. 'We're down to four inches, frozen solid the ground is...there's a queue forming now.'

'Four inches?' said Brum 'not worth bloody going for four inches.'

'The plank you sit on is two foot up you Brummie bastard when was the last time you went for a crap, last year?'

'You won't find me with my pants down in this weather' said Logan before realizing Scouse meant the queue was for the cook tent.

He arrived as the cook was chalking up the menu.

'Soupe surprise' said a voice speaking Franglais 'that's French for soup surprise that is, what's in it chef?'

'If he tells you that it won't be a fucking surprise will it' said Sergeant Head at the front of the queue helping the duff stick back one of his burn plasters.

'What's in the tous dans la soupe' read another.

'Secret ingredients' said the duff followed by the speciality of the tent my j'aime buttay for afters.'

'You wouldn't guess the motto of the Catering Corps is 'we sustain' would you' said Compton taking one of the jam butties.

'The man's tried' said Logan looking down at a mess tin of soup.

'He should be' said Chalkie.

'You got any la sauce favorite de papa chef?' said Compton pushing his luck.

When the sheep floated out from under the broken ice in the stream to the edge of the field clear warning bells started to sound around the camp. Somebody somewhere had to do something. A four inch hole in the ground surrounded by Hessian is not what we call a lav in Liverpool said Scouse on another strop and ablutions obtained through breaking the ice of a stream was not camping as Brum remembered from his youth. At morning parade they split into squads and were allocated jobs dispersed about the camp to keep them from communal moaning.

Jock and the other instructors arrived on parade in heavy para smocks and Snotty had on his sheepskin with a bobble hat and seemed also to have slept well. Chalkie and Logan were despatched to dig a new latrine this time downwind of the cook tent when they passed the officer and NCO tent. Steam was coming through the flap of the tent and looking in they found the source as eight kerosene heaters set between four army camp beds.

'How many tents is there?' asked Logan knowing the answer anyway.

'Eight' said Chalkie shrugging his shoulders.

Digging a latrine proved to be impossible as Scouse had said. Even with a pickaxe the ground was concrete so they found a depression and banked the snow up to make it look like a hole. As Chalkie said he was hanging on until they got back to barracks anyway and they would be long gone by the time the snow melted. Returning back to camp the last of the tents was up and occupied and the cook had started a nice fire which everyone was grateful for even if it was one of the tents. Now a tent short Logan and Chalkie found that along with Ojuku and Compton they had in their absence been allocated space in a smaller tent next to the officer and NCO tent.

By day two they had spent two of the four days in abject discomfort living in permanent sub zero temperatures and it was clear to even the keenies in the troop that the aim of the camp was to teach men to suffer. Less learning how to survive in the wilderness than it is learning how to put up with it was Logan's view.

'They could get the same result if they put us in a walk in deep freezer with a fan' Logan felt.

'This is cheaper' said Compton.

Fearful perhaps of losing some of his men which would have got 'a tad careless' stamp on his records Snotty came up with a brilliant manoeuvre to keep the men warm. Who said the Sandhurst years had been wasted thought Logan taken back to early childhood with a manoeuvre you might expect a six year old to think up. Neither keen on snowball fights Logan and Chalkie had taken to waiting for the first incoming to arrive before shirking off the manoeuvre and making their way back to camp and sleeping bags.

Logan was on one such return when he tripped over what he thought at first to be a red rug in a ditch. On closer inspection he found it to be a very dead red cow.

'It was the horns that gave it away' said Logan, 'that and the tail.'

'That and the fucking thing not moving you mean' said Chalkie.

Extremely dead the poor animal must have frozen to its demise he reasoned in a fate shared with at least one sheep found on the first day and returned to the shagga. In constant state of hunger Logan's initial thought was food but without the means to cook the animal they covered it with snow and made for camp.

The general consensus of the tent was that neither Rarebit or Corporal Jock or indeed any in the top tent would take kindly to men arriving with four prime 16oz rump steaks and asking for medium rare or a chateaubriand in Compton's case but it was Chalkie alone who asked what price prime steak is in the hotels of Richmond. It's a well known truism that you never really know who you're lay next to in a dark tent thought Logan but by happy coincidence he found himself lying next to an ex apprentice butcher by name of Chalkie White.

Ojuku also affirmed skilled knowledge of the cow having spent his early years looking after his dad's tribal herd of two hundred and twenty six such beasts until thirty of them went to pay for the old man's fourteenth teenage wife. What the hell was this man doing in the army when he had all that coming to him asked Logan before discovering Ojuku was sixty second in line to the throne and his dad looked eighty seven when he was only forty two.

They had before them confirmed Compton, the clear basis of what looked to be a profitable venture. Butcher the beef into desirable choice cuts, label up and store in nature's own deep freeze and sell to mutual and opportune profit once they returned to camp.

'And we even save on the abattoir costs, cold storage, vet fees and transportation!' said Compton doing the sums to show a tidy profit.

Short of butchering implements the tent spent the evening sharpening bayonets and honing a Swiss army knife and thinking easy money. Choosing the opportunity well and leaving Compton to cover for them they left next morning's snow ball fight early and headed for the dead beast. Suspecting that bayonets would be of limited use with a frozen animal Logan took the precaution of taking the pickaxe. The move proved to be invaluable in producing meat although it was clearly not the implement to provide the calculated number of T bones and fillets and sirloins anticipated the evening earlier. Nevertheless they left well satisfied carrying four well proportioned legs and some assorted lumps of biscuit or something like that said Chalkie. All in all a remarkable feat in itself considering the tools and Chalkie's eventual admission that apprenticed butchers spend their lives on delivery bikes.

Returning to camp they found the area deserted and sneaking to their tent buried the animal under the snow for safe keeping. As Chalkie said this provided both security and the required temperature recalling the cold of the night before. At least it would have done had not Compton in their absence discovered several lengths of ground drainage piping on a sortie of his own away from camp. Manhandled into camp the pipes were positioned under snow and in a line leading directly to the officer and NCO tent. The resultant warm air heating for the tent was undeniably inventive and would have received full approval even if it was Compton's idea.

It was around mid afternoon with the troop sent on a nature walk by Snotty to find cones and a carrot for Sergeant Head's snowman when a certain appalling odour hit the camp emanating from the area of the NCO tent.

'There is the smell of a putrid and rotting flesh coming through the camp sir' said Head to the lieutenant as eyes looked accusingly over to the cook tent.

'It's that cooking Welshman' said Corporal Jock.

'The fucking Welshman?' said the lieutenant mishearing but getting it right.

'It's not moi soup du jour' said Rarebit defensively before blowing his nose in the bottom of his apron.

'Corporal Jock, go take a look will you' said Snotty.

Maybe he thought Jocks could see smells. At length Jock returned with a twisted face and a report.

'Sergeant ead is correct sir...there is an bleeding orrible pong a coming from our tent...'

'It's not me sir' protested the cook.

'And it ain't not me or Corporal Jock either sir' said Head accusingly.

'Officers smell Sergeant Head they do not stink' said Snotty becoming indignant.

'I think we are pitched over one of those cow pads' said Jock.

Lieutenant Snotty twitched his nose like a man who had smelt cow shit many times before and gave the order to move tent. Remembering the problems of early tent pitching Jock decided an easier solution would be to switch rather than move and Logan and the others returned to find their kit moved to the next tent. After what the cook called the evening meal and everyone else a sandwich they settled in for the last night on the moors.

Unknown to all the mystery stink had been defrosting, putrid and rotting flesh warmed by the introduction of convected hot air and coming from a poor beast that had died some weeks before the big freeze. The stink of an aged dead cow when warmed naturally enough is distinctive and is not dissimilar to that of a knacker's yard but when heated up beneath several kerosene army issue heaters the smell could revive dead flies. It was a life force to be reckoned with.

Tent and bits of cow now abandoned by the cadre they were found the next morning like four fish fingers lying out in the open under a ground sheet. Officer and sergeant in the middle and junior NCOs to the outside and sleeping like a pack of frozen Birdseye. Chalkie approached for a closer look and gently dusted the frost off the sleeping lieutenant's shoulders to reveal his two pips.

'We could leave them here for another two months with a two star rating' said Chalkie to the line of nodding heads.

13

There was a spontaneous euphoric cheer from the back of the Bedford as they arrived back at the lines. The kind of euphoria you have after a fall from a horse to find you have only the one broken leg. Only a cheer for relative suffering it may have been but even Logan felt happy at the return. The feeling was probably close to how a condemned man must feel when his death sentence is commuted to life he felt.

With the queue for a hot bath ten deep and the one for the loo stretching down the corridor it was a long wait but worth it. What consummate pleasure there was from receiving hot water from a running tap. But more than this was the excitement and anticipation of a flushing loo. Plumbing is what separates civilised man from the animals and the call of nature. The first flush of excitement at the return soon faded with an increased level of drill as the troop neared the end of training or cloning as it was proving to be for some who were already showing levels of permanent damage. Just how quickly and deep it had gone in still came as something of a shock to Logan even if he had watched it happen. He was there at the early beginnings as the first of the nipples burned off the toecap and he would be there at the end to put back the pieces. All the Queen's horses and all the Queen's men thought Logan feeling more than a little humpty at the thought of it.

To a man they had all been touched in some shape or form, some however were permanently touched and were already showing signs of being first class arseholes. In just a relatively short number of weeks everyone had changed one way or another. Some metamorphosed into easily identifiable mutant groupings and some arrived already on the brink and were easily tipped over. Down in the miasma of the military abyss they now lay dormant awaiting only opportunity to rise up.

'They are the Corporal Jocks, Heads and Smedley's of this world' said Logan to Compton as he ironed his shirt through his wet hanky. 'Like Alsatians dogs, not that much up top but a good bark and bite on them.'

Alongside these cocooned fruitcakes there had developed another grouping, an obsequious group of brown nosed lap dogs who would spend long evenings curled up before Corporal Jock listening to his records of military bugle calls or his expansive theories on the right turn. Yet another were the super keenies, the irretrievable army barmy who would give over their entire lives and every waking existence to the uniform. With expectation beyond that which the army and life could ever deliver they were on their way to eventual disillusionment and a bunch of pills felt Logan thinking of himself as being in the ever lost doubting dross group and being far from meek by nature would inherit bugger all.

'Like the rest of us' said Compton looking up. 'There was this daft article I read once. Six years service and you have a fifty percent chance of coming out with a split mind, so this quack said.'

'Half of me says that can't be true' said Logan putting a horizontal crease in the back of his shirt that would never be seen.

It was during a barrack room duty sweep of corridor when dross met super keeny and Logan got to know more about the inter-troop competition. Until then he had hardly given it a second thought thinking it little more than the inter troop sports, dominoes and darts that had been running for some weeks. To learn there was a prize of a seventy two hour pass for the winning troop came as a shock and he rushed away to tell the room leaving super keeny to pick up his sweepings from under the coconut mat. He found the room deep in apathy right up until the news of the seventy two hour pass.

The bigger shock came when the results were posted on the troop orders board showing they were running second to eight troop and that the competition included all aspects of training so far. They were being marked but more than this they were losing to the rival eight troop where they had from the beginning of training always assumed themselves superior by simple observation of the other's inferiority. Strange that this should also be the view of the other troop.

There is something particularly off at being last in a two horse race and behind to someone you had spent weeks thinking of as being rubbish thought Logan. The revelations proved true when they lined up for this particular morning roll call. With only the marching competition yet to be judged Corporal Jock was beside himself and almost in tears as he read the end of training reports from his millboard.

'Range scores...Cross-eyes? Fucking atrocious son but not your fault you did your best there.'

'Yes corporal.'

'Bastard weapons training, where's Compton?' He said shaking his head, 'you suffering from dropsy Compton?'

'Sorry corporal.'

'Basketball? We lost Basketball? Top scorer Miller, well done Miller.'

'Thanks corporal.'

'But who the bleeding hell put Hardcastle and Wee Jock on the team...fucking eight troop?'

'The ring was too high' said Hardcastle.

'You's are all crap' he said in that imaginative little way of his 'and now you's official crap.'

He had a way with words did Corporal Jock.

'We have two weeks to pull it together and it's all going to come down to the drill competition.'

Jock's words stabbed deep into the heart of the troop as the arrival of Sergeant Head confirmed life for the next two weeks. Marching the troop off to the far side of the parade ground Head gave them a good going over in his own imaginative little way which went on until dusk fell and he couldn't see what he was shouting at. They arrived back in barracks to find they were all on extra fatigues and Sergeant Head was on duty sergeant. With nothing to do all evening Head called room and kit inspection every hour until lights out and they crawled into bed.

Of particular interest was the drill competition which of all the events took precedence enough to be run as an entire event and placed before a group of learned judges. With the colonel chairman of the panel, Calhoun the adjudicating officer and heavy betting within the camp training cadre the event took on an importance second only to rise of the midsummer sun for the early Britons.

To the military mindless a body of marching men was the most visible indicator of the trained soldier. Useful as marching formations were in the days of Cecil B DeMille and Arthur Wellesley they went rapidly out well early in the 20th century.

'No bugger told the army' said Chalkie, himself not a fan of marching like the majority of the intake.

A closely grouped body of marching soldiers was a bunch of easy targets is how Logan saw it but not unsurprisingly nobody was asking Logan least of all the colonel who was a traditionalist. Like Hague Compton said recalling something his granddad said about generals.

'He's a cheery old soul said Harry to Jack, as they slogged up to Arras with rifle and pack. But he did for them both by his plan of attack...'

'For sure' said Logan 'you sure that was your granddad?'

Who the hell cared how far and fast a man can march in his boots when what mattered was that they were shiny was the ruling of the day. Secondary to firing the weapon was how well he could shoulder arms with it and whether the squad would get straight sixes for technical merit or falter in the lift or worse still fall down on the triple salco equivalent of the 'change arms on the move.'

The days leading to the competition were a series of personal kit inspections in readiness for Calhoun and extra drill in readiness for the overall eye of the colonel and his fellow judges. Come the day Logan was past caring and would have slept through it all had not Corporal Jock arrived at five that morning. Just how much money was on the bloody thing?

In spite of all the bullshit the event did take on a pace of its own. It was the culmination of many weeks endeavour for some and something of a survival for others. This made for a general overall feeling of excitement whichever way they got there. To increase the excitement it was the troop's first official wearing of the number two uniform which rumour had it was a creation of Norman Hartnell the Queen's dress designer. Logan preferred the ones he did for the Queen who must have got a better deal by going private rather than buying off the rack.

The routine of the big parade began with a series of inspections starting with a predawn once over by a roommate and escalated on up through the ranks until the final inspection by Calhoun at noon. By the time they got to the major the process had been through three of the lads, the eagle eye of Chalkie, some picky bastard in room number two who had dressed early and three escalating ranks of non commissioned officer. Logan was more looked at than a page three girl's tits and was absolutely smartness personified. In a word he was immaculate.

Calhoun's inspection was thorough if not thoroughly futile. How is it that a dim witted inspecting officer always manages to find something comment worthy. Why do they do it thought Logan? What can they possibly find of significance that has been missed by a Corporal Jock of this world who could spot a piece of dandruff on an epaulette at ten paces. The answer was absolutely nothing but complete invention of fault in order to point make. What pissed everyone off was that the man in front had a batman turn his kit out for him.

Logan was commended for his brasses and knocked points for his peaked cap not being level.

'Turned out for the twat like an immaculate example to modern soldiery and he dropped me points for having a generic anatomical deviation of the upper cervical spinal column.'

'Oh yeah...it does a bit' said Chalkie rudely having a good stare.

You could feel the tension building as post inspection the troop marched to the parade ground desperate not to scratch their boots. Even without Compton who Jock had ordered to go sick they still had a fair smattering of two left feeters hidden away in the middle rank. Add on the two right feet wonders and the unsure and this one was going down to the wire.

'When it comes down to it some of the intake canny wear a uniform' said Wee Jock standing in front of the lower half of the mirror.

In a dull light and placed under a railway arch Wee Jock could line up for a free bowl of soup thought Logan but kept it to himself. Not everyone can be placed out of sight in the centre rank and so would remain on full critical view to the observant eye of the binoculars. Oh yes, serious money had gone down on this one and the thing was too close to call.

'Can we not try to get any more in the middle' asked Taff struggling with the mathematical concepts of an equal division into three whole numbers.

'No Taff...look, there's two trains coming together on a line OK and each is doing twenty miles an hour...' began Chalkie as they were called out to parade walking like lines of pigeon toed penguins as calls of 'mind me festering boots' echoing down the stairs.

Within minutes they had formed up, received final checks and were marched away from the barracks. Halted and waiting within sight of the square Corporal Jock walked slowly along the line talking in a lowered voice doing his best at what went for a pep talk. He was attempting a morale booster in the ranks and the tension was sliceable. It didn't work at Culloden in 1746 but then.

'This is it men' said Jock feigning a choke. 'Yes, this is the big yin...the day is ere ma braw bonny lads. I did'ne want to tell yous this men but yous here seven troop is Sergeant Head's last troop. He's been retarded...thrown out on the crap heap after twenty two years four months and a bit. Out on his arse the barstets. Let's give him something to remember us by lads. The best present we could give him, to keep by his fireside in the winter months when the winds howl down the corridors at the rehabilitation hospital...yes, he's a sick man alright, let's give him the Champion Troop pace stick with the wee band engraved, seven troop, champion troop. Will you do it for him, will you give it him?'

'Right up' said a voice from the centre rank but Jock missed it.

Going in to bat second was initially thought to be a good thing when they won the toss as it looked like the pitch wouldn't turn or worse still break up and eight troop's marching would wear the patience of a saint never mind the keen eye of the umpire. Sure enough the colonel was still shaking his head even before the front of the squad crunched foot to shale. Alongside the abnormally nice Scotsman Jock now metamorphosed back to big mouth drill pig. Soft Jock had long gone, replaced with vintage arsehole old Jock offering up little snippets of useful tips as they neared the parade ground centre.

'Your right hand side is where the colonel is standing centre rank. Any of yous that turns left when I says right turn will be pulling bits of my stick from his arse for a month.'

Halted and placed at ease and now easy the troop waited as Jock paraded up and down the ranks giving final warnings repeated quietly by some of the more toady of the squad.

'Listen for the piss man, don't move before the piss. Make a big cock up or drop your weapon and you follow it down.'

'Follow it down if you drop one' said the echo of a voice in the middle rank.

'Don't drop one' said another.

'Was'ne me' said Wee Jock.

'Listen up for your piss man' said Corporal Jock.

'Listen for your piss man' said Scouse repeating the order.

'You are the piss man' said a voice immediately behind him.

'Oh yeah' said Scouse.

It was not a good start. Finding someone to take the piss had been a problem for the squad over the weeks and the intake went through several piss men before arriving at the Scouse who with the size of his mouth was a natural. Someone from Wapping had the job before him but couldn't hack it as coming from the east end of London his pssst sounded like he was a purveyor of dirty postcards and he just had to go. Scouse had only been in the job two weeks and the job for him was a personal nightmare but for the rest of the squad the collective nightmare was a dropped weapon.

Of all possible cock-ups on parade dropping a bayonet or weapon cannot be smudged over or missed. General consensus gave only four options for a dropped weapon – break rank shout sorry and stoop to pick it up was a given no, or worse still close your eyes and wait for Jock to pick it up and give it you back. This was not only a no but an oh no. Drop on the move and the dilemma worsens, there is only the go back and collect or hope to pick it up on the second time around and both these options were oh no's!

With those prone to oh no's well pruned and pricked out by Jock to hide in the centre rank with luck even a major cock up might remain unseen in the blink of an eye or sneeze but who can miss an abandoned weapon left on an open parade ground as the squad marches over and away.

Logan's mind was not fully made up on the issue as the troop neared the square knowing that fainting is not a chargeable offence but damage to a weapon is. On the whole the feeling within the troop was to follow the weapon down in a faint as many had before judging from the attendance of the medics with stretchers waiting behind the drill sheds. With a loud shout of 'parade' the ranks stiffened and they were off.

The competition was going well even for seven troop until they came to the drill of unfix bayonets where Scouse missed locating the scabbard with a thrusting blade and put the bayonet through the back of his hand. It was a goodly spurt of blood that splashed Taff who went out like a light followed by the luckless Calhoun watching with his binoculars. On hand the medics appeared stretcher at the ready and the parade was finished with additional stretchers for Calhoun and Taff and for Brum who tripped over Taff and Long Arms Miller who tripped over Brum.

All in all it was turning into a pretty poor to average year on the square for Major Calhoun. Needless to say seven troop lost the marching but not by much so they heard although a rumour went around that they were the worst troop that year which surely came from eight troop and so didn't count.

Whatever it is about competition that turns men funny began to run through the troop like an accusing finger. Suddenly the one for his knob took on real meaning in the crib competition and they even had some tosser from the next room complain people were walking on his clean doormat. Incredibly the competition began to open discussions at NAAFI break rather than the state of the awful tea. Suddenly everyone was into trying one way or another and Logan for one thought it a pain in the arse.

On the positive side the effect was a personal attempt at self-improvement like standing closer to the razor in the morning or an extra five minutes on boots. The negative side came out as being made to try harder by some of the troop. Pressure that on occasion took the form of in barrack bullying which was an unwelcome visitor. Compton was always at risk although he did manage some improvement but not all could.

'Look at it this way,' said Compton responding to a complaint from Scouse about mess on his side of the bed space, 'without someone like me being crap at everything some of you wouldn't look so good would you?'

'That's for sure' agreed Logan as Scouse shrugged and picked up the mess.

Compton seemed to take an inner contentment at his lack of personal pride but for him it was coming to grips with the philosophy of it all, the man seemed to gain strength from it.

'Look at it this way' he said, 'without losers there can't be winners and there's more of us so me I'm a necessary majority.'

It's one way of looking at it felt Logan as for certain there can only be one winner but not all agreed as whatever it was touched each of them in some way. They were all affected by it in one way or another. In seven troop it both unified and divided in one. It set man against man and room against room but most of all it set everyone against eight troop.

Over in eight troop it did much the same but it was their Compton who drank the tin of Brasso.

14

The competition was hotting up with the taunts and jeers between the troops growing into a throwing war. So far this had been the odd NAAFI pie, which was dangerous enough in the right hands, but when the plate came over with it there was a growing need to duck. Then, when someone from down the corridor got worked over in the Harewood club it just had to be eight troop. Hostilities began breaking out all over so when orders announced that the assault course was to be a side-by-side mano a mano competition they were ready to a mano.

Such is the fame of an army assault course that the majority of the troop actually looked forward to having a go. There's no learning some people, although from what Logan had seen of it from across the square it looked benign enough and on the face of it altogether a bit of a dilly. From a distance it had the appearance of a child's play area and was little more than a series of beams, perches and dangling ropes but then so is the hangman's scaffold. They had all heard the occasional shouts and excited screams from the direction of the assault course whenever a senior troop reached that part in the training programme. These had been translated down as shouts and sounds of excited delight as can be heard from school playgrounds. Clearly the obstacles individually just had to be childishly good fun to play on.

Memories of childhood long gone came flooding back as they marched to the area. Lazy summer days of times past and long summer evenings in the park. The evocative smell of newly mown grass and those endless late nights swinging on a knotted rope or climbing on walls until the Parky arrived with his get down whistle. How many times Logan had been told to come down off a wall and three walls were to be seen from across the square as they approached. He smiled at the memory of walls and railings, lost balls in the long grass and the seminal times with Bernice searching for them.

Arrival at the assault course mid afternoon was therefore an awaited pleasure and the casual stroll around the circuit to view and receive an explanation of how to assault each obstacle proved informative. More so felt Logan with each discipline demonstrated so admirably by one of the camp physical training instructors. Supervision of the course was under the eye of the flat nosed Punchy Smith the camp PTI sergeant and his sadistic corporal instructors Bastard One and Bastard Two. Punchy however, was not only a sadist of the Army Physical Training Corps, he was a sportsman too and a great exponent of army boxing and military hockey or jousting as they called it in the middle ages.

Punchy looked the part from levelled nose to cauliflower ears, scars, stitch marks and the constant flinching that years in the ring had placed on him.

'God alone knows what the losers ended up looking like Chalkie?' said Logan at first sight of the man on day one.

'Hammered in pit props' said Chalkie looking the man over.

Punchy was an old friend of the troop from that very first day of training when the squad were dropped off at the gym for their daily dose of pain. It was like Jock dropping his mother off at a euthanasia clinic but it was what the army called physical training or PT. Physical torture or PT was what everyone else called it although it was little more than running to touch wall bars, bunny hops and 'legs raised, hold...and lower' to everyone else.

'Still' said Logan to Chalkie as they walked the course 'we are safer outside and in full view of witnesses now.'

They even allowed a little early go on the knotted rope which had by far the longest queue formed. It required just a modest jump to catch the gentle swing sent by the PTI across a stagnant water filled trench.

The excitement grew as even the vertically challenged Shorty Hardcastle swung majestically across the water to land feather like at the other side and he wasn't only a short arse he was also a fat bastard.

Under more normal circumstances it had all the feeling of a few hours off and free goes on a fair ground. Apart of course from the competition and discounting the high wall which of all the obstacles looked a tad formidable to Logan's eyes. Even Long Arms Miller was showing a level of concern as the PTI's explained the method of assault which is best described as a human pyramid ascent to the top leaving the descent on the other side to the imagination of the squad. Then as Chalkie said it would be a doddle once the PTI's got the ladder up although it had not arrived as they were formed up by Jock and marched back to barracks to kit up.

On the whole the troop were eager to return for a right good go as Chalkie so enthusiastically put it. Scouse too was verbally enthusiastic although being on light duties until his stitches came out he would attend as a supporter cheerleader.

'Knotty rope swing over water, walk along a few poles and a wall or two, clamber up a bit of netting, up a ladder, an under net crawl and ferret down a drainpipe. Piece of piss.' said Scouse managing to sound resentful he would be missing out as he returned his hand back to the sling.

Jock had smirked as he dismissed the troop to barracks.

'Parade in half an hour seven troop, full webbing including backpacks, pouches and your wee tin lids' he said with a second smirk and he didn't normally do smirks did Corporal Jock.

Apart from the days on the ranges they had never paraded in full webbing before and it was something of an event in itself just to get the things fitted and buckled up without getting finger marks on the brasses and grubbing up the Blanco that had taken weeks of bulling.

Jock was still smirking as he handed the squad over to Sergeant Punchy as Bastard One and Two immediately set them to doubling around the course to warm up. Start to finish it was little more than one hundred yards long with obstacles evenly spaced along the route and set between areas of raised banks. Slightly up hill they were well steaming by the time they ran into eight troop at the half way point returning anticlockwise. Perked up by the appearance of the enemy both teams hurled juvenile verbal abuse as they passed. At long last the doubling stopped and they arrived back at the start to be given numbered tops to tie on like a scene from point to point racing.

Now lined up side by side and matched with one man from each troop and with still no sign of the ladder for the wall, the PTI's raced away to man the obstacles. The realization hit Logan and Chalkie alike that the wall was not getting a ladder as the PTI sergeant blew his whistle. It was that short sharp pea-rattling blow that invariably signifies impending pain, hurt or at best a red card. Away in the falling mist of the afternoon the assault course began to disappear into the near distance as the sergeant announced the rules of engagement. To their side came the sound of an approaching siren announcing late arrival of a land rover ominously marked with a large red cross on white background. Medics with bandage bags appeared from inside carrying rolled army green stretchers. Enthusiasm for the event began to diminish as thoughts of summer evenings past turned to gnat bites, hay fever and that lost ball high in the tree and out of reach of anything thrown at it.

'First to finish gets ten points and there's five for each of the obstacles...you're off in pairs at 30 second intervals, right the first two up here...come on, move it!' Bellowed Punchy.

'Stretcher bearers are you ready?' bellowed Corporal Medic as a shrill blast from a whistle sent the first two off like bats out of hell and heading for the knotted rope over the water.

It takes little imagination to realise that the first to any rope swing is likely to get the rope and the second is likely to get thin air or worse still a trailing boot. Being half way down the squad and seeing absolute mayhem setting in before him Logan set to a fiendish plan of skulduggery, bad sportsmanship and some level of psychological warfare.

'Like hospital food do you?' he said to the man at his side before taking an unseen hold of the man's pack.

At the whistle Logan was away first with a tug of his opponent's backpack. Cheered away by the squad and going at full pace he left his man well behind with his mind still on bed pans, flannel baths and tapioca pudding as Logan blistered up the course. As with everything physical, hold back or fear being hurt is asking for a stretcher off and Logan went for it full out.

Suddenly the man was alongside him matching him stride for stride and now gaining until Logan with maximum effort of the sporting man he was deep inside closed the gap enough to trip him up. Down went the man as Logan raced away holding on for dear life to his bouncing tin lid as he went. First to the ditch he paused at the brink with arms ready to receive the swinging rope from the PTI. Now it came. He dived, missed and the water got him. Some plan this was.

Logan surfaced mid water just as his eight troop arrived to find the rope hanging mid pit and limp as a used condom or was until pulled to one side by Logan just as the man ran in. Already committed and unable to stop eight troop left the near bank like he was starting an Olympic freestyle final. He missed the disappearing rope by just four hundredths of a second.

'At this level that's not even bronze' called Logan to the man before wading to the far bank and climbing from the water.

Already the course ahead was flooded with much splash, mud and water from the many who had also missed and was becoming greasier by each arriving recruit. It made the walk along the planks and poles less a race off and more of a slip off. A question of when and how and not if developed a variety of anti slime techniques and all to similar ends. Some went at pace on speedy tiptoe with arms raised like a prancing Nureyev and made a good three or more paces before upending. Worse still was a fall to straddle legs to either side, as the less ambitious went for the bum slide and twirl down under slip off attempt but all fell off sooner or later.

Impossible to watch without a wince, cringe or sharp suck of air though purse of lip the sound of gasps and sniggered laughs from the unsympathetic were everywhere but on the pole. To increase the level of difficulty there now developed a backlog of fallen recruit sent back by the PTI's to try again or sprawled in a confused variable recycled mess of missing kit, tin hat and level of injury lying somewhere within the obstacle. At best accomplished at a brave and stupidly fast run the poles and planks were proving impassable to any man erect as the cries of 'medic' began to come in from around the course.

Logan's eight trooper was lost or could have passed him for all he knew as he arrived at the dangling crawl net hanging down into a deep moat like ditch. Running full pelt up the bank and launching himself off in a blind leap of faith to nothing, Logan hit the net with a bounce and hung on. Snagged like a fly in a web with right leg through up to crotch and left arm hooked to bent elbow Logan climbed out and up and after a good clamber to the top arrived twenty foot up to find Chalkie. Caught by the straps of his backpack and helplessly dangling like a suspended bat Logan came to the rescue and effected a timely release. Judging from the initial scream and foul language the well placed kick was not appreciated by Chalkie who survived the fall remarkably well thought Logan as he raced heroically on.

At the wall without a ladder both troops had gathered in communal mayhem and by the time he hit the wall bodies were already laying in a stack five bodies deep at the base. The result of several collapsed man pyramids it was at best a forlorn hope of a castle siege gone terribly wrong missing only the boiling oil and a siege ramp. Approaching down a bank at warp factor seven Logan was unstoppable.

His back assisted jump off the bodies of the fallen was hardly felt by those at the bottom of the pile as his leap made not for the top of the wall which was the common and painful mistake of many, but for the straddled leg of the man sat on top waiting to pull the next man up. The climb up his leg to screams of mind my balls could be heard well over half a mile away. Up and now over the drop to the other side found remnants of a second failed pyramid coming the other way that broke his fall enough to land him safely to ground. He was swiftly off to the sunken drainpipe going down like the proverbial ferret. By then mostly empty of mud and water by earlier scraping bodies he was swiftly through and making for the barbed wire crawl where snared bodies held in the wire clearly showed areas not to go in. Logan arrived at the finish exhausted but the lone man still standing before painfully limping his way back to the start.

A final blast of a whistle the event was over as everyone surveyed a field looking like Rourke's drift the morning after but it was the cleaning of webbing and scuffed boot that brought tears to many an eye. That and the cries from the man straddled on the wall that had given Logan and the squad maximum points for the inter troop competition.

'Mind my balls, mind my balls!'

'I never even touched his balls' said Logan.

'Find my balls I think that was' said Compton before leaving for a earwax syringing.

15

Nothing if not a planner the colonel's wall chart was covered with a myriad of useless notes to self and lined through marks of obscure placements known only to the colonel. Coloured map pins of varying hue were everywhere but only really important days like the Catterick races and the start of the grouse, salmon and trout seasons got full gold star marking. Useless though the year planner was to man and beast other than those raced, shot or hooked and the jockey Scobie Breasley; to the military eye a full year planner smacked of efficiency. Worthless it may have been but the planner looked the part or so it did for most of the year but for the one week showing nothing but gap. He needed something up there to fill the hole for March as the space stuck out like a sore loser. As was usual with the colonel's dilemmas he called in his best ideas men who arrived in the obese shape of the adjutant and the dimwit Major Rory Calhoun.

'Now chaps, I've been looking up at my hole' was how he began it before turning and pointing at the hole in question.

With a feeling of some relief from the adjutant at least ideas came flooding in from both majors like it was a brain dead daft ideas meeting. Some were average, some typical, some were bad and some were frankly just plain bloody stupid but it was the colonel himself who came up with the idea of a manoeuvre.

'A thumping great bugger of a commando raid on two opposing field headquarters for the senior troops now in training...don't yer know, what yer think chaps?'

'Absolutely spiffing idea' said the adj.

'Yah absolutely yah,' joined in Calhoun.

Toadies both it was hardly surprising the colonel's idea was wholeheartedly supported by the obsequious major's who left with the concept to devise the plan. Spiffing exercises don't just happen even spiffing and bleeding pointless ones.

The colonel's little manoeuvre was born by design to test the fighting spirit and ingenuity of the men in training which, when whittled down to the core of it was little more than moving from A to B over the Yorkshire moors with a few dumb objectives in between and it appeared on orders almost immediately. Short of money to go out but needing to get pissed anyway as it was a Saturday night, Logan was on the Newcastle Brown early doors. When time was called his mission was more than accomplished and being a little worse for wear staggered to the NAAFI loo. He was correcting the appalling spelling of gurlz in trap four when a group of eight troop entered to ease springs. They were in boisterous few beers mood as Logan lay doggo.

'So what's the score with the colonel's manoeuvre?' said a Londoner in a husky high-pitched voice and sounding right up himself.

'It's a field exercise' said another. 'We're up against that seven troop lot.'

'That's easy then against a bunch of bleeding pussies, bet we beat the shit out of them' said the Londoner.

'We didn't on the assault course.'

'Leave it arht John, leave it arht, we was fixed up, those seven troop geezers did us up like a kipper. Out of order that was at the wall. Irish is still on them painkillers.'

'What even now?'

'Oh yes and the bruised nut embrocation cream, extra strength.'

'Twice a day' said another.

'We owes em one for Irish's goolies that's for sure, anyway Smedley says they won't even put a team together' said a new voice 'and he should know...he was their corporal before he moved up to us.'

'Bet they chicken out the tossers.'

'Wankers.'

'Wimps.'

'Ah, that's better...I was dying for that.'

There are moments in everyone's life when a man has to stand up and be counted. This was one of those moments for Logan but caught as he was with his pants down he made do with a metaphorical one. By the time he flushed and rushed outside ready to square up on all four of them they had gone.

'Run off, what a bastard' Logan said taking it out on the roll towel.

Nobody ever hears good about themselves listening to a conversation through a lavatory door on Saturday night after a few beers. The truth hurts as only the truth and nothing but the truth at times can, as the event was broadcast down the corridor to anyone who would listen.

'Even we have our pride.' Logan said to the growing group now gathered before him.

Ojuku Quimbi the Nigerian prince left his room and joined in with some obscure tribal saying about a hyena, two pigs and a group of lions.

'You what? Brum said shaking his head.

'Pride...as in fucking dignity you stupid bloody African...not pride as in lions!' blurted out Logan finally getting his drift before thanking him profusely for his support as he looked to be turning nasty.

Attracted by the ruckus others of the troop now began to appear in the corridor as it was well past chucking out time at the NAAFI.

'And there was crap all on the TV other than some smarmy smartarse with his head up his arse called Frost' said Chalkie arriving back from the TV room with some of room one.

Still fired by indignation and the moment Logan turned to address them as they approached.

'He who has no stomach to this fight, let him depart; his passport shall be made, and crowns for convoy put into his purse.' said Logan still a little worse for wear as he received more and more drink fired support from all about him.

'We would not die in that man's company that fears his fellowship to die with us.'

'Appen' said Chalkie now standing alongside him as Taff arrived straight out of bed and wearing only a towel.

'What's all the bloody noise about some of us are trying to sleep here' said Taff before he was told to bog off as Scouse got into the act.

'I wish I were there like,' he said poking his head out and nose in and becoming heroic 'I would have stood up there and then me like you know.'

Logan thought to say something but didn't want to go there as others now joined in with enthusiastic support.

'And gentlemen in England now abed shall think themselves accursed they were not here...' said Logan still waxing drunk and lyrical.

'See you's in eight troop, you ken them's barstets,' shouted one of the troop's dwarf Jocks.

It was Wee Jock and he was in fighting Kingdom of Fyffe mood. All now agreed with whatever it was he said, as it sounded to be in the spirit of the moment and menacing enough for someone who was only five foot two. Others equally put out at hearing they were wimps and pussies now joined in, as the list of invented and insulting adjectives grew proportionate to the communal support. All about Logan men now gathered with stiffened sinews and summoned blood as a murmur of a winter of discontent went about the block as he switched plays to Richard Three before returning once again to Agincourt and those bloody French.

'Cry God for Harry! England, Scotland, Ireland, Wales, Nigeria and St. George!' said Logan to the corridor before leaving the field for abed.

'How about us Manxmen then?' said a voice.

'And all the tax havens' added Logan apologising profusely to Douglas as he had forgotten the Isle of Man and the lesser islands excluding Rockall.

It was suddenly over and everyone went to bed even if the guitar player was forced to. A day later a Taff from Merthyr in the next room down and known to the troop as Taff Room Two nosed his way into Logan's room.

'Hear about eight troop then you lot see?' said Room Two shaking his head and well gutted. 'Gave one of our lot a right going over in the lavvy see, called him a wimp and there you are see and left him without his pants on...disgusting it was...I know, cos I was there!'

Logan recognised it from the setting. Fact or fiction didn't seem to matter; the effect was to combine weeks of frustration into the one unifying force. In a matter of little over a day seven troop to a man had purpose and had found an identity. They would beat eight troop in the colonel's manoeuvre or die in the trying. Nobody beats the shit out of one of our men and gets away with it was the resolve of the entire troop.

Keen now to a man the troop packed into the backroom of the NAAFI for a briefing on the colonel's little manoeuvre.

'Troop...shun!' bellowed Sergeant Head to the room as the colonel entered with an over expansive wave of his squash racquet.

'Thank you Sergeant Head...have the men sit quietly please.'

'Sarrhh!' shouted Head at the top of his voice 'you all heard the colonel shut the fuck up and settle down quietly...colonel sir!'

'Can we smoke' asked an optimistic voice.

'You will be smoking when me stick goes up your arse!' shouted Head, which was taken by everyone as a no.

Already it was an occasion, you could smell the testosterone as it mixed with the newly laid down lavender floor polish heavily buffed up for the occasion of the colonel who didn't usually go in the NAAFI.

'And it came to pass...'

'Quiet for your colonel at the back!' snapped Sergeant Head as the colonel looked out over his half frames before lowering his eyes to continue the scenario supplied by Major Calhoun.

'And it came to pass...that the Front for the Liberation of Occupied Parts of South Yorkshire...FLOPSY.' The colonel paused for greater affect as the troop looked on with a collective and amazed stone faced wonderment. 'Ever cowering away in their enclaves deep in the Yorkshire Moors some leagues hence and well north of Barnsley in the West Riding. These Leninist Johnnies, these plunderers of democracy, threaten the vast oil reserves of the Sultan of Middlesborough...in the North Riding. In the event of the insurrection succeeding they would without question remove the Sultan's oil reserves from orf of the spot market. The price of a barrel of crude would plunge...up and the world would go...down into irreversible turmoil and everlasting, eternal damnation.'

'Just so' said Calhoun encouraging the colonel from the side.

'Verily, costs of keeping your hunter at lowly stables would go through the roof and the economy of the western world would be undermined. Gentlemen farmers would be forced to cut hedges ruining the rough shoots and the move to chemical based fertilizer would inevitably pollute even the best rivers. Disaster would ensue and your quality salmon reaches would dwindle down to just a few rods worth having and the British way of life as we know and cherish it would disappear...no hunting, no shooting and no fishing...sound' said the colonel clearly into it and himself more than convinced with Calhoun's daft scenario.

Who amongst them could not be moved? A buzz of high incredulity and heavy apathy ran through the room mixed with the odd mumbled coughs turning into a stifled bollocks.

'Settle down for the colonel!' Shouted Head from the back to disguise the fact that it was him that said one of the bollocks.

'All that stands between chaos, anarchy and normality are you chaps here, you few, you happy band thus gathered, to take on wicked FLOPSY and save the world economy' said the colonel before sitting himself down to a rippled applause and to make way for the major.

'FLOPSY? Whispered Logan from the side of his mouth 'the man's a raving loony.'

'I give way to Major Calhoun and your troop officer' said the loony colonel swishing his racquet to display a powerful and cracking backhand that ranked him number one in the regimental squash team, a position that had absolutely nothing to do with his being a lieutenant colonel.

'Thank you colonel' said Calhoun beaming toady like before taking the platform and fighting the map to get it the right way up with Esso at the bottom right and not top left as Lieutenant Snotty had stuck it up.

Keen to assist in front of the colonel the young lieutenant jumped in to assist with a drawing pin and his officer's stick to hold up the top right corner as it peeled from the wall to reveal a squashed and unfortunate spider unlucky enough to be dangling somewhere under Middlesborough.

'The battle plans of the manoeuvre are as follows. Blue army here and there and red army here and here, and there and here, shown in respective colours of...' Calhoun paused to clear his throat.

'Blue and red sir' volunteered Snotty.

'Just so, just so' said Calhoun slightly annoyed at the interjection although he had paused.

'Azure blue and crimson...actually' said Snotty proudly lifting up and showing his set of early art colouring crayons and playing nervously with the end of his stick before sitting back down as the major stuck in a pin to get him out of the way.

'Thank you...' said Calhoun in a tone that said sit down or piss off, as the lieutenant took his seat casting a nervous eye over at the colonel.

'Crimson and blue...what was it? Anyway, red and blue crayon armies muster here and here...and I think also here, have we the right map number?' he said now looking to Snotty for assistance.

'Look at the bottom' put in the colonel agitated at the delay.

'Under the brown rings' said Snotty pointing down and to the right.

'Brown rings?' asked the colonel 'what's the brown here?'

'It's Van Dyke brown sir' said the lieutenant biting his lip and looking on the crayon box to check before nodding an affirmative.

'Looks more like coffee to me sir' said Calhoun.

'Not what's the colour you idiot what's it mean' said the colonel suddenly irritated.

'They're the marked no go areas sir' said Snotty picking it up.

'Do we have no go areas on this map?' asked Calhoun to the room before Logan and most everybody other than Snotty lost him.

'Which finally brings us to the rules of engagement' said the major ignoring his notes and looking to move quickly on.

It was simple enough, number seven troop red army were up against the now hated eight troop blue army. Opposing teams would be dropped off at different locations and make their way across a no man's land to launch an attack on the other's headquarters that would save the world economy. Simple.

'On the way teams will find set obstacles to overcome. Any troops encountering said enemy are at liberty to attack and render them dead by removal and retention of their opponents arm-band.'

'Harm bands is issued after the brief' said Corporal Jock holding them haloft for those bothering to look.

'Winning troop will be the one that gets through all the obstacles in the time set for each and is the first to get one of their men into the opposing HQ still in possession of his arm band.'

'That is your exercise objective seven troop' said the colonel enthusiastically as it was his daft idea after all.

Roughly translated, red army would defend their HQ from the attacking blue army and themselves attack the enemy HQ. Meet enemy, pull off armbands to kill them off and go through a few dopey obstacles. Who needed a two hour briefing?

'Now chaps we need two teams, attack and defence...who wants to have a crack at the elite SAS...the special assault squad...we need ten good men...seven troop...come, come, seven troop?'

It was a big ask but hands began to go up across the room including Logan's who for one thought it would be good fun to get out of camp and drive around in a land rover for a day or so. Driving around in a land rover was his kind of exercise. Teams for defence and attack were quickly picked from an unlikely bunch of misfits before coming down to the last few that nobody wanted. The shame of being last man picked likely brought memories of the schoolyard flooding back for many. Finally it came down to Wee Jock and Compton who found himself by luck and default along with the rest of room three in the special assault squad and anyway they would need a spare driver said Logan excusing the pick even though he knew Compton couldn't drive.

'Distance between HQ will be twenty five miles as the crow flies...and hiking gear and tents can be drawn from squadron stores for the assault teams. Now, any questions?' said the major.

The silence was sliceable; you could have cut it with a plastic butter knife. Interest and enthusiasm died a death at the words hiking gear and went six foot under at the words five and twenty and miles.

'Oh shit' said a mumbled voice speaking for the greater majority.

Oh shit wasn't the word for it felt Logan as the realization of it all struck home. This was not an exercise as in to exert one's rights or exercise as in a lined book, nor was it an exercise as in military training but exercise as in physical exertion. Without question the only question now was who in seven troop special assault squad could walk twenty five miles. Some of them would have difficulty bussing it. It was a big if not impossible ask.

Compton immediately cried off sick and back at the barracks produced pills and cough drops to prove it but all was too late. War was already declared.

'Now is not the time for wobbly knees' said Logan.

Brum however, was as wobbly as he was perplexed and had to sit down just at the thought of it.

'Twenty five chuffing miles as the crow flies' he kept saying from the end of his bed 'that's doing me head in that is.'

'That's like doing a marathon that is' said Taff.

'Craws canny fly twenty five miles' put in Wee Jock and well aware it was further for him than any of them.

With official briefings now over and the colonel well out of it being two points down in a squash court lunch time decider Logan called a strategy and tactics meeting in room three or the war room three as it had become known within the troop. With reports of enemy taunts and threats already coming in from the NAAFI, seven troop self elected strategists gathered in the phoney war before hostilities began.

From a quick look around they were hardly a physical match for a pack of brownies never mind whatever the blue army would serve up. They were troops more shocking than shock but what they lacked in ability they would make up for in stealth, deviousness, outright cheating and animal cunning said Logan as the image of a running chicken flashed to mind. Before him sat the chosen men.

'Brum, Scouse, Taff, Shorty Hardcastle, Long Arms Miller, Chalkie, Prince Ojuku and Wee Jock. God almighty what a team' he said 'Who's missing?'

'Don't you mean what?' said Scouse.

'Hope' said Chalkie hitting it bang on.

'We forgot Compton, he's away at the medics' said Jock.

Hope where art thou thought Logan as the image of the chicken returned, now roasting away on a slow turning spit as the words well and stuffed came to mind.

'What we need is a masterly plan' he said looking around at what fate had dealt him but then he had volunteered.

Logan made a solemn promise with his inner self, 'never' he said, 'will I volunteer for anything ever again, self.'

'I should bloody well hope not' came a reply from deep within.

It was a lifetime promise, second only to the one made to The Almighty shortly after arriving at Catterick, 'never ever will I join anything again, God.'

'I should bloody well hope not' came a reply also from deep within that could have been a bush.

'Not even a Christmas club' said Logan quietly to himself as the strategy meeting ended without one.

By the beginning of the manoeuvre the troop had reached agreement only on the first part of a fiendish plan; they agreed they needed one. Without a plan the defending force fell to a strategy of forming a band of men around red army HQ tent. The plan changed as rain was forecast to be a band of men within red army HQ tent.

'There was always a flaw in that plan Chalkie' said Logan looking around his attacking force. 'Ojuku and Long Arms from next door plus whinging Taff, malingering Compton, two stroppy dwarfs and a fat Brum. Doesn't exactly leave you with a feeling of confidence does it?'

'Still you've got me' said Scouse overhearing.

'So we have' said Logan turning away and raising his eyebrows to the shaking head of Chalkie. Just don't say it, was what Chalkie's shake of head said.

The red army crammed into the back of a three ton Bedford with a reluctance of men going over the top. An early misty frost was forming as the truck set off from camp with a coughing exhaust and a chugging Compton. Already things were looking iffy. Not two hours out Compton lost his armband killing himself off before a shot was fired. How special force is that thought Logan. He was still working on the masterly plan when their vehicle came to an unexpected halt at a deserted unmarked crossroads deep on the Yorkshire moors.

'That's daft look, no road sign...don't you have signs in Yorkshire then Chalkie?' asked Taff poking his head through a gap in the front cover.

'Here's one' said Chalkie sticking two fingers up followed by one finger on its own followed by a left hand to right elbow before running out of them.

Every general needs a little luck as Napoleon said on his way to Elba amongst a lot of other useless stuff about food said Compton and red army was getting their's in the form of a lost Royal Corps of Transport driver. The words 'can anybody in the back read a map?' echoed through the truck before Logan jumped to the warmth of the front changing places with the protesting Brum. An hour later Logan delivered them to the given red army HQ grid reference. Or close enough to it in his opinion to be within the spirit of fair play.

'Is this it then...doesn't look a bit like it did on the map?' shouted Scouse mouthing down the line of men pissing against the side of the truck.

Why is it one out all out and why is it always in a line never a circle or a communal group thought Logan before deciding he really should get out more?

'Yes, this is the place' he affirmed ignoring Scouse and banging loudly on the side of the Bedford.

Away went the truck to reveal the cascading lines of arching urine and steam rising slowly up into the cold of the morning.

'Yorkshire fresh air' said Chalkie taking a deep breath and proudly bending at the knees to see off the last drop before leaving the line.

Shakes over and all put away and with steam still on the rise they moved to dry ground to survey the map.

'Why's we in the brown no go area rings?' asked an overly inquisitive Ojuku.

'That's a coffee ring' Chalkie said immediately getting the picture.

By the time the manoeuvre umpires in the form of Lt. Snotty and Sergeant Head arrived with their hot water bottles the red army HQ tent had been up an hour and the Forestry Commission Experimental Plantation sign had been well hidden further into the plantation. Neither of them being what you might call good readers never mind good map-readers, both Snotty and Head stayed silent believing they must have gone to the wrong place two hours before. At the appointed time red army were released away by Snotty with a wave of his hankie and a blow of his dose.

They were in surprisingly good spirits apart from Compton or they were until they started the walking. Behind them seven troop's beefiest ringed an HQ set in an area marked out of bounds to all but the agricultural scientists of the Forestry Commission.

'If they had wanted people to keep out they should have put a bigger sign up' said Logan justifying the shameful trespass.

'Zackly' said Chalkie agreeing with him.

What a defence. Ahead lay twenty five long miles and the colonel's unknown but 'must be bloody stupid if Calhoun had anything to do with it' series of objectives.

'Not forgetting the approach of the blue army tackling their own version of the objectives and coming the other way' said Ojuku.

By mid morning they reached the first of the bloody stupid objectives and paused to wonder. More obstacle than objective thought Logan but they were right on with the bloody stupid. At first sight the objective showed to be a perfectly crossable rope bridge over an imaginary gorge manned by Punchy Smith the PTI Sergeant. This alone should have started alarm bells ringing although as Chalkie said; Punchy would know all there was to know about swinging off ropes.

The bridge as Punchy loosely called it, was no more than two horizontal and parallel ropes set five feet apart and lashed between two trees.

'It has to be an idea of the barking daft major' said Logan.

'Clearly the idea is to walk on the bottom rope and hold the top one for balance?' said Compton as they stood to give it the once over.

How can anything so simple be made so impossible to traverse? During construction Punchy had managed to make the top rope tighter than the bottom. This meant that the man on the bridge was fine when first on the rope near to the tree but as he neared the centre the bottom rope began to stretch and his hands and top rope slowly rose above his head. It looked like the man on the rope was slowly giving himself up.

At full and maximum stretch this left just the two alternatives. Let go of the top rope and tightrope walk to the end, which was impossible to do because of the slackness of the bottom rope, or dangle like pegged washing from the tighter top rope. Edging forward along the rope and with arms now at full stretch, eventually weight transferred to the top rope in any event. The bottom rope now relieved of any calculable load rose up to meet the top rope as the man's legs bent to keep on.

Now taking all the weight of the man, the top rope slowly came down as the bottom rope slowly came up. That is it did until strength gave out and the man was forced to release the upper rope. The top rope now went up with a spring and, with all the weight now taken by the lower rope it went to earth. Inevitably the man fell off the rope...and, as he hit the ground the bottom rope now sprang up to look like a perfectly crossable rope bridge explained Chalkie who was first to fall off.

'How deep is the imaginary gorge then?' asked Chalkie as he rejoined the group.

'That gorge?' said Punchy stroking his chin and looking down into it. 'A thousand foot...'

'That's dangerous that is Chalkie' said Brum 'you could have hurt yourself.'

'Hurt myself?' said Chalkie sticking his head down into chest 'I could have broken my effing neck!'

Consequently only long Arms Miller made it across and Wee Jock dangled from the top rope for some time before the man's strength gave in. Logan went back on for a hand over hand traverse using only the bottom rope but was disqualified as his feet went to ground.

'Hang on, we have a theoretical gorge here' he argued, 'the ground is not there.'

Punchy ruled that as it wasn't theoretically there they couldn't use it, which was all a bit too subliminal for Logan who gave up the argument.

'How can I be using something if it's not there then?' he said which got Punchy thinking for a time but not about changing his decision.

Scouse came to a very nasty dismount when attempting a top rope slide and pull traverse from the south with a two leg hitch over at the ankles that gave them all a fascinating few moments as he bounced rope to rope until he too came off. Most entertaining of all was an attempt by Taff that began as a horizontal forward pull and push with right knee and ankle hitched over the rope and left foot dangling. It was a death slide without a slide that ended with the man slung beneath like a captured missionary in a Tarzan movie. Only Ojuku thought that one funny as he knew a thing or two about dangling missionaries.

At the end of the impassable rope bridge was a rope swing over an imaginary pit.

'Pretty standard for obstacle courses this one' said Taff spitting into his hands and grabbing eagerly at the rope or he did until Punchy announced it was spanning an imaginary crocodile pit.

'Anyone falling into the pit will be eaten by the man eating crocodiles' announced Punchy enthusiastically and clearly looking to see it happen.

'That's just about as pathetic a metaphoric illusion as you can get' said Logan quietly but keeping well back from the edge.

'Absolutely there are no bloody crocodiles in Yorkshire and I know that for a fact' said Chalkie moving behind Logan.

It took the team one and a half minutes to find some and another two to get Ojuku to let go of the rope. From the screams he had a thing about crocodiles.

'Something from my early childhood with crocodiles' said Ojuku now off the rope.

'Nigeria?' asked Logan sympathetically.

'Prep school in Surrey, we did Peter Pan' said Ojuku losing much of Logan's sympathy.

At the next obstacle they were presented with four planks and the compulsory outward-bound empty oil drum, three pieces of rope and another bloody stupid objective. This time the drum, without touching the ground, had to get to a circle of rocks twenty yards away via a fork in a tree.

'Why?' asked Logan to receive no answer.

What is it about practical problem exercises that insist on there being an oil drum? Why not something small and manageable like a can of WD40 said Logan to one of Punchy's PTI assistants.

'Why the hell is anything served by getting a drum up in the air and over the fork of a tree?' He asked knowing there was no answer but having interest in the likely response.

'For the exercise' was the reply from the PTI.

'Well then' he said 'let's just roll the bastard thing over there and do a few fucking push ups?'

It got him the push-ups but left the drum where it was. An hour later and giving up Logan threw the poles and the rope over the fork and stood back defiantly as the PTI passively ticked a box on his clipboard and stayed silent.

'I think the idea here see, is to do something with them all at the same time' said Taff finally getting it.

'Just where the hell have you been for the last hour Taff?'

'Why don't we just pick it up and throw it over' said Scouse returning to the original problem.

'If we could have done that don't you think we would have already you stupid prat' said Brum having had enough of it and walking on to the next obstacle.

'Watch out for the river' shouted one of the PTI's.

'You've walked into the water' exclaimed Scouse entering into the meaningless spirit of it all.

'He's right' said the PTI 'that's a river is that, you should be in the pretend boat.'

'It's only up to my bastard knees...it only comes up to my knees what's wrong with that, I'm having a paddle, I've pissed deeper than this river.'

'Piranhas it says here' said the PTI reading from his brief.

'Bollocks to the Piranhas' said Brum splashing his way to the bank and losing ten valuable points.

'Don't blame me sunshine I didn't put them in there' said the PTI turning defensive, he didn't want to be out there either.

'How the sodding hell can anyone fall out of an imaginary boat?' Mumbled Brum as they left for the next obstacle.

Arriving at the grid reference they found a land rover parked half the way up a hill and another PTI. Even Compton perked up when he saw the land rover or he did until the rope appeared.

'The land rover's clapped out and for maximum points we need to get it to the top of the hill' said the PTI picking up his clipboard.

'What the hell for if the bloody thing's clapped out?' said Logan looking again for the logic of it.

'How many points do we get if we roll it down to the bottom of the hill?' asked Chalkie.

'Your objective is to get the land rover up to the top of the hill' said the PTI starting to take on a strop.

'Only the army would ask men to pull a perfectly driveable land rover up a hill with a key still in the ignition.' said Brum.

'This is really sad, whatever next?' said Logan.

It was a stretcher carry, another PTI and another hill only bigger.

'Just to the top of the hill' said the PTI gesturing with his binos to a flag some way off that was the size of a flake of dandruff.

This he explained was where they had to carry the wounded man to.

'We haven't got one' said Logan.

'It says here one of you is a stretcher case' said the PTI reading from his board and pointing a finger towards the group. Compton's hand went up for one pointing to a developing blister and followed by several others as the PTI sensed rebellion.

'Man on stretcher, top of hill, in you own time, carry on...go!' said the PTI reverting to gym speak.

'We have come through a world of theatrical imaginary, bastard crocodiles, Brum eating fish, invented rivers and theoretical gorges and now we have to have an actual wounded man?' asked Logan searching once more for the disappearing logic.

Valuable time was lost drawing lots for who was going on the stretcher. It was always going to be Wee Jock. Five hundred yards later they arrived at the flag needing a stretcher each. Not that Long Arms could help it but with him on one end it was like carrying the thing on a perpetual hill even on the flat ground. At the flag stood the camp armourer with a groundsheet spread on which was piled an assembly of broken weapon parts.

'This here is a pile of mixed weapon parts belonging to four different broken down types of weapon' explained the armourer, 'you have to assemble the weapons, load one and take out the sniper hiding in that tree over yonder. No need to duck son, he's not ready to fire yet.'

'Four you say?' asked Logan checking with the armourer like there was some doubt about it.

The objective was to assemble the weapons, load with blanks and prove the correct assembly by firing one of them at the imaginary sniper. With a combined effort the team completed the task well enough but found they had a part left over. Scouse now came clean, he had also trodden on something hard when they arrived which added another complication. At length the decision was their best bet for the fire test had to be the rifle which was loaded with the blanks and given to Chalkie as one of the two best shots. Closing one eye he pulled the trigger to a loud and ominous click.

'Bang?' said the armourer holding up the firing pin and shaking his head 'zero points.'

'It's only missing the firing pin' pleaded Chalkie like it should make a difference.

'That's like an arrow missing only the bow' said the armourer 'if that man hiding behind the tree down there was the enemy we would all be dead now.'

'We were anyway, we've only got blanks' said Logan heading off down the hill.

The colonel's little games over for the day they headed out through no man's land expecting with every step to bump into the opposing army. Eight troop were eventually spotted just before dark doubling away in the distance. Having decided at the outset that fighting to take armbands would be as pointless as the manoeuvre clearly was the team waited for them to get a good bit further away before standing to hurl childish abuse.

As night descended to stars and a likely frost they found a hollow in the ground, crowded round the hexamine cookers for warmth until the fuel ran out and ate heartily of the warmed tins of Irish stew and hardtack biscuits. After a few hours attempt at sleep and with everyone awake listening to Compton cough but Compton the collective decision was to push on through the forest to get warm. At dawn Scouse fell into a hollow, which on inspection was found to be the same hollow from the evening before but at least in the light they found their missing compass.

Finding themselves back where they had started was seen as a bit of a set back to morale, which didn't lift again until they dumped the sneezing Compton off at a road junction for him to make his own way back. Now able to increase their pace to a stagger they arrived mid afternoon at the grid reference of the final obstacle, which the colonel in his wisdom had placed on the opposite bank of a not too slow, flowing river.

One of the few still on his feet Chalkie walked the near bank looking for the oil drums as Logan went in search of a PTI with a make believe bridge. After a half hour's search for the pretend boat or the imaginary helicopter or the Bismarck there came a growing and awful feeling from within. This really stupid obstacle just might be even more stupid than imagined and had been there all along. Clearly it was the river.

With the route lying directly ahead and after several checks to verify the grid reference the obstacle had to be the water. After a quick inspection of the depth observed from the sound of a thrown rock all doubts were removed, this was it.

'What we need is a rope and an oil drum' said Scouse sitting down on the bank.

'And a tree with a branch and a noose' agreed Logan.

'And the colonel's fucking neck' suggested Chalkie.

'I think what we should do here is give up' said Brum joining Scouse on the bank to look at the map.

'No canoe no crossing' said Ojuku clearly fearing crocodiles but really not wanting to get a soaking.

'There's a bridge' shouted Brum looking up from the map suddenly excited until measuring the distance, 'about fifteen miles away.'

'Any more daft ideas?' asked Scouse.

'We could cut down a tree with an axe and make a raft' voiced Ojuku.

'We could use a chain saw it's faster' put in Wee Jock.

'Where the bloody hell do we get a chain saw from?' said Scouse.

'Same place Ojuku gets his axe from' said Jock, which was fair enough as daft ideas go.

Daft ideas were still coming thick and fast but it was cold that moved them to a decision. With the alternative being the best part of a twenty three mile walk back and hot tea two miles across thirty foot or so of water there was no decision. Once getting wet was admitted as an inevitability it needed only an agreed method of crossing but with such a fair torrent running and no rope that would not be easy.

An idea to wade in fully clothed and holding hands in a long line was put forward by Logan and seconded by Long Arms Miller who naturally would be central to success of such a plan. Brum agreed with the idea as he had seen it done once in a jungle film and they almost made it over so it was well worth having a go. There is always someone with a better idea and there was now.

'Right' Scouse said taking up the challenge 'what we do here is strip off to the buff, tie our clothes in bundles and chuck em over the water ahead of us.'

'You can't be serious' said Brum.

'That way when we get over there we have dry clothes to put on see?'

Scouse tapped a finger to his temple as if there was something in there and on a show of hands the team went for it. Within minutes they were stripped stark naked holding hands and shivering in a developing wind.

'It's true what they say then...' said Brum looking over at Ojuku with envy before lowering his head.

With clothes bundled around boots for extra weight the responsibility of throwing them across fell to Scouse who volunteered and was accepted on the proviso put forward by Brum that he could throw his own over first. It was a comfortable enough throw with a decent enough safety margin even for the doubters as one by one the bundles were handed over to land in a crooked line on the far bank. All went well until the last bundle that landed safely enough only to roll back down the bank into the water and away down the river.

'You did that on purpose you Scouse git' said Brum watching his bundle sink as the team made their way down and into the river.

Getting down the bank to the water was hazardous in bare feet but first to the water Logan established a good anchor hold and with a cry bordering pain eased one foot out into the icy river. Once his feet were secure he called down for the next man with some urgency as it was freezing even if the water did only come up to his knees. The second man edged in and past Logan as another quickly followed.

'Let's get it over with' shouted Wee Jock his voice rising an octave and a half as his bollocks were first to the water.

The line now stretched out to mid river and water was growing deeper as hands linked hand to hand in a long and wobbly human chain. With the team now spanning half the river Logan left the near bank to begin his crawl down the line of shaky bodies. There was a general consensus that the water was cold but Ojuku saying it was deep too was ignored by everyone.

Although naturally wobbly due to a river flow that required each man to keep tight hold of the next man's hand Scouse's idea for once was working like a dream. After several traversals they arrived mid river, all arms outstretched, hand to hand and spread out like a human daisy chain. It was at their most vulnerable position not linked to either bank and shivering like the very devil when the sound of voices came through a lull in the chattering of teeth. From over the hill on the opposite bank came the happy sound of singing.

'Faleri falera faleri falera ha, ha, ha, ha, ha, ha, faleri falera, und schwenke meinen hut...'

It was The Happy Wanderer followed by the tops of little brown woolly hats as one by one a Brownie pack came slowly into view.

'Perverts' shouted the Brown Owl pulling the Brownies away and ramming the hats down over the eyes of the more persistent.

'Perverted swine' she called again coming back for another look and to collect her Tawny.

For the school exchange group Brownie pack von Hamburg it was a nature trail to remember and it beat the hell out of collecting conkers and mushroom spotting for young Tawny. The team were on the bank and still dressing when Brum found his bundle held tight against a line of submerged river stepping stones. A feeling of the senseless futility of it all descended on the group. Resigned now to their fate they retrieved the soaked bundle and trudged the remaining miles in an absolute and total silence but for the sound of squelching coming up from Brum's boots at the rear.

It was late afternoon when they finally came upon blue HQ tent and by then they were a pitiful sight even in the fading light. So far they had made it through crocodile pits, an ambulance commando stretcher course, raging river torrents and had been branded perverts by a German Brown Owl and her lovely Tawny. Added to this they had made it twenty five miles through the abandoned wastelands of Yorkshire without bearers, artificial aids and any guides discounting the Brownies. They had survived it all to a man but for the sickly Compton who Logan for one thought likely dead.

'A feat unto itself' said Logan returning with Chalkie from a recce of the area that showed a heavy defending force that ruled out a frontal assault plan.

Second plan was a 'look out there's someone behind you' plan of Scouse's that received just the one vote. This left a 'wave at the defenders and a run off plan to lure them away from the tent and sneak someone in at the back' that got the majority vote.

It was a fiendishly simple plan that may have worked if only the defending forces had stayed ringed about and in their tent rather than ringed around the red army as they now were. After a brief and pathetic fight the attacking force fell to superior strength and the surprise of attack. Stripped of armbands and taken prisoner they were triumphantly dragged into the blue army

HQ tent for a well-received strong cup of Yorkshire tea. At last for them the war game was over. Still it was due to finish in half an hour anyway and it was getting darker with each minute.

Inside the tent eight troop's officer scoffing at the capture relayed the news to red HQ by radio. The news received back advised no sign of blue army likely lost somewhere in the area of the coffee ring felt Logan allowing himself just the briefest smile of satisfaction for that at least. The war game would be a draw and who cared about the obstacles anyway.

They were into the final minutes and someone was firing up a second storm lamp when the colonel's land rover arrived with the colonel and a very sick casualty of war in the back.

'Don't just stand there' said the blue army officer peering out into the gloom as the tailboard dropped to show the prone body in the back. 'Go carry the poor man in.'

Within seconds the casualty was carried into the tent and dumped to the ground as the officer pushed a storm lamp in his face. The man looked green with a tinge of yellow but most of this was due to the storm lamp thought Logan. One look at Compton could tell you he wasn't sick but crying sick. He always looked that colour but in half-light of dusk on a forested track both colonel and his driver the adjutant thought Compton a major percentage dead on his feet.

Counting the seconds down eight troop's officer blew a whistle and the manoeuvre was over.

'Well done chaps,' said the colonel. 'Honours equal and all level with the obstacles but damn bad luck neither side placed a man in enemy headquarters.'

The colonel searched for his hip flask and was about to declare the day an even draw when Compton's eyes crossed. He was about to sneeze; the man really was ill thought Logan. Anxious not to sneeze over the colonel, Compton made a frantic search of pockets for a handkerchief before finally coming up with a red rag just before his sneeze abated much to the relief of those on his side of the tent at least.

That is Logan thought it a rag, but it was no less than the long lost armband hidden away amongst all the pills, tissues and Fisherman's Friends that filled Compton's pockets. The colonel was first to spot it, seizing it on his stick with an enthusiastic grunt.

'You damn cunning little blighters seven troop' said the colonel to the amazed look of all about him. 'Full bloody marks for initiative. You got your man into the enemy HQ still with his armband and before the final whistle...don't you know! Eh? First rate, didn't expect to see it done like this did we Adj? Well I'll be buggered. Well bloody done red army and well bloody done seven troop!'

With that the colonel promptly awarded the day to seven troop and stormed off with the adjutant in tow heading for the mess.

'Bloody damn fine show Adj. first bloody class. To the mess Adj. Jaldi, Jaldi...to the mess!'

Logan was beginning to get a soft spot for the colonel even though the man was a raving loony.

16

Announcing seven troop as outright winners automatically placed the troop top of the points in the inter-troop competition. Such unexpected and weighty success went straight to everyone's heads. For eight troop it got there through their noses. The result turned the planned end of training commiseration piss up into something of a celebration one and after consultation with all the piss heads they decided on a pub in Richmond that needed the trade enough to let them in and a kitty. Chalkie who had experience of these things, said the thing to do is to eat slices of dry bread before you go out as it soaks up the alcohol. It was like skimming two rounds of bread down a slide into a swimming pool. As with any drink kitty the chief objective was to drink more than you put in, the consequence of which ensures you get thoroughly rat-arsed early doors. Corporal Jock stayed with it for the entire event and was the centre pivot of the evening. This was appreciated by the troop almost as much as Sergeant Head not turning up.

Dumped at barracks by an over racy Bedford driver bereft of sleep and concern at the disquiet he was causing in the back of his truck the troop staggered to billets in a haze of alcoholic excess. Fallen bodies lay about the block in an aftermath of drink overdose, some sleeping where they lay as others like Logan made it to their rooms only with support of mates and corridor walls alike. Collapsing to his bed

Logan fell to the sleep of a hibernating bear waking only at the call of nature and the deafening sound of a seltzer in full fizz.

With Jock also suffering, the morning parade was a quiet affair as he dismissed the troop to sign off local issue kit such as sheets and blankets. The form required a release from every department on camp some of which were only found at the point of signature. Only then were they released to well deserved leave. Suddenly it was all over but for the goodbyes.

Chalkie, Brum and some of the others including Compton were to join Logan on the same course of signals training. Nine months of it for the first level and then a posting before returning to complete another six months in another year or so and then another six months after that. It seemed to Logan a long time to learn how to blow a puff of smoke from beneath a sodden blanket.

'No, that's sodden Scouse' said Compton 'not sodding.'

'I know, I know. That's what I said...sodden.'

Mercifully Scouse was not coming with them but was off to train in coding as a cipher operator. How the army could think he was someone to keep his mouth shut is an enigma to me said Logan. Scouse would be missed but not by Logan and Chalkie and Compton and Brum and Taff and Wee Jock as the man hadn't made many friends in room three or in the other rooms either felt Logan and Chalkie and Compton and Brum and Taff and Wee Jock.

Some of eight troop were also destined for signals training and arrived at the corridor to say the war was over. At a stroke them became us in the way it has always happened with foes sooner or later, disregarding our natural enemy the French of course as Compton said.

Passing out parade was no trooping of the colour. The Queen, God bless her wasn't there for one and there was no overgrown hairy dog but for seven troop's standards it went well enough and even Compton managed to stay in step for once or maybe it was twice. The colonel's little manoeuvre had become something of a watershed for the man. It was the first thing he had ever done right in his life and he became a changed man basking in the short lived glory. He would always be Compton but what the hell did anyone care, they were champion troop, and marching to a band all mistakes were placed at the door of the flautist being out of sync with the big base drum anyway as the music played beyond dull care.

Seven troop led the way onto the hallowed ground for the last time as top troop; the colonel took the salute from the podium with his customary squash racquet watched by an agitated Major Calhoun who had double booked the squash courts with the pass out. Needless to say the event was not announced in the papers concerned as they were with the heir to the throne getting pissed on cherry brandy and doubtlessly getting his leg over some horse or other.

High overhead the Red Arrows performed a fly past for some obscure event miles from Catterick and Corporal Jock got a miniature plaque to hang on the troop office wall.

For Sergeant Head it really was his last troop and after an enforced collection he received an inscribed pace stick that Logan was roped in by Jock to organise. You don't get much for one pound four pence, an Irish pig penny and a plastic coat button but it did get an engraved band for his stick. Many including Logan were for sticking it up his arse but made do with a slight modification to the intended engraving before handing it over in a little ceremony to mark the occasion.

'To Drill Sergeant Richard Head from champion seven troop...happy retirement Dick Head, from all the boys in the troop' said Logan reading from the stick.

'Dick Head?' said Chalkie 'I didn't know he was a Dick Head?'

'Where have you been all these months?' said Logan, 'only from day bloody one Chalkie, only from day bloody one.'

Their prize was a rail warrant with an additional seventy two hour extended leave and a posting out of recruit training. What more could a man ask for. Logan had survived it with everything pretty well intact. He was a trained soldier. Why should Britain tremble?

17

It was Logan's very first day of communications training and it began like any other Monday morning. The sun shone high in the heavens but failed to penetrate the British cloud cover and the weather down on earth arrived as rain. Fact was it pissed down. Was this a sign from God or was it a signal? Untrained as he was Logan felt unqualified to have a view either way. He was pondering this very thought as the taxi approached 24 Signals Regiment training camp a mile or so from camp centre. Outside the guardroom on a plinth stood a five foot bronze statue of Mercury the winged messenger of the gods accusingly pointing an index forefinger to the heavens above as he balanced on one leg.

'That's Jimmy said the driver' all knowing of these things and going friendly for a tip. 'Mercury he was to the Greeks and Hermes to the Romans. He was the messenger to the gods that lad.'

'With bloody weather like this the bastard's got the wrong finger up. It should be the middle finger' Logan said sliding from the cab with kit bag and holdall before waiting for the two suitcases to be dragged from the boot.

It was every bit of kit and clothing that Logan owned and it was always the way with a new posting. Surprising as it was to Logan even with the rain he was happy to return. On the whole his leave had been disappointing from day one. So much is that is over anticipated. Logan had arrived home in full ready to party mode and well happy to escape for a couple of weeks. He found everyone else in Monday to Friday working mode leaving only Saturday nights with anything much happening.

The truth of it was that place and times had moved on for Logan. Even after a few short months he found himself a stranger to his past as the world and all around him turned civilian to his soldier. With Bernice a fond memory in an address book full of crossed out names, by the end of the second week he knew there was a need to move on...either that or turn celibate. Back at camp at least there were similar lost souls one way or the other and as names in books go there was always the lovely Roxanne, or the cousin thought Logan as a pleasant afterthought...or both together? He had turned to wish dreaming and erotic fantasies and after a much awaited leave he found himself lustless.

After basic training Logan had assumed that some of the short, sharp shock symbolist crap that had been his lot so far would end when he became a trained soldier. He expected a degree of professionalism and what he found was army. It's like coming of age to realize you still haven't a vote. The taxi had barely time to turn and leave with a squeal of tyre denoting no tip before Logan ran foul of the camp RPs or at least the smug one on lollipop duty at the gate. Hardly bothering to look over his shoulder RP Smuggy used his little RP stick to indicate across the square at a half-mile long Sandhurst block that would be home to Logan for the next nine months. Clutching his bags and noisily dragging the loaded suitcase behind Logan set off wearily making his way across. The RP took Logan's walk onto the parade ground as some kind of personal attack.

'Come back here that man!' called the RP shaking his head enough to dislodge his cap with the ubiquitous slashed peak of the RP that was a sign of the breed.

'You pointed and said straight across the square' said Logan retracing his steps to arrive back at the gates.

'Straight across the square means go around not amble straight over the bleeder! Didn't they teach you bastards anything in basic...you on medication or somefink and stand to attention when an NCO addresses you, come on move yourself!'

For a fleeting moment Logan thought he was going in the nick, as the RP looked him up and down like he had just trodden in him. Logan entered into the spirit of the bollocking by feigning great fear, which went down well with the low life who sent him off after taking his name for his little book.

'Compton' said Logan before being released to the barracks via a route that retraced his footsteps back to the main road and past the RP's little sentry box to begin again.

He arrived at the accommodation block looking like Long Arms Miller. Why is the shortest distance between two points on an army square always a right angle. It's bad geometry. What makes a grown man spend his day protecting tarmac from foot traffic and seeing it as normal and why do RPs get away with slashing their peaked caps? To such things Logan felt there is no answer although he mouthed one as he left the RP with a look bordering on dumb insolence. Jumped up local rank lance corporals, unpaid and unwanted was how Logan saw it as he walked off to the block.

'Fucking arsehole' said the RP behind him as he left.

'Exactly' said Logan overhearing but in a whisper to himself that increased in volume and intensity of foul language with every distancing step.

He arrived at the bedding store sounding like an outraged Tourette. After a search for his name on a list Logan found his room and drew bedding from a reluctant unshaved civilian eating a floppy sandwich who couldn't even be bothered to open the bedding book.

'Sign, name and number' said the man abruptly speaking with a spray of food from an overfull mouth as Logan picked up the pen and wrote on the buff front cover.

'Thank you civilian person' said Logan turning to leave.

'Not on the front, Jesus!' said the man dropping his sandwich and now opening the book at the signature page.

'No, just Logan' he said signing the book and checking for who had already booked in.

Some welcome back this is Logan thought hoping he was catching the place on a bad day but feeling the heavy label of recruit still dangling from his neck. They were in training and all knew it and even if he didn't think so he was still little more than half-baked.

Being Sunday new trainees and returnees could be seen scattered around but mostly the place was dead and empty to an echo. He found Chalkie already in the room as he struggled in with his bedding. Choosing a free bed Logan dumped the sheets and blankets before leaving with Chalkie to retrieve his bags strategically abandoned to the floors below. Chalkie seemed pleased to see him and said some of the others were also back early.

'Ey up, Wee Jock's aboot and Shorty Hardcastle. Still, better than coming backly.'

'Appen thar's rite Chalkie by eck wheer's me cap, English?' said Logan taking the piss but more to let Chalkie know he needed to start speaking English again, 'what's bloody backly? Two and bit weeks leave and you've turned bloody Tyke on me. After all my work with you.'

'Our jolly fain friends short stuff one and two have returned beck...an ave fucked off on a recce to the NAAFI with Brum, is tha larkin art t'nite?' said Chalkie taking the point and giving a bit back before introducing Logan to someone called Jacko.

'Why not' said Logan moving over to meet the man.

'He's on our course and from down south, some island or other.'

Logan knew the man by sight as being from eight troop.

'Wotcha' said the man speaking in a husky high-pitched voice and looking up from a free issue newspaper that looked more like an information sheet than a paper.

'Jackson, everyone calls me Jacko, Isle of Dogs mate' said Jackson all up himself and smiling like it should mean something as it clearly did to him. 'Cockney from the east end?'

'Eh?' said Logan being awkward.

'East end, London? Hello?'

'Oh London, sorry mush, where's that near again?' asked Logan checking out his locker and feigning a laugh that died in both throats.

It was a voice from lavatories past for Logan and he recognized it immediately as kit was dumped in locker and locked for sorting later.

'No locker layouts' said Chalkie 'just works parade eight o'clock tomorrow morning on the square by the guardroom.'

'Know it well' said Logan as the pair left for the NAAFI and more than a couple of sneck lifters.

Morning parade the following day was a raincoat parade taken by a major who introduced himself as Head of Signals. He was one of the old school officer gentleman foppish types with a monocle and a hankie sticking out from the sleeve of his Crombie. The major welcomed them to the school, waffled on a bit about the bike sheds and running in corridors before taking the salute from a sergeant major and leaving for his morning coffee.

'That's him done for the day then' said Compton placing himself in the middle rank out of habit as the parade was handed over to a corporal who was he said their training corporal for the duration.

Corporal Siggy as he was from then on was a quietly spoken man who advised them they were now TG2.

'That's telegraph two' he said explaining before adding he would be taking them for voice communications amongst other things.

Siggy was also in overall charge of admin which translated to Logan as a position missing the title dogsbody but he seemed nice enough once he gave his 'you piss me around and I'll piss you around' speech and resumed to something approaching his natural self. Where have you been all these months thought Logan.

To their side and at the edge of the square senior trainees, some with junior NCO rank attending upgrading courses were clambering up customized metal ladders into the backs of a line of trucks before heading off to training. Ending his welcome address with a roll call Siggy marched them away to their first day's training. Four paces in the order came to lower the swing of their arms from shoulder height to march at a leisurely half way house that made even Compton look good. Pouring rain apart things were looking up.

The training school was set in what must have once been accommodation blocks that were old even when the army was into woad and the Iceni into Italian baiting thought Logan as they came into view. It was a time warp of timber huts set around a central grassed no go area and standing a little back from the road leading to the WRAC camp.

'That's the WRAC camp up there' said Logan calling to Chalkie.

'Yeah, yeah' said Chalkie.

'That's handy then' said Taff at the side overhearing.

'You wish' said Brum.

'Where is it?' said Wee Jock further back and in the centre rank so he wouldn't be able to see anything anyway.

'Keep it down lads please' said the corporal as they neared the training area.

As they rounded a corner to halt at one of the huts Logan for one thought they were entering a POW camp.

'The only thing missing are the dogs, the machine gun towers and a vaulting horse' said Logan looking around as Siggy stood them down to enter the hut.

'Training room five TG2 double phys of E and M theory' said Siggy before handing them over to a man wearing a pinstripe suit he called Johnny.

A sign on the door read CLASSROOM 5 (THEORY). Logan entered a classroom rapidly filling up from the rear. Nothing changes he thought as the instructor moved behind an old wooden desk placed central to a raised platform and picked up a fresh stick of chalk, it was Monday morning.

'Electricity and Magnetism' wrote the civilian instructor on the board before turning back to the blank faces and one gaping mouth sitting at the back with Logan...it was Brum.

Johnnie Boyle their instructor for theory and much everything else, was a man in his early forties and an ex merchant navy radio officer who ran out of ships he said introducing himself as he gave out folded name desk cards calling each name as he walked along the rows.

Returning to the front the instructor observed the names before turning his own name card to face the class. Sir read the card in bold letters.

'Yes gentlemen, I am a civilian instructor...don't look so surprised some of you, it is allowed you know. We are the ones walking around in suits they can't tell to get a haircut. You hiding away at the back with the other shrinking violets Compton is it? Tell me Compton what do you know about electricity?'

'It moves down wires...and also up em.' Smirked Compton at his own quip.

'Does it by God! Electricity moves does it Compton, have you seen it have you? If ever you find any that does move Compton wrap two coils of barbed wire round it, post a bloody guard on it with a sodding great machine gun and you'll make a fucking fortune at the discovery! Got it?'

'Sir' said Compton reluctantly.

Sir stood to move to the board and underlined the word electricity before turning back to the class.

'Electricity! The movement of free electrons. Free Compton pay attention; not three...free electrons through a conductor. Current moves electricity does not...simple. Got it?'

'Yes sir' said Compton.

'Write it down and repeat after me, sir is always right. I and that means you Compton is, or am a bloody idiot. No, correction! I have the makings of being an idiot, as yet I am like a negative charged electron waiting to be positive.'

'An electron waiting to move along a conductor as current' said Compton.

'Yes Compton, by God, yes bloody yes! Sit up at the front where everyone can see you Compton.'

The man came alive at the subject and approached it like a demonic lunatic but he was the best and he and everyone knew it. For Compton it was the first time he had been centre of attention in any classroom to positive advantage electron or not and he savoured the feeling. Compton immediately liked the man, as did all the class even after a morning of amps, volts, ohms and watts and mega piss takes that charged some and challenged others.

It didn't take long to work out that all sir and the army wanted was a weekly pass mark for the basic skills and a line of ticks for the weekly theory and other such tests. All was easy enough once the answers were obtained from the previous intake by Chalkie and the questions obtained from the training office cupboard by theft. Securing the right answers was a way to learning in itself and the months passed by with little technical difficulty for most apart from touch typing for the teleprinter and the Morse code. How anything so easy to see could be such a bastard to learn. Try as he might Chalkie was struggling even from the beginning with the Morse flash cards and, as the group moved from cards to machine generated dots and dashes everyone hit the buffers at some time or other. Speeds were increasing by the week and the weekly timed tests became a major event.

'That Sam Morse' said Chalkie suddenly pensive 'must have been a right sadistic bastard.'

Sending and receiving Morse was like bashing away on a teleprinter for Logan, he had an aptitude for both. It wasn't a clever thing he could just do it but others especially Brum struggled from day one. Able to keep up to speed allowed evenings off. For him and a few others it was a painless enough passage where those failing the Friday afternoon tests found themselves with painful extra evening classes. That said, everyone struggled with what the army termed operational procedure or as Chalkie called it bastard radio speak.

'The uniformity of army radio transmissions for both Morse and voice in order not to give a footprint identity of the operator of use to the enemy' said Siggy giving an official definition.

'Eh?' said Brum.

'Send the same, sound the same and anyone listening in can't track you, even if you are a Brummie. If they can track you, they track the unit you are with...simple. It was idiosyncrasies from German operators that got them into Enigma...at Bletchley?' said Siggy as if everyone should know this.

'It was the Halle Orchestra for The Variations with me' said Compton to much the same look.

The reality of it was learning to speak in something approaching another language where punctuation and sequence rules absolutely and inflection deviation and exceptions are inadmissible. In brief there was only one way as Logan saw it talking to Chalkie as he thumbed through to the back of the book and several pages of corrections to the text of the book until Siggy caught them talking.

'Are you two participating in this lesson?' asked Siggy.

'Sorry corp...I was communicating.'

'Well communicate with the class then.'

'I am wondering where this leaves us with past participles?' Logan asked jokingly.

'Write them in from the back in pencil is what I am doing' said Brum off on one of his tangents and trying to be helpful.

Slowly over the weeks it began to make some sort of sense order for Logan as it is with most languages once you get past trying to understand what's going on then give up and just get on with it but poor Brum battled bravely on. At times it was like watching someone his rub chest and pat head at the same time and neither came easy. Some things some people just can't do said Chalkie talking about Brum later that day adding that likewise everyone has something they are good at. With Brum they decided it was scratching his arse.

'You have a file and your idiosyncrasies are known to the enemy' Corporal Siggy said going on at length about monitoring and returning to the breaking of the Enigma code.

'It wasn't me' said Brum I was nowhere near it.

Corporal Siggy started radio language beginning with establishing communications on page one with corrections stapled in at the back in a large annex.

'Hello all stations this is zero how do you read over.'

'One OK over.'

'Two OK over.'

'All stations this is zero roger and out to you...hello three this is one zero how do you read over?'

It all seemed a tad pedantic for Logan even accepting the need for uniformity of speech.

'Hi there this here's Smokie come on.'

'Roger Smokie this here's bandit, that's a big ten four there big boy, ring a ding, ding loud as a bell come on?'

'Ten four ten four, this here's Smokie...'

'What do you think?' asked Logan turning to Chalkie but largely talking to himself with Chalkie's head deep into the book. 'Works well enough for the teamsters in American don't you think? And the bloody things easier to pick up.'

Chalkie was hardly listening as Logan joined him in revision, scanning his way through the army's version that took twelve full pages for the establish of communications alone.

'Hmm?' said Chalkie not getting a word of it with his mike turned well off as he came to grips with the four pages on 'assuming control of the radio net by use of an authorization password.'

'Bloody hell I'm never going to have a go at doing that and I mean never!'

'Little bloody wonder the signaller always gets it in the films' said Logan remembering Chalkie's earlier thoughts on the matter as he closed his own book with a quick look behind for the man in the camouflage jacket with the black hat and a bloody great knife.

'Talking of camouflage jackets.'

'Were we?' asked Chalkie still trying to revise.

'You wouldn't think all those light and dark patches and the like would be needed in the middle of a thicket, but would make you stand out in the middle of a green field when you need the camouflage. Same as Jock's wee bush in a field don't you think?'

'That's why they wear them, makes them stand out and it looks flash' said Chalkie same as those busbies and red jackets on the foot guards.'

'Bearskins' corrected Compton overhearing, 'busbies are from some other dead creature.'

'Now wearing a dead bear on your head and wearing camouflage, that would really make you stand out' said Chalkie but it was Logan now who wasn't listening.

It had been a long hard bugger of a week in need of a good piss up as Chalkie put it but both he and Logan were stony broke or were until Chalkie produced a crisp five pound note.

'From Jacko' said Chalkie as the pair set off for the Harewood midweek and intent on oblivion 'turned into a loan baron, he's not going out much these days.'

With payday not until the next day the loan was worth the six pound pay back even if it was for little more than overnight. They returned late to find Jacko still awake and making something of an intent himself with a show of intense reading or he was until he rose from his bed and fell to his knees. With face buried into his blankets and fingers thrust into both ears Logan immediately thought the man injured and moved towards him before being stopped by Brum.

'He's praying' whispered Brum pulling Logan away as the man remained motionless.

'Fucking hell' said Chalkie nailing it yet again.

'It's those evangelist sky pilots' said Brum cleaning his teeth at the line of basins 'you know, the one's that come round with the well thumbed Bibles wanting you to go to their Bible classes? I even went myself for a couple of weeks before I saw the light, praise the Lord.'

'Oh those' said Logan squeezing the last of his toothpaste on his brush and remembering the early shock of a man entering the barrack room in pseudo officer uniform and holding a bible littered with paper stuck indices, 'the Bible he had looked more like an Indian chief's sodding headdress than it did a Bible.'

'Say what you like about them, they know their Bible right enough' said Chalkie throwing his towel over the mirror. 'Fuck off I said to one of them once and the man gave me a quote from Genesis...ah you mean go forth and multiply said the man? No I said...I mean fuck off.'

'Give us a go with your toothpaste' said Logan filling his brush. 'And...?'

'You always swear like that asked the man, no I said, then why do it asks the man...I don't know, fucking habit I guess.'

'So what happened then?'

'He fucked off.'

'Really?' said Brum 'any road your cockney's a turned again Christian as of a few weeks back, he's a saved man.'

The return to the barrack room found Jacko off his knees praying over and preying now on Wee Jock who had returned somewhat squiffy from the NAAFI. Something to do with the wages of sin overheard Logan as Jacko posed with the good book open in one hand and pointing an accusing finger with the other that started an argument going nowhere. With neither giving an inch for or against the debate ended with Jock narrowly escaping just this side of an excommunication. Receiving some form of nonconformist absolution and with temptation and the devil blamed Jock was forgiven for not seeing the light and left the room as he was dying for a piss anyway. Good move thought Logan you never win an argument with a bigot.

'Sanctimonious duplicitous bastard' said Logan quietly before slipping under the sheets and calling for lights off at his end of the room. 'The bastards just lent us five quid for six back tomorrow...he's not daft is he?'

'It's a Christian act is Lent remember' said Compton closing his book as Chalkie clicked the light switch.

'Not at twenty percent overnight commission it's not' said Chalkie 'you put my toothpaste back Logan?'

'Toothpaste, what toothpaste?'

After long months there was suddenly an end to it as training hit half way. For some it was break point and as far as they would be going. Happily for Logan and a growing list of others this included the invented cockney and latter day saint Jack the Lad who, as it turned out came from Watford.

'Watford?' said Logan when he was told 'Bloody good hearing he had at birth then? To hear Bow bells from Watford he must have ears like a bat.'

'Leave it arht, leave it arht me old china, strike a light, corr lummy' said Compton who'd suffered the man as much as anyone.

Most of the dropouts were cashiered off to lesser demanding courses and pretty well it was all the usual suspects. All were there including Brum who was borderline as Siggy announced the results to the class and needing resits next time they were all in for testing.

'You have until Friday Brum' said Siggy as printers were turned off for the end of session.

Stay or go for the Brum was coming down to a teleprinter resit of the standard weekly fifteen minutes test. Resits were nothing new for Brum as he had been on them since the start of training but at halfway break point and without a net it became something of a crisis.

Three timed five minute runs was the test for teleprinter, the first two in five unit code left a good run with row upon row of equally spaced five letter squares. With row and line breaks every five strikes the run finished looking like a sheet of stamps you see in the post office or maybe an early Andy Warhol. On a bad run it went the way of a Picasso and at times for some a Jackson Pollack. Final test of the three was a simple copy of plain language and all three runs were calculated to the letter of the required speed.

Now half way through the course this was fifty words a minute and the finished test came off the teleprinter as a four foot long roll of continuous typing. Allowed two runs at the test with only one handed in it was always something of a gamble with both going largely unchecked. As to which was the best run at times was a flip of a coin but the rules of the game for a pass were simple; they required perfect text and no uncorrected errors. With corrections to errors laid down as a method equal to the typing of two extra squares made the corrections directly proportionate to the speed of typing. Too many errors and the lost time required greater speed to finish the test, too slow and you don't make the speed. It was a tortoise and the hare race with an additional problem for Brum.

'My problem is I make too many errors I does, that's one problem and the other is I don't type fast enough. Apart from that I'm bostin.'

Brum had it in one. He was crap at it and as the day of the test approached things only got worse as nerves took him from borderline to certain failure. By Thursday the man was already mentally packing his bags. What they needed was a fiendish plan.

'Here's the plan' said Logan to Brum as Chalkie checked nobody was listening at the door. 'We place a piece of chewy in the window against the lock.'

'Yes' Brum said narrowing his eyes and keen to hear the rest of the Logan fiendish plan.

'Sneak back in later this evening and pull out four foot of paper on your printer.'

'Yeah...and?'

'What do you mean and...you dopey Brummie. Put your name on the top, type the bloody test with one finger and roll it back down onto the roll to the clean paper ready for tomorrow.'

'Do the rerun, bin your crap copy pull up the good one and hand that in for marking, piece of cake' said Chalkie joining in.

'Isn't that cheating?'

'Course it's bloody cheating' said Logan. 'You thick or something?'

'I'll do it' said Brum.

As the clock ticked closer to the go for operation cheating bastard the team sat finalizing operational details in the NAAFI bar. Nerves were jangling with anticipation of what was a bold plan as with a thumbs up and a last swig of Newcastle brown the team left for the training area. Operation cheating bastard was go.

At night and with the lights out the training area took on an altogether eerie feel to it as they made for the teleprinter room keeping well in the shadows. The training huts were a patrolled area for the camp guard but they had all done guard duty at some time over training and knew the routine.

'A quick flash of torch around the huts and get the fuck out of there' admitted Chalkie. 'Who the hell wants to meet somebody up to no good when you're on your own in a dark place and half a mile from the sodding guardroom? It's what I do anyway.'

The other two nodded their own memories of guard duty and a sad reflection of the youth in post war Britain.

'I never even went near here' said Brum 'gives me the willies even in day time.'

True to form a lone torch shone briefly to each of the rooms and after a quick brave statutory shake of the one door handle the man was off heading for safety of the lit up areas before reporting back in. Minutes passed and nothing was heard but the spooky sound of a distant barn owl as Logan checked his watch ready to give the go.

'What the shit was that?' said Brum showing the whites of his eyes like two dinner plates.

'What?' said Logan.

'It's a pigeon' said Chalkie falling in the dark and steadying himself on Logan's arm.

'You what?' said Brum.

'That's an owl' said Logan.

'I know that I just twisted me fucking ankle in it' said Chalkie bending.

'Go, go, go' said Logan having heard it in some daft American war film or other as they left the shadows as one.

Crouching low they made their way over open ground before disappearing back to the safety of shadows.

'Go, go' said Brum also getting into the spirit of things.

'Oh no' said Chalkie now at the window 'the chewy has hardened up in the bloody cold.'

'Bloody Wrigley. It's supposed to survive overnight on bedposts is that bastard.'

'Bollocks' said Brum pushing his way forward and giving the window a hefty thump that could have broken the glass.

'Idiot' said Logan bending double and waiting in the dark with hands cupped ready to give a leg up before realizing the others were already in.

Clambering inside Logan joined them at Brum's printer as all three searched in the dark for the on switch to the sounds of 'get off and that's me you twat' the light finally came on with a noisy buzz as the printer kicked into life. It was a ticking clock.

'The next stag will pass in exactly thirty four minutes at the turn round' said Chalkie in a whisper, 'give or take.'

'Give or take...give or take what Chalkie?'

'Thirty minutes...give or take.'

Logan checked his watch in the light from the printer as Brum set to with a fury pulling up at least half a roll before loudly cracking his fingers and sitting ready to begin.

'I hate it when he does that' said Chalkie, as Logan stood by with a torch.

'Test card' said Brum turning to his side and lifting an arm.

'What?' said Logan annoyed at the pause and in need of a pee.

'Test card, where's the test card then?'

It was a good point said Logan to himself. They would need a test card. Brum was right there.

'Chalkie?'

'Don't ask me I was on guard patrol timings and chewy removal.'

'Brum, Brum?'

Back at the accommodation block they reflected on the overall flaws in the fiendish plan beginning with not having the test card and not knowing which card would be used on the day of the test coming a close second.

'Bastard' said Logan 'we have a perfect plan and the bloody army messes up.'

'Actually' said Chalkie.

'No Chalkie, not just now pal.'

Day of the test Brum was up bright and early. Mostly this was due to the fact that he hadn't actually slept that much after the waking call of nature. Nevertheless he determined to put a brave face on it and after a good breakfast of tea, two sugars and a fag he was ready for the noose and wanting only to get it over with. At the training room he trod in something underfoot. It was the chewy.

'Forget it' said Logan being offered it back.

After thirty minutes or so open practice Siggy called everyone to get ready for a test run before issuing the test cards from an open desk draw much to the shaking of three heads.

'Settle down everybody and keep the noise down if you finish early we have one of you on resits this morning. Whenever you're ready Brum,' said Siggy holding his stopwatch before being asked for fresh paper by Chalkie at the far side of the room. 'Sit your arse at another bloody printer then, what are you doing giving it one or something.'

'Plan B' said Logan settling himself next to Brum and flexing his fingers like a maestro.

'Bostin' said Brum looking over at his name on Logan's printer.

'Ready...and start' said Siggy as the whole room struck up with the sound of a dozen rattling Siemen teleprinters.

Fifteen minutes later to the second Siggy walked to room centre and clicked his stopwatch.

'Time everybody, fingers off keyboards and papers in. Check your names are on the top!' shouted the corporal. 'You too Compton I don't care if you say it looks like one of your's. No names on the papers are resits. Bang on fifteen minutes was that.'

'Are you sure?' asked Chalkie making more than a big thing of looking at his watch as Siggy walked over to show the stopwatch.

Switch made Brum dropped a four foot run on the pile with the others and left without saying a word other than a quick thanks to Logan as he went past.

'And bugger me Brum' said Siggy the following day, 'you only managed a pass run. Slipped up right at the end though with three corrections but still a pass so well done Brummie.'

'Ooh' said the room together.

'Piece of piss' said Brum immodestly taking the applause.

'Right' said Siggy moving on 'who wants to try an assume control of the net...Chalkie, how about you son?'

'Three sodding errors' whispered Brum to Logan as they went to NAAFI break at the Sally Army. 'You could have done me a better run than that don't you think?'

18

It was approaching the end of training. Logan could send and read Morse at twenty words a minute, talk in radio speak and had a spattering of how the universe or at least the ionosphere worked hand in hand with the army to transmit the latter's messages. Signals training ended with a signals exercise where they spent a pleasant enough few days sat in a radio vehicle within sight of Richmond castle sending test messages to the other members of the intake widely dispersed about Yorkshire. All that remained was the end of training final exam and they were out of there with a posting to places ranging from the exotic to the downright punitive and where coming top of the course gave first choice of posting. With an eye on where they would be for the next three years or more and thoughts of days on the beach for some and oriental dusky maidens for others, the competition to do well was only natural and cramming began.

'Singapore, Hong Kong, Africa, South America and continental Europe pretty much anywhere' said Chalkie 'I don't mind me.'

Anywhere but Catterick was how most of the group saw it although for some seeing the world had been their reason for joining. Not so for Logan who for some obscure reason even to him appeared not to have interest in strange and exotic places apart from the dusky maiden side of it. He was discussing this very point with Chalkie in the Harewood bar when Roxanne arrived with news of a posting of her own. The cousins were off to Berlin for three years and waiting for transit. The news was not taken well by Logan and it showed. Berlin after the airlift was not a place for casual visits, Roxanne would be long gone.

Over the months Roxanne and Logan had as they say been seeing each other. Not in any biblical sense however, as true to their first meeting the relationship had remained strictly platonic. It was one of those I will if you ask me relationships that can drag on for years fooling both into a continuing friendship that hides what lies beneath. For Logan at the beginning the truth of it lay beneath his Y fronts but as the weeks turned to months something changed. It's a truism that you never know what you have until you lose it and never having had it in the first place made this true twice over.

'Fond is the word' said Logan talking it through with Chalkie 'that's how it is.'

'Fondled is the word don't you mean' said Chalkie as usual being Yorkshire about it but annoyingly hitting the nail bang on again. 'If you're asking me?'

'Which I'm not or don't Chalkie.'

'If you want my view on it...in my considered opinion.'

'Not really Chalkie.'

'If it were me.'

'Go on then, get on with it.'

'I'd give her one.'

'Thanks Chalkie, that really helps.'

'And her mate.'

'Thanks for that Chalkie, that really helps things that really does' Logan said with a deep sigh of the well pissed off.

The man has got it bad thought Chalkie and as the date of Roxanne's departure neared, things could only get worse. Logan's problem was not the classic feuding of families from Verona but the opportunity. Wisely and slow, they stumble that run fast thought Logan remembering back to the play at school. In brief he was in need of a balcony opportunity and an understanding nurse or he would be worms meat like poor Mercutio. Typically it came to him in the form of a dirty weekend.

'No Logan' said Roxanne 'as a matter of fact I am free that weekend why for do you ask me so my love?' Was how Logan heard it even if Roxanne had stopped at the why?

'Well' said Logan 'it happens to be my birthday.'

'I thought that was four months ago...wasn't it?'

Yes of course it was he had said before moving swiftly on to the central stratagem of a surprise birthday present from an aged aunt quickly adding that it had come late...forgetful old cow that she was. Oh, she had said before adding another oh at the wish of the dear old lady for him to take a long weekend away at the seaside...with someone of his choosing and, naturally enough as they were in Yorkshire the dear old dear had suggested Skegness. Logan paused awaiting a response for the most unlikely of stories.

'Isn't Skegness in Lincolnshire?' asked Roxanne.

'What? Where did I say, Skegness? No, not Skegness, I meant Scarborough...or somewhere I have never been like that, Scarborough is in Yorkshire somewhere isn't it?' he said with the sound of hope in his voice and knowing he was talking gibberish.

'Now that's in Yorkshire' agreed Roxanne 'and no Logan, I have not been there either. Parsley, sage, rosemary and thyme is all I know about it.'

'Yes,' said Logan 'and the fair and all that, me too.'

For a man of Logan's experience his patter not only stank it was painful, it was like pulling teeth but he finally got there. The outcome found him standing alone the following Saturday on Richmond station and looking up at the connections board for trains to Darlington. Roxanne was cutting it a bit thin with ten minutes to go felt Logan as he paced nervously up and down the platform. She was suddenly there and looking the picture of innocent loveliness. Waving and smiling like a child and clearly keen to be going Roxanne joined him with an endearing peck to the cheek. The only thing missing was a bucket and spade and a hankie for the drool, which came as Roxanne wiped clean the lipstick.

'Lucky bastard' said a squaddie to himself standing not ten foot from the event.

She was at once forgiven as Logan rechecked the two tickets and looked to the station clock.

'Do you mind Logan?' asked Roxanne unexpectedly 'only if it's fine with you?'

Turning from Logan Roxanne looked further down the platform as from out of the ticket office walked the other cousin.

'Hi Logan...' said the girl smiling demurely and looking the very picture of loveliness herself to all around but Logan whose face was a picture in itself.

'You don't mind if Susan comes too do you Logan? Can she?'

'Two!' said the squaddie well pissed off and watching on with open-mouthed envy as the Darlington train arrived at the platform just seconds ahead of his erotic thoughts.

'Darlington, the 13.37 train for Darlington' said the voice of the station announcer.

Doors slammed, a whistle sounded and with a wave of a little green flag the train steamed away from the platform. Scarborough here we come said Logan to himself looking out of the window and feeling more than pissed off with events as the idea spiralled well out of his control. Things could be worse he was thinking as the train picked up steam. We could be going to bloody Skeggy.

They arrived at Scarborough late afternoon and after a brief search found somewhere with a vacancies sign and a view of the sea. Unfortunately it wasn't from any of the available rooms but the place looked and sounded the part squeaky floorboards and all.

'Two rooms with two sharing' confirmed the man in a grey striped waistcoat and slicked back hair as he passed over two registration forms. Both girls signed as the desk clerk turned to a key cupboard before returning with the keys.

'One double two sharing and an adjacent single' said the man pushing forward one of the keys that was quickly snatched by Susan who left for the stairs.

'Thank you' said Roxanne trailing behind as Logan picked up the remaining key.

'And early morning calls sir?' asked the desk clerk.

'Thank you porter nothing for me either we will be sleeping in I think' said Logan turning as he reached the stairs. 'I expect to be shattered by the morning.'

'Kids' said the desk clerk as he watched them leave for the upper floor.

Logan arrived at the room slightly behind the girls and entered just as the interconnecting door closed from the other side.

'Drink and something to eat?' called Logan his head to the door as the reply of thirty minutes in the bar came back through.

Unpacking the few clothes he had brought Logan ran a quick bath and was down in the bar early. The girls arrived shortly afterwards and after a short debate all three left for a night on the town beginning with a curry, it was always going to be a curry. Apart from the Indian restaurant Scarborough was at home asleep and even the curry house was empty.

'Have you ever wondered why you never see an Indian eating in an Indian restaurant?' asked Logan scanning the menu and showing off with a chicken Vindaloo that nearly melted his fillings.

After a look at the sea and tour of the bars they arrived back at the hotel late to find their keys waiting for them on the counter. Logan lay in bed reflecting on the futility of a plan that had gone dramatically wrong and helped by an amazing quantity of the evening's alcohol was asleep immediately. He awoke in the night to voices coming from the next room. The girls were having an argument.

Light streamed into his room from beneath the door and, as a shadow moved across the light he had an almost irresistible urge to look through the keyhole. Logan struggled with such a disgraceful and shameless concept and was there in an instant. Drawn as a moth is to candle he stooped placing eye to keyhole and saw only what at first sight appeared to be pink gauze on the other side. An unexpected click at once plunged the room to darkness. Shit said Logan to himself as he crept back to bed with floorboards creaking like a ship at anchor.

'Knickers' said Logan out loud before rolling over and punching the pillow into shape.

The next morning they were not there and neither were the girls as he had clearly overslept. He arrived down to breakfast just as the girls were leaving.

'Morning Logan, bright and early?' said Susan.

'I overslept, the sea air?' said Logan still yawning.

'You need a long bracing walk along the front. After breakfast?' said Roxanne as they passed.

After a long search and a wait to get the cook back in to fry an egg to death Logan finally

223

arrived back at his room and being late knocked once at the girls' door before pushing it open. A loud yelp of surprise came from the bed as both girls drew apart in a scramble of arms clothes and legs.

'Logan' said Roxanne running after him into the corridor as Logan left the hotel in need of a long and bracing walk but now very much awake. She found him after a long search sitting alone and gazing out to sea.

'Don't' he said standing and walking away.

'She loves me...she always has' called Roxanne behind him as he left.

'Don't' he said again.

'But I love you Logan' said Roxanne to the wind but he was gone.

By the time Logan arrived back at the hotel both girls had long since left and packing quickly he settled the bill and left himself for the station. Dropping his bag at left luggage and with some time to wait for the late afternoon train Logan set off for the nearest pub and then a second. He arrived back at the station just in time to see the rear of the last train to Darlington.

'What on Sundays? Nowt now until the morning son' said the station porter agreeing to hold the bags until the milk train.

'Thanks' said Logan heading off to find a café until opening time.

After a restless night on the waiting room bench Logan caught the first train out, missed the connection to Catterick at Darlington and arrived back at camp exhausted. More importantly he had missed morning parade and was hardly in happy mood as he walked to the training huts. Inside the training office he found a sympathetic Siggy who had just twenty minutes earlier handed in the morning roll call with the one missing name.

'Sorry' said Siggy genuinely appearing to be so as Logan heaved a heavy sigh and mouthed something suitably obscene. 'Nobody knew where you were Logan.'

'At the mercy of British Rail is where I were' said Logan.

'Anyway, back here at eleven hundred hours, you're up before the OC' said the corporal. 'Automatic charge of absent without leave. AWOL. Blame it on British Rail and you will be fine, slap on the wrist. You will need to change into number two dress, web belt and beret.'

Siggy raised his eyebrows. It was as much a pain in the arse for him too he was thinking.

19

Corporal Siggy was already waiting in the training room office as Logan arrived for OC's orders to find Chalkie and Compton there as escorts to the prisoner. Siggy went through the procedure for orders that would be a left wheel quick march into the room, a right wheel before the desk and a mark time before the order to halt.

'Then a left turn and remove berets and remember if he asks will you accept his punishment say yes.'

Logan must have looked confused as the corporal spoke quietly into his ear.

'You're up before the OC Logan. A junior officer can only award minor punishment like a fine or extra duties, say no and you go on up to the colonel for a flogging, for giving him the bother?'

'Good luck' said Chalkie behind him in the line as the corridor fell to an ominous and expectant silence.

'Here goes a day's pay' said Logan as the OC's door opened and the SSM entered the corridor in a get it over with mood.

'Ready? Prisoner and escort...shun! Quick march, left wheel, right wheel...mark time. Halt! Left turn. Hats off!' shouted the SSM snatching the beret from Logan's head.

'State your name rank and number' began the captain.

Five minutes later the office sounded to the same shouts and stamps but in reverse as Logan was marched out to find Siggy outside and waiting.

'CO's orders' said the SSM to Corporal Siggy.

'CO's?' questioned Siggy sounding surprised.

'The colonel's seeing all AWOLs, says there's too much of it about.

'For twenty minutes adrift?' said Siggy.

'CO's at twelve hundred hours sharp corporal, you've got an hour...to get a haircut if I was you.'

'Sir' replied Corporal Siggy.

'And Siggy?' just watch yourself with the RSM' said the sergeant major offering a bit of advice. 'He don't much like Mondays.'

Neither do I at the moment said Logan to himself as he was marched off to regimental headquarters in the all-telling line of three marching soldiers, escorts front and rear with naughty boy in the middle. He didn't even know where the bloody place was until they arrived outside. All of them, prisoner and escorts both received a customary dressing down from the RSM beginning at the boots and moving on up to the length of hair. Even Siggy got a lashing for his boots and he was the charging corporal.

It was immediately clear to Logan that the RSM had achieved the exalted rank of warrant officer first class by shouting at people and being an all round first-rate tosser. He was a man out of place in any real world and without any use or function in a training regiment other than to be top dog. Untrained from the look of his badges to any level of real worth to the corps he was without technical function other than to see to the admin and absorb himself in matters of military discipline. The brightest thing on the RSM was his belt buckle and it glistened in the sun like the rest of him, but what was between his ears you could make chips out of thought Logan and it stuck out a mile. He certainly scrubs up well felt Logan as the man strutted up and down the colonel's corridor like the peacock he was.

Having chosen this route to the very top of the non commissioned ranks the man was no idiot but once you were past the parade ground and into the man there wasn't much in there. Mouth and trousers thought Logan and that was the best of it. Logan took an immediate dislike to the RSM as the warrant officer did to Logan but that was far from his mind as with a slide of the metal peephole and a click of a turning key, the door to the guardroom cell clanged noisily shut.

*

'Far too much of this going on' said the colonel in a squeaky voice and hardly bothering to listen before interrupting Logan's account of events with something he had prepared earlier. 'Three days detention, march him out RSM.'

A cell was a new experience for Logan although he had slept in one before when on guard duty but being banged up in one with shoe laces and tie removed at the door was altogether entirely different. It was a place forlorn. Before long an eye appeared at the peephole and with the sound of a sliding bolt and turning key the door opened to none other than Logan's favourite RP.

'On your feet you' shouted the RP throwing Logan his laces with an order to lace up.

'Staff' said Logan remembering back to an earlier RP and an ose pipe in basic training as he threaded the leather laces.

'I knows you from somewhere doesn't I?' asked RP Smuggy.

'I doesn't think so Staff.' It was a stupid reply thought Logan but it went way over the man's head and was still rising.

'I knows your face from somewhere. Never forgets a face I doesn't, where you from Logan?'

'I lives here in the camp staff.'

'Outside and have him line up on the road with the others Corporal Kinnock' came the voice of a sergeant RP from somewhere down the corridor.

It saved Logan as he left the cell to join a line of three other prisoners waiting in the roadway.

'Move yourself, move yourself,' hassled Kinnock behind as Logan passed through the guardroom and out into the road.

All three now set off in line and at quick march heading for the accommodation block. The voice of the sergeant bellowed after them from the guardroom veranda.

'Double those bloody prisoners Corporal Kinnock!' said the sergeant suddenly aware of the approach of the RSM.

'Prison detail, double time' shouted Kinnock from the rear of the men who within seconds had left him far behind.

'That's cos of that bastard RSM' said a voice behind Logan.

'Mark time!' called Kinnock holding back the squad to allow him time to catch up. 'Keep your legs up, higher, higher! You're not going to lose somefink.'

The march to the accommodation block was for Logan to change uniform to fatigues. Once in his room they found Chalkie and Compton also changing before heading for an early lunch.

'What are you two doing in barracks?' demanded Kinnock before standing the other prisoners at ease as Logan changed uniforms.

'We were escort to the prisoner corporal' said Compton.

'Staff!' corrected Kinnock.

'No talking to the prisoners there' he shouted as Chalkie whispered something to Logan before moving away to his own locker. 'Eating irons and mug with wash and shaving gear in your small backpack. Change of socks and shreddies. We don't want you honking out the guardroom does us.'

'He can borrow my aftershave if he wants staff' called Compton turning Kinnock's head to look down the room as a packet of cigarettes looped behind the RP's head to be deftly caught by Logan.

Chalkie gave a stupid grin and a thumbs up as Logan stuffed them down his trousers.

'No he cannot...aftershave's alcohol, no alcohol in the guardroom.'

'So how do you get to be an RP staff?' Chalkie asked like he really wanted to know.

230

Kinnock's head turned back as Compton now threw over cigarettes followed by a bar of chocolate.

'Apply to the RSM but they don't take just anybody you know. There's a lot to learn...you got to have your wits about you with this lot' said Kinnock as the contraband was dropped down through waistband to Logan's legs.

'Oh I can understand that staff, it's a select few right?'

'Many apply but few are chosen, right staff?' said Compton.

'Correct' said Kinnock preening a fleck of something from the lapel off his tunic.

'Correct' said Chalkie dropping his bottom jaw as the man turned back to Logan.

'Right you lot form up outside we haven't got all day' he said as Logan walked stiff legged ahead of him before stamping his feet as the half empty packet of smokes dropped further down.

For God's sake don't let me be frisked thought Logan as they arrived back at the guardroom via the mess and an early lunch. Sat apart on a separate table in the mess Logan met his fellow inmates. They were all AWOLs although the big West Indian serving five months said he went on the run after someone had planted something in his locker.

'Someone left it in me locker to drop me in it' said the man as the prisoner to his side stuck his tongue in his cheek.

'It was a wallet wasn't it Charlie?' asked the man as Charlie reluctantly nodded. 'And some other fucker's wristwatch got left in there as well didn't it?'

'Right you are and the bastard ting never worked man, wasn't worth finding it lying around' said Charlie laughing away to himself and thinking it well funny.

'Watch yourself with that twat Kinnock, he's a vindictive little bastard' said a Geordie sat opposite. 'Only got six weeks this time as I came back on own accord but he got me extras the bastard. I would be out now if it weren't for him.'

'Shouldn't have come back you Geordie man' said Charlie.

'Away man, that twat Kinnock's on his way over.'

'How long you got?' asked the third prisoner now arriving back with his pudding.

'Three' said Logan lowering his voice and clearing his throat as Kinnock neared the table.

'Months or weeks?'

'Days?' said Logan with another cough.

'What you do rob a fucking piggy bank?'

'Keep it down you lot, you got five minutes left.'

'Staff' came the immediate joint response and the silence that spoke volumes.

Arriving back at the guardroom Logan emptied his pockets of all personal items into a plastic bag and signed to agree the list. After a pat down of his pockets the sergeant removed Logan's razor to a locked cupboard before pointing him to his cell.

'No cigarettes on him corporal Kinnock we've got a non-smoker.'

'I am now' said Logan as the cell door slammed shut behind him.

Logan's eyes scanned the cell for likely hiding places. The cigarettes were proving more a problem than a relief. Climbing to an air grill he found the remains of earlier contraband in the dust behind and quickly inserted most of the cigarettes before climbing down to check they couldn't be seen from the floor. Chalkie had been overgenerous making the hiding of almost a full packet of cigarettes difficult. It was a nice thought but being only an occasional smoker Logan had enough to last for weeks, which is what he would need if they found them on him he thought. His mind went back to the Geordie's comments regarding extras. For sure said Logan to himself he would watch the little shit and at the same time watch his own arse.

Ever the thinking man Compton had included matches in with his pack and a tightly folded page of a magazine that unfolded to a smiling face and a magnificent if over ample pair of pendulous breasts. On the back was a rear view of the same girl in suspenders and stockings. Very thoughtful of the man felt Logan to have it all covered in the one hastily ripped page. Above all a nice face and legs, firm bum, strong thighs and nice breasts. As a face bum thigh and tit man with a predilection for the stocking covered leg he'd got the lot. What was the man trying to say thought Logan as everything went to every inventive nook and cranny of the six by four foot cell.

Climbing to the window ledge to hide the chocolate Logan's hand felt the rustle of paper as he landed down with a dated portion of Tit-Bits for June 1953. June is busting out all over said the headline and she most certainly was. Nice to know your mates see you as a heavy smoking wanker with a stocking fetish and a love of chocolate thought Logan as he settled back down on his bed for an afternoon nap. The sound of sliding bolts on metal echoed down the corridor and his door opened with a loud bang.

'You!' came a shout from outside his cell as Logan jumped to his feet. 'Out now!'

'Sir' said Logan now at the door.

'Work detail, camp litter run and haircuts Corporal Kinnock' barked the sergeant as the detainees lined up outside the guardroom. Somehow the words work and detail did not compute in the Logan mind as he thought detention more or less a lock up and a daily circular walk around an exercise yard. He'd been reading the wrong books.

The litter run began immediately they left the guardroom with Kinnock pointing his baton at whatever took his eye as litter or as being out of place on the road. To his sides left and right they ran ahead like sniffing dogs back and forth to collect whatever had been thrown to ground. Paper, cigarette butts, twigs and an occasional blown leaf, all were collected and held in hands before being dispatched to the next litter bin en route to the barbers.

'Staff, staff, here' shouted Charlie excitingly pointing to some missed piece of litter like they were in competition. Clearly they were; a competition to please felt Logan but with only three days ahead of him he for one wouldn't be playing and that was for sure.

'Here staff here!' called the third prisoner finding an old discoloured spent match.

'Good one Smithy, have it in the bin' said Kinnock spotting another one and prodding to it with his stick.

It was like taking dogs for a walk and missing only a long running leash and a pee up a tree as Logan stooped to collect a discarded piece of silver paper.

'You get training for this or did you just pick it up?' he asked the Geordie who of them all showed an obvious dislike for the game.

'He had us picking the adjutant's dog shit up the other day the bastard. Fucking animal...'

'Which one?' asked Logan.

'Both of them' said Geordie before being called to a cigarette packet.

They arrived at the barbers to find the place empty and both barbers finishing a tea break. First to enter Logan was directed by Kinnock to one of the chairs as the barber waited with sheet poised ready. The man liked his guardroom cuts, it was a sort of pay back time and he went to it with a fury of a man not looking for a tip. It was always going to be short back and sides and he needed no direction. At length the barber finished and smiling the smile of the sycophantic twat that was his nature he reached behind the chair to hold up the mirror. With no tip coming for sure and knowing Kinnock of old what he gave was a shearing.

'Sir?' said the barber sarcastically taking delight at the white skin of the scalping.

'Who are you, the last of the Mohicans?'

'Shut up Logan' snapped Kinnock 'or you'll get another one.'

'Can I have a bit more off the top' asked Logan.

'Give the bastard another one' said Kinnock as the next man up sat ready in the next chair and Chingachgook set to on Logan for the second time. With little to no back and sides left to remove the barber soon finished and the chair was taken by Charlie.

'Same for me Barbie man, like that one no back, no sides with a bit off the top' said Charlie 'don't matter to me I got three more months left in the hole. You can take it all off for all I care Barbie.'

'You wouldn't have all your hair off' said the Geordie quietly waiting his turn behind.

'Bet me then!'

'Go on then, all your hair off for a fiver.'

'What?' said Kinnock looking up from page three and looking only slightly interested.

Kinnock shrugged his shoulders. The idea appealed to the sick humour in the man as he nodded for the barber to go ahead.

'A number one, yes!' said the barber eager to start and clicking his demon clipper to maximum revs.

'You're on' said Geordie sitting back and folding his arms.

The sound of the clipper changed as teeth cut deep into a thick head of curls, ploughing through in a furrowed line from brow to nape of neck. Clumps of hair began to drop to left and right as the barber shook the clipper clean with a practiced flick of his hand. In less than two minutes the West Indian was done to the bone as the barber removed the sheet. Charlie left the chair rubbing his head and turning to the line of smiling faces behind, even Kinnock was smiling.

'No hair, five quid man!' said Charlie pointing up to a head of nothing.

'Oh no' said Geordie 'all your hair was the bet. Eyebrows, eyelashes, ears, nose, chest, legs and arms and bum fuzz.'

'Bollocks!' said Charlie.

'Yeah, bollocks as well' said the Geordie.

Even Kinnock thought it funny as he recounted the event to the RP sergeant back in the guardroom after the evening meal run.

'Fags up' shouted the sergeant down to the cells as a line quickly formed at the door.

Opening the locked cupboard the sergeant dispensed cigarettes from the prisoner's marked packets for those who had them as those without cadged a drag.

'Don't suck the guts out of it' shouted Geordie as the other sucked heavily at the weed.

On the stroke of six o'clock the corridor door between cells and front of guardroom was locked and the guardroom handed over to the oncoming duty guard commander as the RPs left for the night. From his cell Logan listened as the guard mounted on the veranda outside. After some time came the sound of the outer door being unlocked and the detainees were stood to in their cells for inspection by the duty officer.

'Four prisoners on detention present and correct and nothing to report sir' said the guard commander as the officer walked slowly down the line of open doors before pausing at the first.

'Who's this' asked the captain.

'Cell one is a Private Smith the cook sir, HQ squadron, in on a charge of mass poisoning sir, ha!' joked the corporal.

'Everything all right Smith, still here I see?' said the officer looking in and clearly knowing the man from a previous guard duty.

'Yes sir thank you sir' said the duff smiling before his face turned back to his normal churlish self as the duty officer walked on.

Reaching the next cell the officer paused before deciding to enter inside. He found Logan stood to and blankly staring out to the corridor. Logan was surprised to see the troop officer but the officer clearly expected to see Logan.

'Cell three is...' said the corporal before pausing to look down at his handover sheet.

'Logan' said the officer.

'Yes sir' said Logan flatly.

'Should have telephoned in Logan, you knew you would be late.'

'I was busy trying to get back sir.'

'No excuse Logan remember next time.'

'There won't be a next time sir.'

'That's the spirit Logan, that's the spirit.'

'That's the truth' said Logan as the officer left the cell.

'Good man, thank you guard commander, seen enough. I will be in the mess if you need me.'

'I will keep bloody running next time' said Logan quietly as the officer left and the outer door clanged shut.

Try as he might Logan was unable to sleep as the cells were locked down for the night after a call for last ablutions and brush of teeth which was more a stretch of legs for some not liking the confinement of the locked cell. The evening had been noisy with the guard commander keeping the cell doors open to allow the run of the corridor to the detainees. Friends of the Geordie were on duty guard and passed cigarettes through the grill on the outer door as the corporal turned a blind eye to what was going on until he had enough of it or the smoke and called a halt.

Being awake all night was always the lot of the guard commander who, apart from a middle night pee call from Charlie and a later one for cell two that woke them all up had a nil return for his incidents book. At six the doors and bolts clanged open as they filed out to receive their razors from the cupboard before being taken by the guard and second in command to the guard commander for early breakfast. Without the noise of Kinnock it was the best meal of the day but soon over as they returned to the guardroom only minutes behind the RSM and the sergeant RP. The RSM was fitting his Sam Brown and left without speaking as the breakfast run entered. It was then that Logan saw the locker in one of the open cells.

'Used by the pigs as a storeroom for their personal gear and changing room for the RSM. We all take turns batting for the bastard. Bulling his belt, boots and his hat' said Geordie. You don't think he turns himself out looking that shiny do you?'

With much of the day spent clearing a stagnant firewater tank and after three sweeps of the camp area including one with brushes Logan for one was glad to arrive back at the guardroom. At least he was until being awarded the prize for the lowest collection of dog ends by Kinnock. Amused at his inventiveness Kinnock gave him the honour of shining the arse of Jimmy. Five foot of stature takes a lot of Brasso and supervised by the RP Logan was kept at it until the call for evening meal came from inside the guardroom.

For some unknown reason the day had been fractious. Something of an argument had broken out between Charlie and the cook Smith. Tension had been building since the day before and Logan could sense it. Some things don't need reason. Some things lie there dormant, just waiting to happen and even the largest bomb needs only a small spark.

Bang! It started as Logan entered the guardroom. Geordie saw it too and got between them just in time to stop the blows. All over in a second or it would have been had not Kinnock jumped in. Looking to make an issue more than anything and having a personal down on Charlie the West Indian was the one to get it.

'Black arse always does' said Charlie later that seemed the way of it too from how Logan saw it but then he should have buttoned it as he was told to, only his chip just wouldn't let him.

A charge from inside the nick is the worst of any events and it was always heading for tears as the next day Charlie was marched off to regimental HQ in the all-telling line of three. He arrived back later that morning with something in his eye that made it water and looking a broken man. Kinnock locked him up for the day before briefing the sergeant, coming on in a serves the bastard right mood as he busied himself with a mug of tea.

'Fourteen days extras to detention and on a warning' he said like he was proud of the event.

There was a waiver in Kinnock's voice that laid bare the man's real thoughts felt Logan. Even bastards recoil when the knife goes in.

'That would have been it then,' said Kinnock pausing to take a drink. 'Then the RSM had him up for back chat, wouldn't shut up even then the thick arse...so the RSM had him back in...gave him another seven. Thought for one minute we would be booking him in for Christmas dinner. RSM went bleeding ballistic, never seen him that bad before and that was it.'

The guardroom went stony silent but for the whining coming from one of the cells. The sergeant RP only shrugged his shoulders.

'You get his tie and laces?' he asked as Kinnock threw them over the counter. 'Good man.'

It was a long day clearing rubbish until returning back to the guardroom they found Charlie scrubbing away at the floor and in seemingly happy mood.

'Mind me bleeding floor with your mucky boots!' said Charlie.

'You OK are you Charlie?' asked Logan surprised at such a dramatic change.

'Never better man, clear in me head I am now man, clear in me head. Anything else' he asked shouting through into the front of the guardroom.

Guard mounted to the same noise of stamping boots outside and the evening passed slowly with the guard commander choosing to keep everyone caged. It made for a quiet night and after slipping his fags to Geordie and the others at last pee Logan slept through until first light. Next morning the cells honked of cigarettes and the guard commander flapped about opening doors and windows to clear the smell before handover.

At around eight o'clock the RSM and the sergeant RP arrived within minutes of each other as the guard busied with a show of cleaning the front of the guardroom aided by the detainees when Charlie appeared from his cell with the RSM's bulled gear. Awarded duty batman for the night the man had worked hard as Logan could see his face in the leather of the Sam Brown and the peaked cap was circular brushed and polished to perfection. Placed proud and ready for inspection was the truth of it and even in the dim light of the guardroom they shone reflecting the hours of work as the West Indian lowered them slowly to the counter before leaving for his cell. He was a changed man felt Logan and it was sad to see.

'Morning sir' said Kinnock to the RSM arriving at the guardroom and immediately entering the main cell area to hassle the morning clean up as a cover for being last in.

Not all saw it but they all heard the cry of pain from the RSM as the shiny peak of the cap came off in his hand and the rest disintegrated into many segmented parts. Louder still was the cry when the Sam Brown fell to pieces as the picked stitching fell away and the belt dropped to the guardroom floor.

'Which bloody idiot gave that mad fucking West Indian me fucking best bits?' yelled the RSM before the slightest of portentous pauses.

'Kinnock! Your stupid little twat get your fucking arse in here...now!'

Three full days to the very hour Logan was released back to training and still smiling. He arrived back to a letter placed centre bed and bearing a local postmark. Logan came back to earth with a crash as he opened the letter to find a note from Roxanne.

'Shit' said Logan quickly changing to civvies and running from the block by the back way so as not to pass the guardroom.

He was on the road within minutes and hailing a passing taxi sped off for the station. The train and Roxanne were both long gone and he knew it even as the taxi slowed to a stop but Logan still ran to the platform. Soundless, as only empty stations can be but for the sparrows fighting over bread on the line, Logan was desolate.

'You all right mate?' asked a ticket collector reading Logan's face as he left the station 'missed it hey pal?'

'Her' said Logan heart on sleeve as he walked to the line of waiting taxis.

'Sorry' said the WRAC sergeant on gate duty explaining it was against standing orders to give out the names of the girls. She was very sorry and even managed to make it sound so and no she had never met anyone by name of Roxanne.

'What if I am pregnant then?' said Logan out of frustration, which the sergeant did not respond to positively.

'So don't waste your time writing in' she said which sounded very much like I've had enough, now piss off to Logan.

'Cow' he said as he turned and walked away although he himself thought it stupid he didn't know Roxanne's surname but then why should he.

'Must be a rookie with that haircut' said the WRAC sergeant to herself as she watched him leave the gates. 'Don't dawdle there you two, move yourselves!'

'Sergeant' said the two girls walking away.

'So what happened then?' asked Chalkie at an impromptu mid week post release piss up.

'Well' said Logan taking a long swallow of Newcastle brown. 'You know how berserk and scary that reject Sergeant Head could be at times?'

'I did' said Compton reflectively.

'Well him and Corporal Jock together compared to the RSM going at Kinnock were like a couple of pussies.'

'So what happened to that Charlie feller?' asked Brum.

'I don't know but you can bet he's off batman duties that's for sure.'

'For tonight anyway' said Wee Jock.

'Reminds me of the sticky rock manufacturer in Scarborough' said Chalkie, 'had to lay off the man who put the letters in the rock. Gave the bugger two weeks' notice.'

'And?' said Compton.

'Got left with a million and a half sticks of rock with bollocks written through em' he said as the joke fell flat with Logan at least.

'Whose round is it?' asked Compton knowing damn well as Logan left the table with unwelcome thoughts of Scarborough.

'Remember me to one who lives there, she once was a true love of mine' hummed Logan as he walked to the bar.

20

The return to training for Logan was hardly that as it was the final week and every day held a stumbling block of the trade boards. Feared by some and at best to be got through by most the test week arrived as unwelcome as two weeks on the Costa del Sol for Dracula. Monday morning first light Siggy posted the timetable up outside the training office. It read like a hangman's roster. First up came the written papers with end of the week heavily loaded on skills. This said Siggy was to give more time to practice but for some it was just prolonging the torture and delaying the inevitable. Although Brum had improved he said.

'What do you think Brum, jokes apart, no names no pack drill, all up and all that, what do you think to your chances?' It was a fair question four months or so on since the last meaningful test thought Logan. Had the man improved sufficiently to take his own test and would he pass out by his own efforts? Simple question, simple answer.

'Ah, you are into multi choice questions here now, I have to think about it.'

'Fifty-fifty, touch and go, sixty forty, evens, odds on or what Brum, give it me straight?'

'What was the first one again?' said Brum.

The decision to go for a rerun of fiendish plan B and a straight switch as previously was decided at the cheaters' meeting held in the NAAFI where Brum as benefactor would feel obliged to get a round in. Chalkie agreed to throw a diversionary wobbly as a distraction to allow the switch of papers.

'I'll go for a coughing fit this time' said Chalkie having a practice run.

'That sounds nasty' said Jock passing the table.

Even with Chalkie's chest it still required the switch to work again not to discount the fact that Logan needed to have a good first run for his own result. By the time Friday arrived nerves were more than a little jingly as the time came for the test. Tension mounted as Corporal Siggy settled the class down with a threat of reduced play time before issuing the test cards and with a click of his stopwatch the room deafened to the busy chatter of a dozen machines. Fifteen minutes and some seconds later due to a problem with the stopwatch the test was over. There would be no second test run. Logan and Chalkie left the test room with a man dejected. It was a Brum.

'How were we to know that?' asked Logan defending the fiendish plan.

'That's unfair that is, how can they expect us to pass out with a good mark and only give us the one run to cheat at?' asked Brum.

Maybe Siggy and the army were not as daft as they appear to be thought Logan. Trade test week over, the following day the class gathered eagerly outside the training office as the test results were posted. Choice of first posting went to Compton who passed out top of the class. Ever the pessimist Brum didn't bother to turn up but somehow he had managed a pass along with the rest as the postings split the class from Benghazi to Singapore and to all parts Europe. For the greater majority this was with the British Army of the Rhine.

With choices narrowing quickly Logan found himself with a split decision and holding back to think about it missed his choice and was flung to the far off reaches of Salisbury Plain and a place called Bulford. He found himself to be going with Chalkie, Wee Jock and Compton who came from Hampshire and chose it as being virtually a home posting. Left with a choice of take it or leave it Brum took Germany and BAOR but on the whole everyone just wanted to leave Catterick.

To be finished with Catterick was a pleasure to be savoured for Logan too, as Salisbury Plain was from all accounts a beautiful neck of the woods even if it hasn't got any said Compton.

'Not many trees left standing but it has some stones and tank tracks' said Compton before explaining the location of Stonehenge to more than one disinterested ear.

Seemingly in the know Siggy only shook his head when the name Salisbury Plain and Bulford came up like he knew something about the place.

'Carter Barracks Bulford Camp, three years, good luck' said Siggy making it sound like a sentence.

'Stonehenge, men in pointy hats and white bed sheets' said Logan looking to make the best of it.

'Thought that was the KKK' said Chalkie.

'Druids' said Compton 'Celtic pagans.'

'Celtic?' said Jock sounding like he was going home.

At least he did until the taxi abandoned them at the gates of Carter Barracks. A sign read 3 Division Bulford.

'Looks more like Conference than division three' said Logan looking past the sign to the guardroom 'and destined for relegation if you ask me.'

The camp had an overall deserted feel to it missing only the tumbleweed and a sign with a struck through population count but in reality it was just another God forsaken isolated army camp. Not a happy prospect for three years felt Logan as the RP in the guardroom pointed away from the road and past a line of garages to a felted timber hut with a veranda.

'New arrivals, report to the squadron office' said the RP not bothering to look up.

At the office Logan handed over their posting documents to a clerk who was expecting them.

'White, Compton and yourself and Sinclair are billeted together; on up the hill alongside the square and in the second spider on the left if you follow me' said the clerk locking the office and setting off up the hill at a pace that left them struggling behind with their kit.

Stopping outside one of a line of half a dozen identical timber barrack blocks set alongside a road the clerk waited for them to arrive before disappearing through a door. Inside was a square circulation corridor set about a central ablutions area. Barrack rooms edged on to two sides of the square as the clerk held the door to the middle room of three.

'Choose yourself an empty bed, you have missed evening meal but the NAAFI is up the hill on the other side of the square' said the clerk pointing absently on up the hill.

'Bit desolate here isn't it?' said Logan looking out through a window.

'We call them spiders' said the clerk ignoring the remark, 'there's six legs to each spider.'

'Doesnae a spider have eight legs?' asked Jock which threw the man into a search for logic before giving up and leaving them to the room.

All things considered the place had a homely feel to it if you grew up in an overcrowded shack and liked fresh air, rain and cutting winds howling through the windows and coming straight off Salisbury Plain was Logan's view of the place.

'Those Druids must have been right hard bastards to walk around in bed sheets round here' Chalkie said sorting himself a bed and checking the locker. 'No bloody wonder they worshipped the sun.'

'And the radiators' said a corporal getting off his bed and introducing himself as Geordie.

With the only empty beds away from the radiators getting a bed close to one would be like putting your name down for Lords felt Logan as he nodded over to whoever bothered to look up before taking the Geordie's outstretched hand. Geordie said he was from Gateshead and had been at the camp doing nothing for two years and saw the place now as a way of life.

'The place works like an open prison. Providing you turn up before they find you missing and don't offend you get made a trustee.'

'That's nice then' said Jock.

The rule in this working unit was not to hang around unless you want to be given some work to do explained the Geordie.

'Keep moving about' he said 'look like you're doing something and you won't be given something to do.'

The man had clearly become institutionalised Logan felt listening to the brief and getting the low down as Chalkie put it later.

'So why is this called a working unit when there's no one actually working?' Logan asked thinking it a fair question.

'You a trouble maker?' said a voice further into the barrack room.

Next morning they paraded with others in three ranks on the edge of the square and met a sergeant who introduced himself as Sergeant Tomas. He was in charge of number three troop, which is what they now were the man said. After a short roll call and distribution of what appeared to be the odd regular job about the place that scampered men off they were immediately stood down until two in the afternoon.

'What you on Geordie?' asked Tomas as he dismissed the squad to duties.

'Garages serge' said the man before joining a small group heading down the hill and making for a line of old corrugated buildings.

'What are you new blokes on?' asked Tomas like they should know.

'Garages' said Logan following the Geordie as the others joined on behind.

With seemingly nothing to do but hang around the garages and make yourself scarce as the Geordie told them to do until the afternoon parade at two o'clock and forbidden to enter the barracks until noon, they followed a long line walking up a rough track heading for somewhere called Tin Town. This leave of camp at NAAFI break and other such times was allowed in Bulford and it was either this or the NAAFI said the Geordie raising his eyebrows.

'Get your drift' said Chalkie 'went there last night, so what's at Tin Town?'

Tin Town turned out to be in a place everyone went to when sloping off and making themselves scarce. It was skive centre and had survived two world wars with little alteration other than a change in management and the move from gas to electric lighting.

'Tin Town' said Geordie proudly pointing ahead as they approached the lines of tin huts.

An explanation of the name was not needed. The place had begun life as a hurriedly put together early military shopping area somewhere around the time the Mahdi was chucking spears at Charlton Heston thought Logan. The entire complex was little more than crinkly tin nailed to a wooden framework to form sheds housing outlets vital to support army life, and the place thrived.

Catering entirely to military necessities it had everything needed including shops, a greasy spoon café and a menu that hadn't changed since 1895 and the invention of HP brown sauce. Top of the list ahead of the sausage sandwich were bacon butties served with pint mugs of steaming hot tea or camp coffee for those into that sort of thing or short of money as Nescafe was extra. Chalkie was immediately taken with the place when he saw it sold Bovril.

'Class place this and it's got Marmite on toast.'

'Oh God' said Logan at the thought.

Around the corner from the café was a dry cleaners with long lines of uniforms paraded in the window; rank and file order with officers on a separate rack.

'Bet they get cleaned together' said Logan 'tomato ketchup and cold Windsor soup what a mix.'

'Bog standard service is a brush and dry clean or you can have the deluxe gold service' said Geordie pointing to a sign.

'What's the difference?' asked Compton.

'Half a crown' said Geordie 'special service for mess dress.'

'That Windsor soup must be a right bastard to get off then.'

'Somewhere around here is a tailor for taking off and putting on stripes and there's two barbers and that's about the short back and sides of it...add a newsagent, and that's Tin Town!'

Geordie made back for the café as the others followed, once around Tin Town was enough for Logan who thought it a depressing affront to modern life and out of place with the times.

'The place is a time warp of single socket, multi plug adapter' he said 'what it needs is a bloody good bulldozer.'

'Or a fire, the tailor's iron plugging into a swinging ceiling light did it for me' said Compton as they entered back into the café.

'You would be hard pressed to find that anywhere else but Tin Town' said Geordie waiting for the groan.

At odds with the overall squalor of the place stood a line of flashing pinball machines. State of the art and acting like a magnet to some and a noisy annoyance to others the queue to get on one and lose money was three deep. A sanctuary away from camp and a convenience and a blight Tin Town was all three along with being an insult all at the same time but nobody minded, least of all the squaddie screaming tilt at his chrome sided machine.

'Something to do with the real world a bus ride away unless you count Salisbury and then it's ten miles' Geordie said who after two years had the place more than thought out.

'And that' said Chalkie noisily finishing his Bovril 'is a bloody long way to go to get a stripe put on.'

'You wish' said Compton.

'Or off' said Geordie looking down at his own arm.

'It says here...' said Jock his eye taken on something in the paper before realising the others had left for the exodus back down to the camp.

Back at barracks they were immediately called to the squadron office and arrived to find half a dozen others waiting on the veranda.

'Major's briefing is in the back room no smoking' said the clerk opening the door to the veranda before returning to his office. Called through into the office by a sergeant major they lined up in a semi circle before the OC's desk. Minutes later he entered from a rear door.

'Off to Norway' said the major who knows where that is, anyone?'

'Scandinavia is it sir?' said a voice.

'Well done that man, does anyone know where Scandinavia is?'

'Near Norway' said Geordie clearly joking.

'Where it's always been sir' said another voice which received a watch it look from the SSM.

'Exactly!' said the major but deciding he was going nowhere but up his own arsehole with his condescending geography lesson for idiots he gave up.

'Detachment with NATO's Allied Mobile Force upcoming exercise Winter Wonderland, to provide communications for the first battalion the Barthshire Light Infantry currently based down in Gravesend Kent.'

'That's nowhere near Norway sir' said a voice.

'You will be with my boot up your arse Grogan' said the SSM having enough of the piss taking. 'Now listen in.'

21

Chalkie was almost beside himself with excitement at the prospect of Norway and the detachment to Kent as was Logan but for him it was to escape from the nightmare of Bulford.

'What's so special about Norway? They are a nation of anoraks that can't sing.'

Coming from Viking raided Yorkshire Chalkie wasn't to be put off, as he was convinced of some early Nordic connection in his family genome.

'It wasn't someone called big Sven was it?' said Logan.

'Eric the leg over more likely' felt Compton much to Chalkie's disgust.

'A slow running female ancestor somewhere around the ninth century is a bit obscure as a connection if you ask me' said Logan.

Chalkie was impervious to barracking. Calling up to Odin somewhere in the ceiling rafters was all they got out of the man for a good hour or so as he repeated the name like a mantra whenever anyone passed his bed space.

'Do you really have Norse blood in you somewhere then Chalkie?' asked Logan, like the man would know this.

'Appen and it explains a lot' Chalkie reflected 'like I have always had a thing about blondes with pigtails.'

'You can't be serious. The whole of the bloody camp has a thing about blondes and pigtails Chalkie and gymslips too likely but that doesn't make them Vikings. I happen to like Diana Ross and the chicken Supremes but that doesn't make me African does it?'

'You doesnae sound much Norwegian' said Jock.

'Your problem is your female ancestors couldn't run fast enough like Logan said' put in Compton.

Clearly Chalkie had something deep going on about Norse mythology and Vikings and Odin that must have gone way back. After another hour calling to Odin from his bed it turned out to be back to 1958 and the film The Vikings with Kirk Douglas.

'He was American you tosser' Logan said. 'Real Norwegians wear woolly hats with bobbles on them not cow horns. They were a Hollywood invention like the yodelling cowboy. They are all phoney apart from Trigger, he was for real.'

'Yes' said Jock who reckoned he knew a bit about films 'he was a real horse Trigger...definitely a real horse. The Lone Ranger and Tonto...faster than the speed of light!'

'Real Indian as well Tonto' said Compton joining in 'Jay Silverheels he was called although he wasn't an American, he was a Canadian.'

'Kemo sabe' said Jock.

'And Odin wasn't a phoney of course' put in Compton 'he was a mythical Norse God.'

'God of war was Odin, he was the one with the hammer' said Chalkie displaying his genetic pig ignorance.

'I think you'll find that was Trini Lopez' said Geordie getting the wrong end of the stick as he entered the room.

'Thor' said Compton becoming frustrated, 'he was the one with the hammer.

'Outer Hebrides have a thing about Vikings' said Jock.

Suddenly they were all at it especially Jock who warmed to the talk of pagan ritual, burning longboats and wicker men as the conversation turned silly.

'Do all that stuff in Kirkcaldy then? Bit of disembowelling and burning of wicker men with animals in baskets Saturday nights?'

'Chicken in a basket, yes' said Jock as Chalkie's face went into a contorted memory scan.

'Famous Norwegians' he said suddenly 'Anita Ekberg and Ingemar Johanson.'

'Swedish, and Johanson was a boxer, not a dog but Trigger was a real horse and the Lone Ranger's horse was Silver' said Compton losing everyone but putting an end to it even for Chalkie.

The journey to Gravesend took the best part of a day and was by the circuitous lost route courtesy of a misread London underground map and British Rail. They arrived late afternoon in fading light and found the camp was within walking distance of the town. Milton barracks as the place was called had been built by the Victorians and looked it with a typically overstated ornamental stone entrance and swinging gates that creaked in the wind. The kind of entrance you see at municipal parks that leads to keep off the grass signs and swings and roundabouts felt Logan.

Set immediately behind the gates and to the left was the guardroom. Keep off the grass said a sign. Knew it said Logan to himself looking for the keep dogs on a lead sign as he walked over the grass to the guardroom.

Expected by the guard commander they were taken down past a parade ground eventually arriving at a block of empty timber huts to the rear of the camp. Abandoned for the night they found the barracks freezing cold and filthy like it had not been used for some years but it did have hot water in the bath area piped into the place from the boiler room said the guard commander.

'And central heating' he said with a laugh before leaving for the warmth of the guardroom.

'Grave is this place, Gravesend' said Chalkie speaking for all of them.

'If you ask me' said Logan 'this place is not a place to come to in the depth of winter.'

'Or summer either' said Geordie lifting the lid of a round cast iron stove set in a raised square hearth in the middle of the room.

There was a sudden rush for the beds nearest to the eventual source of heat as Geordie peered down into the empty black hole as if looking for a switch or inspiration. A fagot of wood and a bucket of coke to the side of the stove said there wasn't either as Geordie took it upon himself to be the maker of fire. The man hadn't got stripes on his arm for nothing. After two attempts it was clear the stripes were not for fire lighting and with wild animals closing on the hut and night approaching he gave up and handed over to a joint effort before Logan took it on.

'Boy Scout fire lighting badge second class' said Logan stretching his arms.

Three more aborted attempts later and after a sacrifice of Compton's broadsheet, the stove finally sent smoke and flame to the room. Thirty minutes later the damp air in the flu heated and the smoke was at last drawn up through a six-inch pipe and away to the ether.

'Fire is man's greatest achievement' said Logan immodestly taking full credit for the third attempt.

'Has anybody seen my newspaper?' asked Compton returning in from the ablutions as flames and sparks now rose from the stove like a burning volcano.

'No' said the room as one and sounding like a male voice choir.

'It had the solutions to yesterday's crossword in it.'

'Don't look at me sunshine I never did it' said Chalkie 'especially not with the crossword clues still in.'

'Appen not...you of all people Chalkie' said Compton taking the piss.

By ten o'clock they were in bed to a man seeking warmth of their blankets and by two in the morning the cast iron stove glowed a dangerous red in the dark. By morning and out of fuel the stove and hearth was full of cinders and as cold as the grave. Without the Telegraph and wood to relight it Logan went for a bath to warm up but decided instead on two jumpers.

Milton Barracks was from an age before civilized living and had clearly seen better days.

'Likely around 1860' said Compton coming back from finding the cookhouse with a steaming mug of tea. The 1st Battalion Barthshire's Light Infantry were light of foot and light in hospitality felt Logan feeling well pissed off and wishing for the warmth of Salisbury Plain.

At around eight o'clock the barrack room door opened to a gust of cold wind and a sergeant. It was Tomas who had arrived some days before to arrange their reception at the camp which for Sergeant Tomas was a faggot of wood and a coal bucket.

'Everything all right here is it then lads' said Tomas to the circle of men grouped around the cold stove and wearing blankets Indian style like they were in a pow wow.

'We are waiting for the Red Cross parcels' said Chalkie.

'Why the fuck don't you light the fire' said the sergeant to the line of dirty looks.

'It's hiding the entrance to Dick or is it Harry' said Logan unsure which of the escape tunnels of Stallag Luft 3 began under a stove.

'Harry' said Compton.

'Briefing by the RSO at noon over in the main building across the square. Regimental signals officer' said Tomas seeing the blank looks as he was leaving for the warmth of the sergeant's mess, 'and don't be late you lot.'

'Or zerr entire camp vill be punished' said Logan as the door closed.

It was a day full of blank looks as the RSO a second lieutenant in the regiment who got all the useless jobs, enthusiastically welcomed the detachment to Milton Barracks and the 1st Battalion Barthshire's Light Infantry.

'Raised in Madras by the East India Company the 136th Regiment a Foot served in the Indian Mutiny of 1857 and was placed under command of the Crown in 1858...' was how it began before Logan for one dropped his jaw and switched to a deadpan look mode and blanked the rest.

'I wonder if the Kent Yeomanry are based in Bombay?' said Compton as they left the briefing.

The 1st battalion it transpired were the British contingent of what was called the Allied Mobile Force by the officer.

'Allied Command Europe Mobile Force brackets land is NATO's quick reaction force' said the young lieutenant before turning to a blackboard.

AMF (L) he wrote before dropping the chalk and missing it on the way down. This obscure international grouping was officially a rapid reaction force for NATO and got together every now and again to give the Russians something to have a bloody good laugh about. The every now and again timing came from their joint exercises involving all fourteen members of NATO and not surprisingly the things were an organisational nightmare.

Subsequently they took much of the intervening months for the exercises to be set up although Norway was a gimme for winter and a likely soft line of attack should the Eastern block cross the Norwegian border with Russia where Norway just had a keep out sign.

'Not even a beware of the dog' said Logan.

At the height of the cold war this loose level of the unready would have impressed King Ethelred and been very comforting for the man in the street and the Russians both felt Logan as the officer explained they were now on a permanent seventy-two hour standby.

'Scary' said Chalkie as the lieutenant went on to say they only had five weeks to prepare for the exercise which is why they were brought down to Kent early.

'No Chalkie, that's scary' said Logan speaking for the man in the street.

The Force had as its badge two clenched gauntlets on a metal shield said the RSO holding up the one-inch shield before passing it to the front row for a look and pass on.

'This is the only extraneous badge army command allow to be worn on British uniform' said the RSO.

'It's clenched fists on a yellow shield' said someone in the front row now he could see it closely.

'Two clenched gauntlets actually' said the RSO correcting the man. 'Gauntlet without the fist and arm.'

'What is it' shouted someone at the back who couldn't see.

'It's a pair of old gloves' said Jock.

'Woolly gloves?' asked Chalkie.

'Gauntlets' said the lieutenant.

'Old gauntlets' corrected Jock.

The AMF they were told acted as a rapid reaction strike force for NATO in the event of an unprovoked act of aggression against the freedom of the western world by the communist block. At least that was what the lieutenant of infantry had said or something like that. Theory was that this multi national ever ready force would mobilise early thereby allowing NATO time to get their act together.

Back in barracks Logan looked at his free issue shield pinning it to the left breast pocket of his uniform before returning to the circle grouped around the stove and a fading radio Caroline.

'It looks like a medieval arm wrestle' said Chalkie having a closer look before placing the shield in his locker and snatching Compton's Telegraph. 'Now then today's crossword, how are we doing?'

'Hard one today' said Compton in a supercilious tone.

'Ooh' said Logan 'one for the fire then.'

'Easy or hard it's all the same to me Comps' said Chalkie turning to the crossword and ignoring the sniggers.

'Give me a hard one' said Logan.

'Here's one then, five down, four letters ending in UNT applicable to women?' said Chalkie to the turning heads. 'Easy one that is...aunt isn't it?'

Chalkie threw the paper over to Compton's bed and warmed his hands at the stove as Compton hurriedly retrieved his paper to scan the clues.

'Bollocks' said Compton throwing the paper back down.

'Shield with clenched fists inside a gauntlet I hear you say' said Logan out loud and searching for the meaning of the interlocked clasp of gauntlet.

'Nay hands remember just the gloves' said Jock.

'Probably some obscure esoteric meaning in there somewhere, fucked if I know' said Compton.

Esoteric meaning or not it seemed to be a tad provocative for such an unorganised and small a force.

'Clasp of a handless glove. I wonder which bright spark in an officer think tank thought that one up? Appertaining to a junior officer in a think tank...ending in UNT again' said Logan.

'How many letters?' asked Chalkie.

'Four...and it isn't aunt.'

'Runt' said Compton.

Exercise Winter Wonderland was designed to test the AMF's capability to stop the Russians coming down through Norway they were told at the first briefing. Why the hell NATO thought they ever would was a mystery to Logan as it likely was to the Russian high command. Likely it was a northern most point perimeter defence thing in some obscure strategy worked out on the playing fields of Eton but what the hell he thought, it was character building.

With weeks to wait until the start of the exercise and nothing to do but sit around waiting for the snow to deepen two hundred and fifty miles inside the Arctic Circle it was plain to Logan they were being acclimatized for sub zero temperatures sat where they were in Kent.

A sort of step down variable leading to cryogenic he felt.

'Shit doesn't just happen in the army man, they plan early for it' said Geordie poking life back into the fire and pulling his blanket round his shoulders.

What was coming out of the briefings was the AMF was like NATO and Europe in general.

'One united mess of political self-interest with the only thing in common being the agreed 7.62mm size of their bullets.' was Compton's take on it all, 'multi national forces are always asking for cock ups, look at Waterloo.'

Only Wee Jock was listening, 'I had an uncle at Waterloo, my uncle Jock, never met him...he was in the ticket office.'

'Where the hell were the Prussians at the kick off?' Asked Compton continuing with his version of events. 'The biggest most important battle in the history of Europe and the bloody Germans didn't get their boots on until half time.'

'Bastets did'ne even bother you ken' said Jock 'and where were the fucking French as well hey?'

'Jock?' said Compton.

'What?'

'Never mind.'

The truth was the AMF couldn't have stopped a bus but the Russians probably knew this Logan felt but then the Soviet Block was also a multi national force and probably in a worse state than NATO, as they had to watch their front and their backs or so it was rumoured.

'At least we have a united Europe with NATO discounting the French' said Logan.

'All the AMF is doing is playing a holding game' said Compton. 'Until they load up the Vulcan bombers and bomb the shit out of them...and us likely.'

'The strategy is sound enough' said Chalkie wanking his hand and mouthing wankers.

'It's the theory of it that scares the shit out of you if you think about it' said Logan.

'A great asset to the non thinking man at times is a theory' said Compton.

Exercise Winter Wonderland said it all really and involved most everyone in Europe discounting France and De Gaulle who wasn't playing with NATO anymore and had taken his boule back. A big fan of cryogenics and fish fingers Logan for one couldn't wait for life under canvas in the Arctic Circle and Compton was right but then nobody ever listened to him not even himself at times thought Logan.

It came as something of a shock to learn that as part of the exercise they would be required to learn to ski, which raised something of a question over the words first, rapid and reaction to Logan's mind. Cold though it was in Gravesend skiing on rain would be difficult even for the best of them. The army must have looked on skiing as a sort of issue thing like cold weather kit. As usual the UK was out of step with the rest of Europe Logan felt as skiing for the average Brit was out of the question unless you were royal or knew someone you could bunk up with at Kloisters.

'Surely someone at the exercise set up meeting should have put his hand up when it came to supplying ski troops from the UK don't you think?' said Compton.

'Achtung gentlemens, zer exercise Vinter Vunderland vill be mit zer skis' said Logan. 'Up jumps our man, actually Wolfgang sorry and all that old fruit but the UK hasn't well...got any ski troops...fact is old thing, we haven't actually got any skis either. That said, you can take it from me that all our men will be fucking good on slush.'

Funny though this was to Logan's mind nobody questioned it as everyone wanted to have a go on skis without it costing an arm and a leg – although it likely would for some of course thought Logan. Even Chalkie was still up for it even after being told that going on the piste was not what he thought it was.

Later that week the BLI kitted them out with Arctic Warfare gear, which was really warfare gear with woollies. What a marked comparison it was to the year before on the Yorkshire moors when it was pick and mix warfare from Woollies felt Logan. It was damn decent of the army to kit up for it as Norway in the months around February was from all accounts bastard freezing or so Tomas said. He seemed to know all about the place and how cold it was from his old man who had been there as a merchant seaman.

'In the far north you might only get an hour or so of daylight in winter months and in the south only five or six, and cold like you never knew it. Don't know how cushy you have it here you lot.'

'Pass me another blanket Chalkie my legs just frozen up' said Logan.

'Sat around moaning to me all the time about the cold. Wait till you girls get over there. My old man said he went there as a lad and nearly froze his bollocks off' said the sergeant before leaving for the tropical heat of the sergeant's mess.

'Pity it wasn't the year before he met his mother if you ask me' said Chalkie.

The issue of winter warfare kit included with it a much needed demonstration of how to put it on by the quartermaster sergeant who had been to Norway some years before and was introduced by the RSO as being Barthshire's expert ski man.

'Of some years now quartermaster sergeant?'

'Two stints in the Arctic sir' said the QMS coming to attention and thrusting his chin up with a look of self-satisfied smugness like the smug git he was.

'There's not much the quartermaster doesn't know about skiing, right QMS?'

'So they say sir' said the man brimming with false modesty 'I know a little bit I've picked up...over the many years.'

Don't you just hate that felt Logan as the quartermaster began a thirty minutes lecture on putting on a pair of trousers and a heavy woolly. The kit began with standard looking granddad long Johns and string vests onto which went under and over trousers, shirts and jumper's light and heavy and some chunky knit socks. Then came Arctic boots, thermal under coats and a special furry hooded outer coat called a Parka. This was a knee length quilted coat with wired furry hood and a tail that buttoned between the legs to form a thermal seal beneath your best bits. With all the layers on you looked like a Weeble and sweated like a pig indoors even without the gloves and scarf.

'Some swear by ladies tights' said the QMS 'next to the skin to give another layer.'

'Any particular colour or will tan do?' asked Logan keeping a straight face as the man ignored him.

'But get the right size or they chafe your willy.'

'It's stockings and garter belt for me every time' said Logan.

'Thank you for those valuable tips' said the RSO 'and the sergeant will be going out early to recce the ski routes for us will you not QMS?'

'Always do sir, check them all out for the lads being expert on em as they say and I never ask the men to do anything in the snow I can't do myself sir...oh no.'

'Admirable, very commendable and thank you' said the lieutenant ending the talk.

'What a load of bollocks' said Chalkie.

The meeting over everybody made their way around the square and back to the billet and arrived with a full sweat on.

'The only downer with this lot on is the time it takes to go for a pee' said Compton finding the thought hilariously funny until realizing he needed one.

He left the room stiff legged and walking like the monster in the film The Mummy and was gone for some time before arriving back walking like someone who had pee'd down his leg.

'Four minutes thirty seconds' he said shaking his leg.

Why if they had all this was it not issued for the camp on the Yorkshire moors asked Logan?

'What is death at minus forty something in Norway that isn't death at minus twenty in Yorkshire?'

Logan was beginning to get a feeling about Norway that someone somewhere knew something and it wasn't old man Tomas but thoughts of Norway disappeared completely when he was called to see the RSO. The man had unfortunate news was how the lieutenant had begun and within two hours Logan was packed and heading home on compassionate leave. He arrived with arrangements for the funeral well underway.

22

It was a simple ceremony as despatches go and well attended although most of the people were strangers to Logan, adopted late in life as he was. Cousin met cousin and friends alike renewed acquaintances long neglected until the next one. Suddenly it was over but for what went for a wake down at the pub. The queue not to get the first round in went right back into the room and was heading for the loo until somebody stood and bought his own. God this lot are boring bastards said Logan to himself and God before thanking him that he was actually not related.

Seeing them together in a massed lump of kith and kin was not a happy sight. Adam and Eve were about as close to this lot as Logan wanted it. For sure he felt with his all round good looks and strong masculine form he was clearly no relative of this lot. Pretty much this was how the rest of the assembly saw it also particularly when they staggered back to the house and it came to the subject of the will or as it transpired the lack of one.

'In simple terms...' said someone introducing himself, as a long lost unrelated second cousin, connected by Logan's adopted mother's second marriage through a half sister, who expressed concern as a fourth or fifth claimant to the estate, 'that the will had not survived the deceased.'

'What?' said Logan but stopped the man from going through it all again 'you mean the will's gone missing?'

'Zackly' said the man stuffing a sausage on a stick and spiking a cube of loose cheddar.

After a sordid few more drinks Logan had seen and heard enough and moving to the solace of the front room laid claim to a photograph from the display cabinet. It showed happier times and was all Logan wished for. Placing the frame into his bag he left the house to the vultures kissing his inheritance and the nicest looking of the cousins goodbye before heading out into the rain of the night.

Cold and miserable Logan's head was in turmoil of loss, self-pity and cursing his luck and all his lousy non relatives together but not the cousin called Anne with an e who the best of them attached though she unfortunately was. He had decided on an early train back after a final beer and was on his second final beer when a voice to his side turned his head.

'Sorry to hear' said the voice. It was Mrs Wellfitt, Bernice's mother and showing real concern about him, asking how he was and how he had been and inevitably when he was going back until noticing the bags.

'So soon' said Angela Wellfitt getting some but not all the story from Logan as she sympathetically bought him a cheer up drink.

At length it was obvious to Angela that in his sorry state of mind and grieving as he was he could not travel back tonight, of that she was adamant. He should stay at least until the morning and would not take no for an answer before gathering him up bags and all and ushering him out of the pub like a mothering hen.

'Thank you Angela' said Logan in one of those over sincere self-pity moments when drink takes over and you resign yourself to the inevitability of whatever and wherever.

The wherever was with Bernice and her mother as there was bags of room at her place since the divorce last year from Bernice's father that bastard Jim.

'Long coming it was too Logan' she said asking if she could speak plainly as Logan nodded.

'Of course' he said as he was going to hear anyway.

'He was an arsehole and a right miserable bastard, pardon my French.'

'Oh, sorry' said Logan 'I didn't know.'

'Fifteen years I stayed with that rat, married at sixteen we were. It was too young Logan...but listen to me going on' she said as they passed the Bombay Palace.

At once they were hit by the irresistible smell of India coming direct from a Pakistani restaurant.

'My treat' she said pushing the door to the Bombay Palace to an over the top welcome from Ali who was on one of his quiet nights.

'Midweek United game on bladdy BBC, nil, nil...for both of them at half game time' he said explaining the empty seats as they slipped into the dark of a side booth.

Ali lit the Tea Light candle with a practiced click of his lighter before dropping two menus and leaving for the requisite lagers as Mrs Wellfitt left for a requisite powder of nose. Strange thought Logan watching her walk from the table how similar to Bernice she walked and for that matter looked.

'How similar Bernice is to me don't you mean?' corrected Angela when she returned well powdered, combed and with freshly applied lippy. She looked the very epitome of the young mum that she was.

'Of course' said Logan loudly crunching his complimentary big crisps with lashings of onion and lime pickle before setting into a steamy vindaloo.

The meal over and after an argument to pay that Logan was never going to win they left for the side streets and home.

'Shhh' said Angela over loudly as the door sprung inwards and they stumbled in both more than a little worse for wear.

Closing the door before turning on the hall light Angela made her way down the hallway and into the dark house clicking lights as she went.

'Bernice?' she said shouting upstairs but it was clear the house was empty from the note left on the hall table.

'Is she not back yet?' asked Logan acting like he was stupid.

'Not until tomorrow' said Angela without looking at the note and removing her scarf.

Dropping her coat at her feet she moved to the window drawing the curtains before turning back to the room. 'Now Logan, how about a nightcap?'

'Never wear one' said Logan flashing his eyes as Angela tapped his nose with her forefinger.

'Now that, is naughty' she said before they came together at a rush.

'Very naughty' said Logan as he was pulled down to the settee in a sprawl of arms and removal of everything that could possibly get in the way of the action.

'Yes, yes!' screamed Mrs Wellfitt in an explosion of unrestrained mouth watering lust.

For a few moments everything was frantic panic until, with a scream and grasp of his shoulders it was suddenly over but for the little bit of remorse that would come later. Although there was little of it showing that night until in the early hours and with a final peck to forehead Logan was tucked safely away in Bernice's room. The light clicked and the door to the landing was quietly closed.

'I'm done for' said Logan feeling like a sucked out prune but had little time to reflect on the day or night as he was asleep before the door closed to Angela's room further down the hall.

Logan awoke with a gasp. It came from Bernice as she peered round the door to her bedroom.

'Angela' he said to the dim light coming from the landing as his eyes strained to focus on the figure framed in the doorway.

'Logan?' said Bernice in what went for her what a pleasant surprise voice before closing the door and with a bound was in the bed and on him in a second.

The next morning everyone had slept late and last to dress Logan arrived downstairs to find both women having breakfast.

'Morning Logan sleep well' said Angela Wellfitt winking at him across the table 'how many eggs Logan my love, one or two?'

'Er...two, two?' said Logan somewhat shocked at sitting at the table between them in what was the most bizarre of breakfast atmospheres.

'Oh give him another one mum' said Bernice smiling over with the sweetest of innocent smiles as Logan jumped at the thought. 'Go on give him another egg, the poor lad looks shagged out.'

Once is cool twice is kinky said Logan to himself as the taxi left the house heading for the station.

'They'll damn well kill that weed Billy Drinkwater' he said as the taxi drove off down the street.

'What was that guv?' said the driver as Logan realised he could be heard through the glass grill.

'Sorry mate I was rambling. The er game last night driver, know what the final score was?'

'Three two after extra time' said the cabbie 'what a night that was.'

'You betcha' said Logan yawning all the way to the station and sleeping most of the way back.

Arriving back at camp Logan found preparation for Norway had moved on a pace and he returned to a line of newly painted white land rovers fitted with bolt on cab heaters. The detachment to battalion level would mostly use voice communications and required fitting the land rovers out with suitable radio sets. These were bolted onto an angle iron rack screwed down into the back of the vehicle directly behind the driver's head. Hessian sacking had been taped everywhere to form a second inner skin inside the soft top rover. To the sides and back the floors and overhead, everywhere had several layers and behind the radios Hessian hung down curtain like to cocoon the driver in his cab from the radios in the rear. Once inside and with heat from the radios and body alone the back was cosy enough until someone poked a head through and the cold came in. At least it was parked in a heated garage in Kent with the land rover engine running and the radios loaded up.

As the nominated driver Geordie seemed always to be working on some part of the land rover or other to make it Arctic ready and as the chains went onto the wheels in a practice run Jock just shivered at the prospect along with Compton. Only Chalkie seemed oblivious to the cold walking around in just a jumper even if it was his heavy knit Arctic jumper.

'Don't you feel cold walking around in just a jumper?' said Geordie.

'Cold? I don't feel the cold, must be my genes.'

'The genes and the one piece woolly long johns, string vest and thermal undies and the scarf likely as well Chalkie' said Logan.

'Only trying them out, only trying them out.'

With mechanical and anti frost activity seemingly never ending the days went quickly

278

for Logan and evidently too quickly for some as life in a four star freezer loomed ever closer.

One of six vehicles nominated to fly ahead of the main party to set up communications they left early for Brize Norton before driving into a Hercules C130 and heading off for Bergen. Chalkie was still going on about Vikings as the Hercules landed on the snow covered runway before coming to an eventual and slow stop. Chains were already applied to the wheels before the cargo doors opened on the Hercules and they disembarked to find a waiting matt green Norwegian army coach. The advance party set off for the long drive north in convoy following behind the bus and a trailing shroud of swirling dry snow.

'Which way's we heading?' asked Jock nervously looking through the misty windows as the bus left the airport.

'Er, up?' said Logan.

23

Logan's innate sense of danger went into the red two steps out of the aircraft when the hairs in his nose froze lolly solid. Norway was there somewhere beneath a blanket of white snow and the air was as cold as an ice skater's pond.

'It's bastart freezing' said Jock zipping up and drawing in the hood of his Parka to form a horizontal peephole.

'Way down below freezing' said Compton 'it's frozen.'

Semantics apart it was altogether a different dry type of cold and Logan was glad of his own Parka even for the minutes waiting for the transport.

'I'm not getting in if it's a sled, man with a red coat or not' said Jock peering out through the hole from somewhere deep down inside the quilted jacket which stopped mid calf.

With the tail dangling in the oversized coat Jock looked as ridiculous as everyone else looked envious.

'You look like one of the seven dwarves' said Compton being more than a little indiscreet but fortunately for him the comment escaped Jock's ears deep inside the jacket.

It was always going to be dopey for Logan until Jock turned grumpy which shut everyone up 'in case he became stroppy' whispered Chalkie behind his back just as the man sneezed.

'Don't say it' said Logan mouthing he needs a Doc and looks far from happy.

'That's only five' said Compton 'stroppy doesn't count.'

'I can hear you know' said Jock shutting everyone up.

Without any real clue as to where they were heading other than up as established by Logan earlier, attempts were made to map read from what looked like an Esso map found on one of the seats. With not one word of Norwegian other than Quisling Chalkie took the job on some time after the bus left and was many minutes searching the map for two adjacent towns having the same name.

'Logic?' said Logan moving to look over his shoulder at the map.

'We just passed two places with the same name...they do that do Europeans you know. What's that place...Baden Baden?'

'That's one name Chalkie believe me' said Compton overhearing. 'Stick with East Riding and West Riding of Yorkshire, Baden is a bad un mate.'

'Oh yeah?' he said like everyone on the bus was a dope before he spotted another one. 'There's another of em!'

'The sign's a bloody road sign you thick arse!'

Before long all signs began to disappear down into the snow until veering off the main highway the driver seemed to be following little more than a series of thin poles sticking up through the drifts. Driving down between the poles was like following a ski run until even they at times disappeared and the driver seemed to be playing it by ear heading for the hole between the lines of trees and the occasional house. Only Jock was out of it spreading himself along the back seat and sleeping like a baby.

'Ah, sleepy' said Compton as the search for the remaining name continued.

After an hour a small village suddenly appeared as if out of nowhere 'which is actually where it is' said Logan before the bus turned and skidded down through more houses.

The driver was into his poles again only to run into lines of ropes slung between them.

'That's a line of washing' said Compton able to see at the front 'they are clothes props!'

'Unless the bra on the wipers are his' said Chalkie as the bus found the road.

Knickers on the bus wing mirror were a giveaway for Logan unless they really were the driver's. Eventually the bus chugged out of the side roads and gardens and found the real markers, which was fine for the first hour until the snow either got deeper, or the clothes props smaller. When they disappeared altogether the driver went back to going for the gap between the trees.

'The bastard's driving on a hunch' said Logan amazed at the man's innate sense of lostness that somehow found the way.

Chalkie was raving about the beauty of the country the moment they left the clothes lines although how he could tell under all the snow was a mystery to most on the bus. At long last and after some hours and with dark approaching they arrived at a Norwegian army camp. Well knackered out and fluent in Norsk for get out and push the convoy entered through a snowdrift into a large fenced off area. A Norwegian lieutenant with Sergeant Tomas in tow met them just inside the gates of the camp. Tomas had flown in the day before to prepare things for the advance party. It made army sense to get someone there early to act as a liaison officer with nothing to do but say here's the lads now in English to the Norwegian authorities.

The convoy arrived at the gates looking like an iced up line of snowballs behind a white forty-foot snow splattered sausage but for the wipe of the wipers and the smoke and steam from the exhaust there was no sign of life.

'I think this is your men coming now sergeant' said the lieutenant as the bus entered the camp and slowed to a halt by a Norwegian flag.

'Are you sure?' said Tomas as with a discernible cracking of ice sealing the doors the snowballs cracked open and men began to emerge.

'God dag og velkommen til Norge' said the lieutenant, 'Velcome to Norway.'

'God dag, take me to your leader' said Logan as they grouped around the flag expecting prayers and a naming ceremony.

'Who got here first' asked Compton leaving the bus late, 'the Norwegians or us?'

'They did' said Logan pointing up at the flag.

After the horrors of the journey Logan was really looking forward to a nice hot bath as they were taken first to a tented area to drop off their kit before following on to the main army barracks for a briefing on cold weather safety.

'What a journey, hot soak in a bath, wrap up well and a couple of beers down the nearest pub.'

'Pub?' said Tomas 'there isn't a pub round here lads.'

'Shit, you mean there's nothing near then?' said Chalkie showing a justifiable Yorkshire concern.

'No' said the lieutenant showing little to no concern at what he was saying 'there are just no pubs in Norway gentlemen.'

You could have cut the silence as the room went silent to a man and the words sank in.

'That Kirk Douglas is full of shit' said Chalkie almost in tears at the let down.

'What's nay pubs?' asked Jock of the man so alien was the statement to the Scottish ear. 'Where the fuck do we get pissed then?'

'Nobody ever died from non alcoholic poisoning Jock' Compton said.

'How about trauma to the liver then?' said Logan.

It turned out that the question wasn't where to get pissed but when and was confirmed as likely in three months time when they returned to the UK looking like dried prunes. The thought immediately turned everyone into deep gloom until told that you could buy beer in Norwegian cafes by the lieutenant.

'That's something then at least' said Chalkie much relieved.

'The beer is a full two percent alcohol' said the lieutenant but adding cheerily that there was a pub in Tromso attached to the sole brewery.

'That's something then' said Chalkie 'and where's this Tromso place?'

'Tromso?' said the lieutenant 'maybe sixty kilometres or so north from here.'

'Fucking doom and gloom merchant that bastard was' said Jock as the man moved to the front of the room to begin the briefing.

'Two percent alcohol! Gnats piss three percent' said Chalkie finding his voice again after the shock.

'Oh it gets worse than that' said Tomas sat behind them, 'the law only permits two bottles per person.'

Logan was about to say something on the lines of I told you so to Chalkie but thought better of it as a genuine feeling of a deep sadness fell on the group. It was as if a descending fog had fallen to obliterate the sun from the civilized world for the rest of time.

'Or at least three months' said Geordie arriving from the land rover park.

'Bloody Vikings' said Chalkie 'no bloody wonder they went on the piss when they raided to the UK, they were let out.'

Turning on an overhead projector and taking the lights down the advance party were taken through the safety rules for happy camping in the Arctic. They do say good presentations start with a shocker to get the attention and the lieutenant certainly did that. Slide one was a scary.

Rule number one – never ever pull out all your pecker when taking a pee. Two – never piss into a Norwegian northerly full on and watch out for the ice droplets when you do the shake and pack.

'They go everywhere, freeze immediately and then melt when in the warm hours later' said the Norwegian. 'For some this would of course be only a little problem but some of us Norwegians have to be careful.'

'Bet they are all called Sven' said Logan.

'Big Sven' said Compton as the lieutenant clicked the projector.

'Why don't you both piss off and listen in' said Chalkie still irked at the missing ale.

'Chalkie's right, keep it down Compton, the man's not just talking willy-nilly here...nilly-willy maybe.'

'Just chuck it' said Chalkie as the lieutenant clicked the projector.

Overhead three was never, never, never, never forget to zip back up. It was just something else to think about for some but pissing down wind was well established with Logan having gone into his cerebellum early in formative life along with rule number five never piss down your leg and never letting go of appendage mid leak. Nothing worse than losing hold of it thought Logan and with everything freezing in seconds out here the consequences would hardly bear thinking about.

Safety slides on the pecker over and well and truly noted Big Sven zipped up and moved on to the next slide. An image of a large round tent with a chimney now appeared on the screen.

'We have here a big Svedish eight man tent.'

'I've heard this about the Swedes' said Compton 'wait till he gets to the bit about birch twigs.'

Shaped like a twelve sided three penny bit with a wood burning stove in the middle and a central chimney they were big tents.

'It's like a small yurt' said Compton to the blank faces either side of him.

'Hate that stuff, its sour milk is that' said Jock pulling a face.

'A yurt is a Mongolian tent dip shit' said Compton.

'That's right, you dope' said Logan 'how are you spelling it?'

'Y and a URT' said Compton.

'Ah, same as me then.'

'Everyone in zer tent,' continued Sven with his briefing, 'sleeps feets to zer centre.'

There now came another major warning slide. They would be sleeping directly down on compacted trodden down snow he explained onto which was placed straw and on top of that the hide of a reindeer.

'But, when doing zer manoeuvres in the forest and away from camp and straw vie use pine needles...and birch twigs' said Sven.

'Told you' said Compton with the tone of a man vindicated, 'they're into all this sort of stuff are these Scandinavians.'

A fire safe one metre circle is drawn around the stove said the Norwegian. This, he said was kept clear of anything that would burn like straw and sleeping bags and feets by the man on night fire duty as there was a natural tendency for the body to involuntarily move away from the tent walls and towards heat. Temperatures tonight he said were anticipated around minus thirty give or take ten degrees. Not to worry said the lieutenant sensing concern from men who would get cold licking an iced lolly. With regular feeding of logs the tents would warm up well enough and the stove would glow red hot with the heat.

'So it was not a job to fall asleep on as with the dryness inside your tent will completely burn to the ground in less than two minutes.'

Fearing fire above everything the rule was for each man to sleep with a bayonet tied to the tent wall above his head.

'With a live fire central to zer tent your only way out is through your hole' said the lieutenant sounding cheery enough before adding 'or up zer chimney with zer smoke.'

During your fire watch he said continuing with the briefing the man on duty heated water on the stove and shaved and made a drink for the next man on shift. This was done to allow your face time to recover before next morning.

'He's heard about your tea then Jock' said Compton.

'In zer Arctic zer rule is either full beard or no beard.'

'No beards is the rule for us' said Tomas receiving a groan from the room.

'Stubble hair traps ice and frost and chips off with a piece of face if you rub when it freezes and it vill freeze!' he said before showing overheads of men with black noses, fingers, toes and chins and gaps where each had once been.

'That's why you never see Vikings with designer stubble and red braces' he said thinking it well funny before moving to the final slide as the lights clicked on to lines of men checking crutch and noses.

The Arctic he said 'works on zer buddy system' where you team up with a friend to watch and check for signs of early frostbite such as white patches 'or something fallen off.' If you cannot feel you must rub immediately.

'What if you've just had one?' said Jock at the back thinking it funny before being invited down to the front as a guinea pig.

He was still smiling as the Norwegian removed his boots and socks to bare feet and asked Jock to sit on the floor and open his parker.

'The procedure for frozen hands is rub and place zem on your stomach, under armpits is better' said Sven as Jock followed the lieutenant's actions finding his own hands chilly enough even inside the barracks.

'And for the feets' said Sven with a thrust that placed both feet under Jock's armpits to his cry of alarm.

Jock did not find this at all funny as Logan looked around undecided in a choice between finding a hairy armpit or someone with warm feet before thinking it would be the Norwegian in another ten minutes or so. Returning life back to frozen hands and feet was always with rubbing and body heat said Sven and never by a heat source like a fire.

'Zer pain of returning circulation to cold and frozen parts is excruciating if it is done too quickly' he said allowing Jock to get up and stagger back to his seat, 'so in Norway nobody is bashful.'

'Bashful, that's the one we missed' said Compton quietly.

Excruciating was a big word for a Norwegian and it was a big point to make. Other rules now followed with slide upon slide of warnings like keeping hands and feet moving or stamping and control of sweating when skiing he said. Many were common sense but mostly it was about thinking differently Logan felt, such as slowing down before a long halt to arrive sweat free, the exact opposite of the hurry to get home of the UK. To arrive at an overnight halt sweating freezes the sweat to body and as the temperature drops so do you said the lieutenant. Keeping moving or even skiing further to cool down was a strange concept for everyone.

'Until it becomes second nature' was how the lecture ended with lessons half heard and some never to be forgotten as Jock let it be known later.

Get it wrong in the Arctic and you die was the message and that is not funny said Sven asking for another volunteer to the lines of men stamping feet, wiggling toes and turning well away from the big Norwegian and none more than Wee Jock.

After a long think on the matter Logan decided to announce he for one would ideally be looking for a sweaty female buddy with hairy armpits and warm feet.

'An anthropomorphic impossibility that, a female with warm feet' was how Geordie saw it.

'Me I'm going for a bird with hairy armpits' said Chalkie.

'Hirsute' said Compton.

'She would' said Chalkie 'I just said that. What do you think Logan?'

'There you have it' said Compton jumping in to rationalize the options, 'hairy armpits for the warmth and accept the cold feet or look for a girl with warm feet and accept the lack of body hair. Assuming finding a female with hairy feet is out of the equation...what do you think?'

'I'll go for one with big tits every time' said Logan.

'Sound' said Chalkie 'can't fault you.'

One thing for certain, choice of buddy for Logan wouldn't be a cross-eyed Smith from basic training, as Logan was well intent with holding on to all his bits in all regions nether or otherwise. Leaving the briefing well concerned and full of a stew best described as hot, wet and Rudolf they joined a queue for reindeer skins. Poor Rudolf was having a bad day in the office and so were Prancer, Dancer, Donner and Blitzen from the size of the stew. After stamping down the snow inside the tent and lighting the stove they spread the straw as directed by the lieutenant and throwing down Father Christmas's little helpers they got into their sleeping bags for the night.

'The stink of these skins is something awful' said Chalkie in the dark 'there's bits of meat still on my skin from the skinning.'

'Ugh, not tried mine yet' said Jock.

'You're not chewing it are you Jock?' said Compton, 'only an idiot would think of chewing it.'

'No' said Jock, 'but I'm thinking about it.'

'Thinks he's lying on a Donner Kebab. You're supposed to be lying on it not having it as a bedtime snack' said Chalkie, 'hang on, found a chewy bit.'

At length the tent calmed to the flickering light of the stove and the one torch of Compton trying to read. Once inside his bag and lots drawn for the one hour fire stag everyone settled for the night. The relaxing atmospheric crackle of burning wood and rotting reindeer bits pervaded the tent and before long it was warm enough to remove some clothing. For Jock it was his beret until even he had to unzip his Parker.

Lying there in the dark took Logan back to the moors especially with the smell of straw and the rancid odour of dead animal remaining on the pelt where the Laplanders had missed in the rough skinning. We could be in Yorkshire right now he thought with the temperature outside below minus twenty something.

'The only difference between Yorkshire and here in the Arctic is here I'm sweating like a bloody dog' he said.

'Yorkshire terrier or Lap dog?' asked Compton to his side.

'Never thought I would sleep with a bayonet hanging over my head' said Chalkie 'a noose, yes.'

'Or with your life in the hands of someone chewing on his bed roll' said Logan, 'it's like sleeping under the sword of Damocles hoping whoever is on fire stag will stay awake, and I don't mean the bayonet' he said to Chalkie as the tent settled to sleep.

'What I'm wondering' said Chalkie to the silence of the tent 'is what you do at minus forty as you stand there in your socks in the fading glow of a smouldering burnt out tent clutching your bayonet in one hand and your nuts in the other?'

Logan gave a bit of a nervous laugh as the sound of zips came from around the tent to all segments but Wee Jock's.

'That comes in lesson two' said Logan getting out of his bag and putting some clothes back on.

'Oh shit, bloody shit, bastard, shit bastard' said Chalkie in that expressive way of his. 'I only need a bloody pee.'

'Shit, bloody bastard' came the calls from around the tent as they were all up and dressing but for Compton who was already up and loading the fire with yet more Norwegian wood.

'I doesnae need one yet' said the voice of Jock before being forced out of the tent to have one anyway by an angry mob.

24

The following morning Logan awoke to find he had survived the night and as the sun came out to a beautiful and clear blue sky he crunched his way over the snow to the queue for breakfast. At the duff tent they were offered a full Norwegian breakfast, which looked remarkably like a full English breakfast in Norway, which is what it was, but with real coffee and Frosties.

In the full light of day Logan found the camp was a gathering of nations' advance parties turned out in a noticeably variable collection of Arctic uniform. With all the accents around it gave the place something of an international feel to it much the same as the winter Olympics minus the cow bells and those annoying whistles Logan felt but without the dope testing although there were a few of them around the place. Top of the list for Logan were the Italians who were fielding a company or so of their specialist alpine ski troops wearing what looked to be Robin Hood hats but with black chicken feathers sticking from them.

'How ironic is that' said Compton voicing the thoughts of many including Chalkie who felt Alpine was a breakfast cereal with nuts and raisins.

Largest in number and naturally enough scattered liberally around their own camp were the host nation's military who appeared to be dressed the mirror image of WW2 Germans even down to the coal scuttle helmets. Something to do with kit left around at the end of the war felt Compton which had something of a ring of truth about it.

'They are even wearing those metal half moon necklaces you see in the films' said Geordie 'you know, the ones around the necks of the motorbike and sidecar drivers.'

'The ones that always drive down the centre of the road going the wrong way from the retreating lines of French civilians and making everyone get out of zer vey?' said Logan.

'Them's em' said Geordie.

'Nay wonder they always got strafed by a lone Spitfire in the films' agreed Jock 'that kind of driving gets right up everyone's tits.'

Compton remained convinced with the theory that the German look was stolen from them along with the uniforms and other bits of kit found lying around at the end of the war.

'Unless they were big into army surplus' he said taking a lot of interest in a BMW tracked vehicle and looking for a painted out swastika.

There was also a lot of hair about the camp Logan felt. This they learned was because the Norwegian army was largely conscript and also unionised. You can't tell a man to get a haircut if he's allowed to go on strike was the general consensus. The net effect was that many of them looked like they should be wearing one until a duty guard at the gate turned up in a cute honey blonde one under his tin hat. Everyone felt this a little weird but preferable to probably having it up in a bun or worst still plaits and a couple of ribbons thought Logan immediately going off the idea.

Apart from the guard that day on the gate everybody immediately took to the Norwegians. Largely this was due to their long hair and the smoking on guard duty but mostly it was the scruffy bastard look of a conscript army. Combined force or not, from the outset the nations were kept apart by the AMF and were split into different camped areas which was probably a good thing as it was immediately obvious there were major differences.

Nowhere did this show more than how each nation treated their troops. Ever the talker and smelling freebies a metric mile off Chalkie was amazed to find that the American field issue compo rations included packs of cigarettes and chewing gum. How nutritious is that Logan asked Chalkie who went around the American radio vehicles openly bumming unwanted packets of Lucky Strike from non smokers. For some reason they found the Americans were not in tents with the logic for this being given by one of them on an exchange visit looking for his Scottish ancestors.

'Why suffer in a tent if you don't need to. Come a war you gotta have to do that kinda shit so what's the damn point when we ain't got no war.'

'It's good training and very healthy and we love it' said Logan defending the British high command's uncaring attitude to UK soldiery.

'Only a dumb arse goes looking for pain soldier' said the dumb arsed American looking for anyone called 'Macgregor living near Edinborrow in the early part of the last century.'

'Are you sure he was a Jock' asked Logan quickly checking behind in case Jock was close.

The blank looks from the others probably said it all although Chalkie said he would ask around for him when he discovered he was a non smoker.

'You guys don't not get no smokes in your ration pack? You want that shit come and take it' said the American 'even a bum don't not get no smokes in his ration pack.'

Thinking it through Logan felt it probably had something to do with some amendment or other in the constitution like the right to bear forearms or kill with smoke. Although they didn't say, it must have tested the constitution of the Norwegians too as they vacated their barracks for it to happen or so rumour had it.

Line up for the exercise proper proved to be the Norwegians, Canadians, Americans and the Brits, joined together in one large command said the RSO arriving at the tent from the Norwegian officer's mess and smelling of bath loofah, sauna steam and birch leaves. How big or where this command was nobody had a clue, for as usual all that was seen in the field was a small part of the big picture. War is always a yard wide for everyone but the general staff where it's a mile or so back and more if you are a three star general. For the one commanding the forthcoming battle with a whole country to play with war was a green mobile home the size of a large removal van with triple glazing and central heating and a large wall map with little coloured stickers and pins that made sense and nonsense of it both at the same time.

'Ski training' said the RSO getting everyone's attention for once would begin at 1400 hours with the sizing and drawing of skis and would be delayed, as the Barthshire quartermaster sergeant had not yet returned from hospital.

'There is something entirely disconcerting about drawing skis from a skiing expert with a broken leg' said Logan as he queued up for the issue to find Sven in charge at the store and shouting the ideal size for both skis and poles as each man approached.

Somehow Logan had assumed it was a one size fits all approach for skis until Wee Jock picked up a pair of ski poles that went over his head. Tomas and the RSO had already been issued with their's some days before along with the quartermaster and were already proficient in the fall on arse but the quartermaster sat this one out with a pot to lower leg and looking less smug than Logan recalled from the last time he saw the expert. Word came down the line that he had slipped on the sergeant's mess step. True or false there was not one man in Norway who believed it.

'Ooh, bet that's really painful quartermaster sergeant' asked Logan as he signed for his skis in the silence of a no reply, 'is it?'

Split into teams for training the detachment joined the RSO and Tomas to find their group instructor was none other than Sven. This was a pleasant surprise to all of them as the Norwegian was more civilian than lieutenant and more than proficient on skis but then so were the kids of every age who packed the high ground either side of the field ready for a good laugh. There is something entirely off putting for a grown man to fall on his arse in the snow watched by a bemused two year old who has arrived at speed by doing a series of Telemark turns.

'Turning around one hundred and eighty degrees on skis' said Sven sounding very positive before demonstrating the act with an easy swirl of his body.

The squad followed in an ugly mess of arms and angled leg and might have made it had not Compton fallen inwards to the line from the one end. Down they went to a man falling in sequence and much to the amusement of the onlookers including the Italians who had paused their patrol to watch and jeer from the higher slopes. Some days later and after much practice they were more than proficient at the fall over remarked Logan.

'It's the getting back up that's the problem.'

'Lost somewhere in all this is a misunderstanding of Newton's theorem of revolving orbits and gravity' said Compton referring to the standing turn during a smoke break 'or it could be his first law?'

'You what?' said Chalkie.

'Objects in motion stay in motion unless an external force acts upon them.'

'Can't fault you, sounds right enough to me.'

'Equally a stationary object at rest remains at rest unless an unbalanced force acts upon it...I'll have to look it up.'

'It's about falling on your arse and not skiing into bloody trees Compton' said Tomas overhearing and wondering what the hell the bloke was on.

'I think he's on another book' said Chalkie.

Newton's laws apart only Chalkie had the ability to lose control in a spin half way down a hill to ski the next half backwards and yet arrive at the bottom ahead of the others. It was a feat he alone had perfected and Logan for one felt it would be in the Olympics one day along with other missing British sports like darts and snooker. Norse blood or not, on skis the man was at best a trier and at worst a tosser.

'Langlauf skiing' Sven said on day one 'is little more than walking on skis with poles and differs greatly from zer down hill skiing.'

For starters it knackers you out Logan decided not twenty feet into the first walk attempt to the hills in a line following a trail made by Sven.

'Langlauf skiing' said Logan 'is shuffling through snow on your arse with two planks on your feet.'

'It wouldn't be half as knackering if it wasn't for the bloody skis' said Chalkie who after two days was more a slider on bum than a skier but had the fall to left and right nigh well perfect.

Falling was something that came naturally to all of them and painless enough in the snow but getting up was tricky for everyone but Wee Jock. The man had a natural ability to fall and get up quickly to the point of being good at it.

'Something to do with his arse being nearer to the ground' said Compton showing more than a hint of green eye.

Clearly the man was envious for his own trail in the snow resembled two parallel lines with every six feet an impressed bum print or shape of prostrate body to left or right with what can only be described as evidence of a personal struggle to attend verticality. From day one of ski training both Compton and the RSO jockeyed for the worst skier in Norway title and if anything they were worse after two full weeks than when they started, although Compton had perfected the fall over and arse sit down slide stop worthy of a six point nine even from a Russian judge. With the group showing overall improvement Sven moved them on to larger slopes and faster turns. It was what Chalkie termed broken fucking leg territory.

In some ways the move from the nursery slopes to infant one took the pressure off as once the whole group was falling to snow again nobody seemed to notice Compton and the officer of infantry. Try as he might the Barthshire lieutenant was even worse than Compton and being an officer hated coming last in clear sight of the men or being the one likely to fall arse over tit in an undignified pile of snow, crossed ski and officer. Unable to swear in front of the other ranks and incapable of improving his lot on the slopes, the man took to wearing a red silk neck scarf. This and a strong stink of Brute would serve to separate officer and gentleman from base, common and popular. As ever Logan was sympathetic to anything with a pip and felt for the man as he helped him up yet again.

'You don't think it's the red scarf do you sir?'

'In what way Logan?' said the lieutenant narrowing his eyes.

'Well sir, Wee Jock over there is a whiz on skis and if I am allowed a modicum of immodesty here, so sir am I...and he and I both, do not have anything round our necks?'

'My hands will be Logan if you don't shut up and join the others.'

'That's not very nice' said Logan quietly leaving to catch up.

The arrival of the battalion took the pressure off everyone including the RSO who left the group to join them already some weeks on and something of a whiz himself relatively speaking. Logan watched him go. In the kingdom of the blind the one legged man is king, thought Logan as the lieutenant sped slowly away.

As the crowds of kids and the Italians now flocked to more amusing sights and with Lieutenant Touchy with them Sven decided it was time to go faster and the morning started with the issue and application of a new ski wax. This said the Norwegian would help the glide through of the skis although the technicalities of each wax type were lost to most including Compton.

'Hard and soft, glide or kick or whatever he is calling them' he said 'it's all slip, slide and fall over wax to me.'

Cross-country skiing is like running felt Logan, at best a three on a desirability scale of one to ten until you reach a point when it suddenly becomes fun and you are hooked.

'On a scale of one to ten I see skiing as a number two' said Compton 'always a number two.'

Before long the woods and frozen lakes surrounding the camp became a maze of crossing parallel lines as teams formed into patrols and ventured further out. On each of these loops from camp a close eye was placed on the temperature with the imperative being to keep a constant body heat of neither too cold nor too hot for fear of becoming sweaty. This could be done in a flash or with one by having a pee but was largely done by removal of a single glove for periods sometimes for only seconds at a time or by unzipping the Parker and always the rule was constantly to keep toes and fingers moving. Forget the one and the sweat froze on you; forget the other and getting the feeling back to hands and feet was agony to the point of grown men crying. Mostly it was feet and almost everyone was caught out at sometime over the weeks including Logan as the tears of pain came to his eyes as slowly the circulation returned.

'My God Chalkie what an arsehole you are, you just don't know how painful this is, you do this again and you can stuff your feet up your own armpits.'

'Sorry Logan' said Chalkie apologizing to his buddy with just a hint of enjoyment showing between the protests of Logan's pain mixing with those of his own.

As the skiing improved the group took to making ever-longer trails to the outlying country. Now skiing with Bergens and reindeer skins lashed in a roll across the top and wearing white camouflage smocks they at least looked the part. Always following the trail of Sven and taking turns as point man whenever they found the deeper snow they were suddenly skiers.

'Must have happened twixt cup and lip' said Logan, as it was a shock to all of them but none more than Compton when Sven called him forward to take his turn at the front.

At length they were trekking for most of the daylight hours before returning to camp late afternoon until one day they arrived at a forest clearing to find other patrols assembled and unexpectedly a horse and sled.

'Food!' announced Sven.

'A fucking horse?' said Chalkie arousing concern from the animal lovers until the rations were seen on the sled alongside bundles Sven said were tents.

'He did say tents didn't he?' said Jock with a heavy heart.

With darkness falling fast the small conical tents looking like American Indian tepees, were pitched down into two foot of snow in a frenzy of eager activity spurred on by the usual thoughts of approaching death. Logan immediately took charge of stamping down and clearing the snow from inside as others set to with bayonets cutting blocks of frozen snow and piling them igloo style around and against the tent walls.

Choice of snow proved critical for the blocks explained Sven leaving with his bayonet to find snow that held the correct texture. Sods law said it had to be some distance away as others in the patrol scoured the immediate forest area for anything green, soft and on a branch. Soon pine leaves several inches deep formed inside the tent as skins were thrown on top and sleeping bags unrolled ready. First in Logan found it was surprisingly warm under the snow as any bunch of snowdrops and the Inuit will bear witness and the fight to form a protective cocoon around Logan was touching he said although a little embarrassing.

'Thanks buddies' said Logan as bags and bodies moved ever closer.

'Something to do with you getting to the middle first?' said Compton annoyed at being two bodies out.

'Look Comps, we can't all be in the middle in a clutch of buddies can we, I am at the central mass and pivotal to our survival here look. Someone has to be on the outside, that's physics' said Logan 'look the bastard up.'

Light filtered down through the trees as dawn arrived on the body mass piled in a mid centre log jam of rising steam. Outside heavy snow was falling and it seemed some hours before the voice of Sven called the patrol to break camp. After several calls they emerged like ferrets from a hole to a scene unrecognisable from the day before with several inches of fresh snowfall blanketing all but the deepest of tracks. Sven had been up some time even before the snow had stopped falling and had something approaching tea made from pine needles that surprised everyone. First to try was Chalkie.

'Looks funny, what's it taste like?'

'Funny' said Chalkie dunking his hardtack.

Breakfast over the tent was collapsed and gear packed ready for the off just as the sled arrived.

'Oh look a norse' said Compton to the amusement of nobody and not understood by Sven who simply nodded agreement.

'Ja it is a Norse...vie live here yes?' he said.

'No an orse as in orse' said Compton feeling the need to explain, 'not a Norse, a horse. We sometimes drop an aitch in English...like the French do?'

'Ah,' said Sven nodding politely but not fully understanding.

'Like hotel and homme, you do not pronounce the aitch in French?' said Compton nodding at the puzzled Norwegian and raised his eyebrows like he was talking to an idiot.

Likely he will be raising his voice next thought Logan but the penny had already dropped for the switched on Norwegian.

'Ah now I see' said Sven 'comme en Français and in English words like zer cart orse. I did not know this and what others?'

'Ankerchief and ard tack biscuits' said Chalkie walking past.

With an eye on keeping warm they were eager to set off when the sound of an engine was heard approaching from some way off. The long search in the pine for Jock's torch and loading the tent on the sledge was completed just as a white painted half-track snow vehicle arrived that Sven said was a Veasel. Compton thought about it but kept his mouth shut and the Weasel driver greeted Sven with a wave of hand somewhere between a salute and a howdy.

The half track was their lift for the five miles back to main camp as the vehicle set off at a pace towing a line of men desperate to hold onto the trailing line and at times the pole of the man in front and even more desperate still not to fall and be ploughed into by the man behind. Inevitably someone did and fun though it was for a time with wind chill from the speed of the tow and less body movement keeping them warm they arrived back at camp like a line of frozen icicles looking for an armpit.

Daily the parallel lines got exponentially longer and bum prints fewer until one day they were almost gone. To escape the camp as much as anything Logan had taken to spending evenings at a café at the top of a hill overlooking the village. Although there was rumour of a second place out in the forest it was said to be some distance from camp and with the only way there being on skis in the first weeks everyone stayed in the village. Not that being accessible by foot and a short distance from camp was the only attraction of the café, for it held greater delights than open top obscure meat sandwiches and inedible cheeses.

These and the beer were served by the fair hand of a plaited blonde by name of Frida. The lady's desirability factor grew as the weeks passed to levels measured beyond the bounds of reality. In the first week Frida was a straight ten in many books and by week three in a village largely bereft of females other than the odd lady moose and an ageing postmistress she had risen beyond an out of ten classification to a crawl naked over broken glass level. Not unnaturally the lone lady Viking became the focus of much disgraceful and undisguised lecherous attention. Testosterone, sweaty palms and dirty thoughts abounded and all of it seemingly wasted, for the maid was an impenetrable fortress with knickers to match.

'Tostesterone?' said Jock 'love em, triangular they are.'

'That's Toblerone Jock you want your ears de-waxed mate' said Compton.

Inevitably rumours began circulating about lights coming on when Frida opened her legs and there was even one that she had a preference for women.

'There's nought wrong with that' said Chalkie 'that's the same as me then.'

Whatever the truth Frida was branded an Ice Maiden and off limits even to the Norwegians who had all long since given up trying said one of the conscripts from the camp who hung around the café practising his English. God only knows what he got out of Chalkie thought Logan or Jock for that matter but Geordie found more than the odd word between Newcastle speak and Norwegian that had the same meaning. This was discovered by chance from the overnight in the forest when the Norwegian sled driver threw over a tent peg mallet to Geordie's shout of 'hey hinnie, hoy yer hammer ower' and when gan yam translated as going home in Norse there was no stopping the man's enthusiasm for the language which bored on for weeks. Teaching English and learning the odd useful phrase in Norwegian like 'where's the nearest fish canning station' moved quickly on to more useful phrases like 'can I take you home' and 'do you have a big sister' plus a list of foul swearwords that would blush a strip club comic.

'Gan away zer girls frigid mon?' said Tor one of the Norwegian conscripts teaching Norse to Geordie 'ye got nay chance with that hinnie. Knaa what ah mean leik?'

Poor bastard if he ever comes to the UK thought Logan, the man's got nay chance outside Newcastle.

'You do know Geordie's a monkey hanger don't you Tor?' Logan said when Geordie went to the netty 'I mean lavatory...the bloody man's got us all at it, he's infectious.'

'Whey aye from Toon leik...and it vas the South Vellians what hanged zer monkey.'

Too late thought Logan, the man's gone over to the dark side, as Geordie returned and Tor continued with tales of his own and others' many failings to pull with the voluptuous maid Frida. Not that it helped with her not speaking a word of English apart from the odd word of Geordie and a well practised icy no given with the sweetest of smiles. At times sign language alone is enough but not here, as all failed that would venture in and hope was abandoned.

Weeks were passing and Logan found he was getting quite a taste for Norwegian beer, which seemed to grow in strength as real ale faded into memory.

'It's either that or I've lost some of my taste buds.'

'The reaction's psychosomatic. If you ask me we are suffering post alcoholic withdrawal symptoms' said Compton looking over at a table of Norwegians drinking the same stuff who managed to leave like newts on some nights.

Was it possible thought Logan that his body was actually getting used to the low percentage and remembering falling around as a youth on two bottles of ginger beer? It was Chalkie who noticed the topping up from beneath the table and it was Geordie who got the source from his Geordie cloned mate Tor.

'Moonshine leik' said Tor explaining quietly.

Norwegian moonshine was like Norwegian sunshine, a wondrous thing like water in the desert, your first kiss and first real love, the love of a football team like Accrington Stanley or memories of the bike sheds with Bernice and one of her mates felt Logan.

Heimebrent Tor called it sliding the bottle from his pocket and translating the Norse as 'home burnt and for short Heimert or wine of the forest.'

Tor poured a thimbleful using the top of the pop bottle.

'What is it?' asked Compton before dumping it into the remains of his beer and raising his glass to look at the rising smoke before trying some.

'Something local' said the Norwegian, which suggested he didn't know to Logan as Compton managed to swallow before going into a long silence as he fought for breath.

'One hundred eighty proof' said Tor waiting for Compton to recover.'

'How is it?' they asked as the man tried to speak.

'Anything that shuts him up for two minutes can't be all bad' said Jock declining the cap as it passed to Logan.

For all they knew white spirit was what it was but Tor explained it was distilled from the forest, maybe wood maybe pine maybe potato, maybe all three.

'Maybe fucking turshpentine' said Compton finally able to speak.

'No,' said Tor defending his nation's illicit hooch 'not any more, only sometimes in zer past maybe but not here. This is best quality Norwegian made...with full guarantee from maker.'

'Guarantee for what?' said Compton still recovering and wiping his runny eyes.

'He guarantees it will not make you blind' said Tor like it was a declaration of the maison or a Norwegian appellation controlee.

Everyone liked the sound of Heimert and liked what it did better but as to calling it wine of the forest.

'Er no' said Compton passing on a top up 'I think it needs a little more time in the barrel ageing, or decanting through a sock or a sump or something to catch the volatiles.'

'Volatiles can't live in that stuff can they?' said Jock looking down into the drink.

Whatever it was thought Logan it was not something to smoke near or splash onto your boots and was best described by the words spirit and white. Heimert defied all attempts to remove the taste whatever was put with it, demolishing coke and all manner of juices at whatever parts per million. The taste always came through. Real scotch Tor explained was available in hotels, but at prices approaching the best part of a day's pay for a measure heimert had a lot going for it not the least being cost and availability.

Under the haze of illicit moonshine the world and the hours in the cafe were seen in an altogether different light. With fear of rejection drowning in something approaching 180 percent proof Logan for one was spurred to greater efforts to defrost the lovely Frida.

'Liten gutt oppfører seg' said Frida ruffling Logan's hair before turning and leaving for the counter with the empties.

'Listen good what?' asked Logan patting down his hair and turning to Tor with an am I in with a chance look 'what did she say?'

'Liten gutt oppfører seg.'

'Yes?' said the table to a man.

'You don't want to know.'

'Yes we do' said the table as Tor reluctantly translated into English.

The sounds of laughter could still be heard coming from inside the café as Logan left for camp pausing only to dump all their skis in a snow drift.

'Little boy behave...cheeky cow' mumbled Logan as he clipped into his skis and kicked off down the hill heading for the camp.

Smarting from the put down and with some parts per million of Heimert inside him he arrived at the camp still mumbling on and travelling at quite a speed. Unable to turn Logan sped on past the gate and further down the hill as the road dropped steeply away. Skiing still at a pace the hill took him away from the village and out into the clear night. Soon all lights were left behind until they were suddenly gone and the sky lit up with the twinkle of countless stars and a strange glowing light far away to the north.

Logan stopped to wonder at the beauty of the aurora. It's the kind of thing women and wood spirits can do to a man he thought before turning his skis to head back to the village. Beautiful though the night was it was stupid to be out alone and he turned to retrace his tracks back along the road when a light caught his eye coming from somewhere deep in the forest. It seemed to be at the end of a track showing recent vehicle traffic and intrigued to know what it was Logan stepped into the ruts and made for the light.

Within minutes the trees opened to a wooded glade and before him stood a small cabin with smoking chimney and an open railed veranda. A number of skis lay propped against the rail and some like his own were painted military white. Yet more lights now appeared around him as he approached and he was about to ski back when the beam of an approaching car moved him off the track and into the darkness of the trees.

Logan watched unseen as the vehicle drove past before stopping to park by the cabin. Three girls now noisily left the car to enter the cabin through a side door. The faint sound of distant music and dim light came from inside as the door opened and closed until all was again quiet. Moving from the dark and over deeper snow Logan cursed as his legs straddled a painted wooden sign until realizing he had of all places found the second café. Skiing over to the cabin he excitedly removed his skis stuck them into a drift kicked the snow from his boots and walked onto the veranda. The wooden latch of the door clicked noisily turning all heads as Logan entered the dim light of the cabin.

Inside the place was a room no larger than two billiard tables with candles placed on small trestle tables set against the walls and was full to heaving with female Vikings. All conversation stopped and eyes followed as Logan made for an open serving hatch at the far side of the room. To his surprise he was joined at the hatch by one of Geordie's English students who produced a thimble full of the real stuff for him to choke on first and a thump on back to help get his breath back. When his sight returned Logan had grasped a beer and following the Norwegian joined a group of four conscripts. Around him and to his happy amazement sat a fair proportion of what were the missing village maidens. Not even a Viking but an Englishman and the Gods had granted him all this. He had found Valhalla. Yes, thought Logan to himself, there is a God. Thank you Odin, thank you.

25

Invited to sit Logan was formally introduced with much handshaking and not a word of English to each of the conscripts and missed all names but Eric as he link associated the name with the man's red hair. Formalities over and the word for cheers well established as skol the table fell to an embarrassing silence.

'Skol' said Logan again after a pause beginning another round of raised glasses before another long silence.

'The Queen' said one of the Norwegians raising his glass as all around joined in with the toast.

'And the King' said Logan guessing they had one, which from the raised glasses affirmed they did before with the toast of Olav the conversation or lack of one fell to yet another silence.

Rapidly running out of royalty other than the hangers on the lack of conversation drifted into another nothing until with a raised finger a topic arrived from Eric the Red.

'Manchester United' he said as the table began nodding affirmation of a shared knowledge of football team names before descending to Liverpool United and unintelligible names of the Norwegian game, which Logan politely nodded to without having a clue.

'Bobby Charlton' said another voice beginning another round of naming someone everyone knew.

Quickly out of players' names the conversation thankfully left football after what appeared to be a history of Bergen Boys' second eleven but then nobody knew Accrington Stanley either.

'Queen Victoria' said a voice but nobody wanted to go there although Robin Hood had his supporters along with the Sheriff of Nottingham and Winston Churchill and for Norway someone put up Greig and the painter Munch but who was Olav the Fifth again Logan asked?

'The King' said a voice to his side beginning a new round of song naming that died a death with Hound Dog and Blue Suede Shoes. It was the wrong king.

Thank Odin Logan said nobody but nobody put up Cliff Richard, which summed up the all round good heartiness and enjoyment of the evening. Why had the Vikings not told them about a place full of local talent Logan asked himself before answering? Would he tell?

Being the token Brit made Logan something of a celebrity if not for himself then for rarity value. He was a one off and immediately aware that this increased his pulling power by a goodly factor and likely considerably more than at any previous time in his life. Not since that time with a mix up in dormitories on a school hiking holiday when he was ten thought Logan. What a waste of a lifetime opportunity that one was he remembered looking around the small room. In short he said to himself and in all modesty there was a fair bit on offer.

About him lay a superfluity of Norwegian maidenhood metaphorically speaking and with good odds in his favour he felt sure of pulling something. Hopefully it won't be another muscle he said to himself recalling the earlier straddle of the café signage. Not surprisingly Logan reasoned that two hundred plus miles inside the Arctic Circle in February the café wouldn't get many overseas visitors. If only people knew places like this existed away from the beaten track maybe they would he was thinking and it was well worth the bang in the groin to find the place.

Logan was happy with what he saw and it was clear to him that Norway was an amazing nation of clean-cut female beauty with minimal makeup and natural colour hair – at least as far as he could see it was. Something to do with the clean air or the national gene bank of the Viking he pondered until hitting on the Viking penchant of abducting females. They would hardly come back with the ugly ones would they he reasoned sticking with the gene bank theory. Either way it made for very attractive looking women and supported the theory of natural selection.

With hope and expectation gaining as the evening and moonshine wore on Logan genuinely felt his chances were good. Even Chalkie could pull in a glut he was thinking although modestly admitting to himself the reality of the situation that placed his optimism into some level of reasonable perspective. He was in fact the first overseas soldier to enter the place since November 1942, only then the man had come in waving around a 9mm Schmeisser machine pistol looking for British paratroopers. It pissed the locals off considerably at the time as the area was overrun with the bastards...Germans that is. Consequently that man did not pull.

By ten o'clock the Norwegian conscripts had run out of money and had left for camp leaving Logan to sit the evening out alone. With only a tent and minus thirty or so outside the choice was a no decision for him as he elected to stay where he was until chucking out time. At length he was approached by the tallest of three girls sat away to his left who had been looking over for most of the evening. In fact all the girls had been looking over unless he was being paranoid but then people do look even at the paranoid.

The maiden had to have been six foot four in her fish nets with broad shoulders like a hammer thrower and would likely have killed Logan without proper rests. After a few checks behind to see if it really was him she was heading for he smiled all the way up as she approached. Still not sure what was happening as she arrived at the table Logan beamed up and smiled hopefully. Entirely committed to pulling for England and beaming like an idiot he invited her to sit before he got a crick in his neck. Her eyes flashed azure blue in the light of the candle as her hand moved gently across the table and closed Logan's mouth.

Behind her sat two ash blonde mates also smiling and nodding encouragement as the girl leant forward to the light and in sexy English asked if Logan was British soldier. Sat as he was in British army uniform with a three inch square

Union Flag over his right breast this was on the face of it a really dumb question but it was a good enough chat up line for Logan who nodded modestly pointing a finger at the flag and stiffening his upper lip.

'Oh then, you like to come with a party with me' she said quite matter of fact about it all and in such a husky voice and foreign turn of phrase that melted his iron will to resist as both legs turned to wobbly jelly. Logan thought about it for a nano second before remembering to close his own mouth and nodding an affirmative followed her back to the other girls like a dog at heel. For sure he was panting like one as he arrived at the table.

'Sit' said the girl as Logan sat waiting for a pat on head.

Never having been picked up by a trio of gorgeous women before Logan thought it was how a dog must feel when his owner places a collar around his neck and leads it away to perform on a lady dog. It's like being asked up by a girl at a dance in front of your mates or suddenly finding someone's tits pushing into your arm in an art gallery. Do you move, stand still, push back or just say something nice about the picture. Good innit thought Logan as he waited for the next move. It was an 'is that a pistol in your pocket or are you just pleased to see me' moment and Logan was simply just not in control.

Now at her table the girl introduced herself as Elke and her two friends as Bjorg and Valgerd. Logan sat transfixed as the conversation now moved to a discussion in Norwegian before Elke turned to face him.

'In England for your party is your liking to drink the brandy?' she asked.

'The what?' he said before the words sunk in and he shrugged agreement to whatever they liked as he would drink whatever they wanted him to...and whenever.

Elke went to the hatch leaving him alone with the two girls thinking he was either in heaven or hallucinating. With not a word of English or Norwegian passing between the three of them Logan went for a practice name and point with finger session before the Elk returned carrying a bottle of obscure fruit brandy and standing as she arrived they left the café heading for the girls' car. A thought went through Logan's mind that he should perhaps pinch himself to see if it was all a dream but decided against it in case he woke up.

Collecting his skis he gave them to Elke before climbing into the back and settling himself thigh to thigh between the girls as Elke tied his skis to a roof rack. After something of a stutter the car started and as the windows misted Elke turned the heater to full boost and settled behind the wheel. To his left was the right thigh of the lovely Bjorg and to his right the left thigh of the gorgeous Valgerd. Or was it the other way round thought Logan to himself as one of the girls now crossed her legs. Which one did that he wondered as the size of the small car forced his arms up and around both girls.

He was doing his best for England and hoping he would have the strength of character not to give in too easily as an unseen hand fumbled the front of his Parka before there came the erotic sound of a zip in the dark. The Parka came apart about the same time as Logan did with a gasp and help of another unseen hand. That wasn't me thought Logan hurriedly biting off his gloves as visions of armpits and body hair flashed to mind. Not having a clue where he was being taken and hardly caring Logan relaxed back listening to the girls' chatter in Norwegian as a head now gently nestled into his neck and the smell of perfume rose up faster than the swelling in his groin.

Hardly believing what was happening Logan sat transfixed as the car slithered and crunched into the ruts and with a bit of a giggle and clunk of a missed gear they left the track and joined the road for the village. Speaking between themselves and Logan not having a word of it made the moment even more bizarre. They could have been saying anything as Logan's mind raced with erotic and disgusting possibilities as both now took to patting and rubbing a thigh each. It beats the shit out of Sven's buddy system does this said Logan to himself and that's for sure and who the hell cared what they were saying he was thinking as the driver's eyes found him from the mirror.

'Are things good for you on the back?' asked Elke dropping her hood and partly turning her head to look behind.

'Anyway up is fine with me' said Logan surfacing for air and suddenly startled as an arm made its way about his back coming from his left he felt but not caring one way or the other.

It was one of those once in a lifetime moments you just hope will be twice or another of those ten things to do before you die he thought as his mind and the car raced on. Reality at times is hard to believe and he was still doubting what was happening as they entered the sparse light of the village. Still, who would believe there is an organisation called Surfers Against Sewage or that the Vatican actually signed the Nuclear Non Proliferation pact he reasoned. Some things are beyond belief thought Logan squeezing both girls to keep it fair and still clueless which one had undone the zip when a thought came to him coming in like a bolt of lightning.

'Both!' said Logan as the mucky side of his mind got the better of him.

Amongst other things he was giving himself a stiff neck moving from blonde to blonde when, with a sudden slide of snow chain the car came to a sliding halt. Skiers were crossing the road ahead. Looking out through the misted windscreen Logan could see Chalkie and Compton on their way back to camp. They must have found the skis then he said to himself, that's good.

'British soldiers' said Elke rubbing to demist the windscreen as they passed to the front of the car.

'Really' said Logan showing a genuine disinterest 'Oh yes, so they are...drive on.'

Chalkie peered inside the car just long enough to realise just what and who was in the backseat before the car left him at the side of road thrashing away at a drift with his ski poles.

'Temper temper Chalkie' said Logan before resuming where he left off.

'Ah Chalkie's is friend, no?' asked Elke as the car started to move away.

'No...who?' said Logan waving with his hand for her to drive on but it was too late as the girls went into a girly discussion that didn't need Norwegian to know was something to do with simple mathematics.

Behind them both Chalkie and Compton were now furiously chasing after the car and going like a pair of champion skiers as Logan questioned the justice of it all.

'Play fair Odin' pleaded Logan, 'why couldn't they go and find their own women?'

What kind of a world do we live in Logan asked himself. Envy, greed and injustice everywhere you look. Elke seeing all through the rear view mirror immediately hit the brakes and the car slid to an eventual stop. After a decent pause the boys slammed into the back of the car with an anticipated two thumps and after a brief discussion with Elke they also wanted to party.

'Surprise surprise' said Logan as Elke wound back up her window, put the car into second and continued on down the road.

Hooked by the baskets of their ski poles to either side of the bumper the boys followed in tandem as the car now pulled away...and so did the girls. What a fickle world said Logan zipping back up and resigning himself to his burst bubble as the dream of a lifetime faded into the never, never. After a brief drive through to the far edge of the village they stopped before what looked to be a timber latticed single story house raised on stilts with wooden steps rising up to the entrance. Dropping everyone at the steps Elke drove on down beneath the house and parked the car as the others made their way up the steps kicking boots free from snow before entering through the door.

'Took your bloody time stopping didn't you?' said Chalkie getting out of his Parka and kicking out of his wet boots as lights came on inside.

'Couldn't see out of the car Chalkie, thought you were just a couple of lost skiers training for the winter Olympics...and the girls took a bit of convincing, practically had to fight two of them off me before I could get them to stop.'

'We saw the struggle' said Chalkie moving on in, glad that he had put on fresh socks at the beginning of last week as he said to Logan.

'It's Saturday night, that has to be a good two weeks ago Chalkie' said Logan moving away.

They entered to a large open room with a glowing log burning stove set in a hearth to one corner and a pine floor. A door to one side led off to a kitchen area and what Logan presumed would be bedrooms. Moving to the fire Elke opened the glass front before placing in more logs as Bjorg set to opening the brandy. Valgerd now arrived from the kitchen with a chopping board and an entire smoked leg of some beast or other that was dark purple looking before dropping both down onto a coffee table with a loud thump. Taking a Lap knife Valgerd sliced off a fair piece placing it into her mouth with the one deft movement of the blade before reversing the knife and stabbing it a full three inches into the meat.

'Fucking hell' muttered Chalkie under his breath as she turned from the table and removing a headband shook her hair free before leaving to help Elke chop wood for the fire.

'I'm on her side' said Compton trying to get the knife out and failing miserably.

'What is it?' asked Logan as Chalkie tasted a piece before whispering whatever it was it's well fucking dead now as Valgerd returned from the stove to remove the knife.

'Eat' she said slicing some off and stuffing it Compton's way.

Compton ate it like a lamb although it was clearly another Rudolph. There was something entirely Viking about eating chunks off a dead deer and driving a knife in it down to the handle thought Logan as brandy was poured by Bjorg and something white in a coke bottle emerged from beneath the wood pile. Elke now joined them and helped Compton with the knife which to be fair to him had gone through the bone this time. The evening or night as it now was had all the makings of being a thoroughly excellent party although the brandy was best described as typical Norwegian, like staying up long into night in the long darks of winter said Elke and in summers too also she added 'because of long lights of summer night.'

Chalkie took over bar duties and the brandy began to take on a funny taste, which went funnier as the night wore on. That stuff would take the colour out of cola and whiten plum brandy and not much can do that felt Logan. Several skols later Compton had gone missing with the gorgeous Bjorg and Chalkie was dancing cheek to elbow with Big Elke. Never was a girl more aptly named. They made a lovely couple but looked more like one and a half. This left Logan with the lusty Valgerd who Chalkie the daft bastard had managed to get so rat arsed she had collapsed dead to the world on a settee.

Such is fate thought Logan. Two seconds earlier leaving the café in the car and we would never have even seen them and two seconds later they would have been road kill. If only thought Logan. What a pity. Instead one of them's being hand fed lumps of something to keep his energy up and Chalkie looks to be getting away with the one of the Valkirie.

'And me?' said Logan looking over at the prostrate Valgerd. 'I end up with a ratarsed Viking.'

Everyone had something to do at this party but himself he was thinking before taken by a surfeit of something local or heat from the fire he too fell sound asleep alongside the remains of the dead Valgerd. He awoke to an empty room and the sound of a turning latchkey.

Stretching and turning to face the door he found himself looking up at the shocked face of none other than the lovely Frida. From the look on both faces it was hard to know who was the more surprised at seeing the other, her him or him her. Throwing her coat to a hook by the door Frida flashed her eyes about the room before kicking off her boots and entering.

Obviously at home Frida immediately began clearing the place up, punching at cushions and throwing them to a rightful place. There was a definite feeling Logan was part of the process as clapping her hands she ushered him away from the debris and down to the settee with a push in the chest. A natural survival instinct borne of moving away from a cleaning woman came to Logan as he stretched his feet out to the coffee table as Frida's icy gaze froze onto the outstretched feet and chunky socks. A look that was Norwegian maiden for get your dogs off my coffee table and plant them on the bloody floor hit him like a strike of lightning. Onto the oiled pine went his socks as the girl's eyes flashed a cutting look that clearly said dickhead in both languages.

Frida now went on a quick recce of the other rooms returning moments later in a bit of a huff having found all well occupied. Seeing the bottle Frida helped herself to what was left of Chalkie's concoction draining a tumbler of the stuff without flinching before slicing off a chunk of meat and ramming the knife back in down to the mandatory hilt or until it hit bone or maybe it was the table this time thought Logan.

'Liten gut' said the girl shaking her head and turning to put on a record.

He knew what liten gut was and was still hurting from it, little boy he most certainly was not he said to himself as he swiftly sat his arse down on a cushion by the fire in case he got it smacked or worse still got it picked up and thrown out through the door. Logan liked his arse being inside and behind triple glazing at minus something incredible outside.

Music from some unknown and obscure Norwegian pop singer came from the speaker and for a nation of nil pointers it wasn't that bad if a bit atmospheric. A bit what you might call mood music Logan thought as he toasted his toes, forgetting for one moment that she was there when a hand tugged his arm and he was pulled to his feet. Logan felt for sure he was heading for the door until he was suddenly dancing or more accurately being pushed around the floor like a rag doll. This wasn't dancing, not as he knew it, more a control of his body thing and wearing woollen socks on an oiled pine floor he followed the lady's lead like a dog.

Inevitably he slipped but was supported by Frida. Then again with a stagger. Frida gave a loud discernible sigh with an annoyed shake of head before resuming the dance. He slipped again. This time she took his slip as some sort of personal attack, showing her annoyance by jerking him upright as Logan slipped yet again this time holding tight to her arm. She must have assumed he was trying to pull her over for without warning, she suddenly grabbed an arm and turning to her side went to throw him over her hip. Logan had done some judo; the move was an ogoshi and countered by a bending of the knees or it is in the dojo when not wearing woollen socks on a slippery pine floor. The slip moved him forward and spun him side on to Frida who unbelievably to Logan went to throw him once more. What is it with this girl thought

Logan as Frida tried again when, without thinking Logan's leg moved instinctively to the outside and swept upwards. It was a harai-goshi throw going for a full ipon and the result was catastrophic.

'Oh my goshi' said Logan.

Frida went legs akimbo heading for the ceiling as she rolled high over Logan's trailing hip. She was at once heading for solid pine. Frantic now to save her Logan held tight to her blouse and hung on for dear life. An almighty shriek came seconds after the sound of ripping cotton as blouse left ample breast and cloth ripped from shoulder to hip. Logan released his hold and stood back stunned at the event as the girl regained her feet. Arms now slowly rose to cover her naked breasts as hands clutched at what remained of the blouse. Hardly daring to look other than to catch a sneaky one he made to turn and was heading for the door. It was too late! With a cry of something sounding most unladylike Frida lunged forward and was on him in less than a second.

He tried to turn again but it was too late as her arms clasped tight around his neck. Suddenly he was being showered with kisses. Eyes and lips, cheeks and neck, anywhere and everywhere skin was exposed as he fell backwards to the couch under a frenzy of abandoned raw Scandinavian sex.

'Liten gut' said Frida pausing only to sit up and rip away what remained of her blouse before falling on him again like something uncontrollable.

'That Norwegian mood singer?' said Logan sometime afterwards. 'What was his name again?'

He arrived back at the camp a shadow of his former self and after a late breakfast as it was Sunday, he went straight into his sleeping bag and was asleep at once dreaming of dripping taps and waves lapping on the sea shore, waterfalls and flowers opening in slow motion and something obscure about a very dead snake. The sound of banging brought him back to life in the tent. It was Chalkie clanging a mess tin as everything else had failed to get through. Chalkie was in an excited state.

'There's a taxi at the camp gates...driver wants to know when you want picking up?' He said sounding really pissed off, as he and Compton didn't get one sent for them.

Thus began the happiest and most completely fulfilled period of Logan's life until then including the bike sheds. Life became a series of parties. Anytime and whenever he left camp there was a taxi and party in waiting. All Logan had to do was to turn up and they would throw a party. With an eye to regular business in a one taxi town and assured of a fare from Frida the driver took to regular parking at the gates ready and waiting to take him to Frida and the girls. At times this got a little confusing with even the taxi driver forgetting if he had been booked to go get him or if he was hanging around on the off chance.

Most evenings when Frida worked were now spent resting in the café until closing before a quick ride to the girls for the night and a lift back to camp early the next day. It was altogether a good thing on more than one count and with the alternative being a night in a tent under a bayonet there was no decision. Nightly they would stay up until the early hours before returning to camp and a few hours sleep until the morning ski lessons or preparations for the exercise. Life was pretty idyllic and was for something approaching a month.

Now the brain of man is a wondrous muscle said Compton going on to explain that it has the ability to adapt to most anything including high mental activity, stress and even low sleep levels that would normally be categorised as borderline sleep deprivation. Although true for man it is not necessarily true for all of the man he considered continuing on with the topic although he had lost most of the tent by then.

'That is to say not the whole of the man' he said, pausing to throw another log in the stove and stamping on a rogue spark before resuming his seat. 'Consequently the libido, which is what we are discussing here, does not always go hand in hand with the rest of the body.'

'You what?' said Chalkie nosily listening to what was now turning into a private and sensitive conversation with Logan.

This Compton explained, is not necessarily true of all mankind either but is apparently true on both counts for only one half of it, that is to say womankind.

'Where, surprising though this may be to some of us, not only does the female of the species adapt measurably well on the one hand to the mental excess thing it also adapts measurably well to things on the other hand.'

'Eh?'

'In brief where the appetite and stamina in the one falls short with excess, that is to say deflates, the opposite is the case for the other. Viz. activity increases appetite in the one and reduces appetite in the other. Or put another way I think you've worn your dick out.'

'Have you tried exercise?' said Chalkie zipping his Parka and leaving for the mess tent.

After one month of it Logan could feel positively ill just at the sight of the taxi and knowing it was waiting for him by the gates was a form of female stalking. The sound of an approaching diesel engine was enough to turn him limp and break Logan out in a heavy sweat as the taxi turned from passion wagon to passion killer. Not so of course for the other two bastards Logan felt, as partying at a lesser frequency than Frida had appetite for pushed for party after party after party after party.

Entirely unhelpful and not fully understanding of the situation whatever Compton had said Logan escaped to new haunts of the café in the woods. Rather than ease matters this opened up to a much wider range of Viking maiden, and always the taxi followed him like a four-wheeled hunting dog. Pressure and strain began to show as the constant goading of the tent to get the party on the road at Frida's increased. There just had to be a way out and as fate would have it, the way out came in a most unexpected form.

The biggest charge ever placed against Logan when out on the pull was that his patter used to stink. I know this reasoned Logan to himself; I am my own worst enemy. In truth he just wanted to be understood and had over the years talked himself in and then out of many relationship opportunities including many a mess but having not a word of discourse with the lustful Frida other than a long list of words to look up privately in the library, Logan had at last found someone who couldn't understand him. It was a fatal combination where his every word was translated as words positive and Frida's eyes glazed to thoughts of life in swinging sixties England. Yes, it was serious but was it love?

'And moreover' said Compton continuing on regardless of any interest 'clearly what we have here is a lack of communication.'

Alongside this great personal revelation of the bleeding obvious Compton told Logan there needed also to be an understanding of the macroeconomics of the Norwegian economy.

'In short' said Compton, 'apart from a few Christmas trees and canning factories the Norwegians have much of their GDP hooked up in the sea and in fishing if you pardon the simile.'

'You've done worse' said Logan wondering where this was going other than over his head.

'This and feeding whale meat to the Japanese nation' felt Compton was at the crux of it.

'Correct' said Chalkie listening in again, 'they like their fish big in Japan.'

'Thus,' said Compton before pausing to shake his head at Chalkie 'with the majority of men away at sea for most of the year the nation's females are left abandoned or put another way...without.'

'What?'

'It' said Compton resting his case and making a mental note to discuss what is and is not a fish with Chalkie some time in the future...'plus, if you haven't noticed there isn't that much to do around here.'

'Apart from freezing your bollocks off' put in Chalkie.

Sod me said Logan thinking it through; he was a diversion from the cold winter nights and an escape from domestic boredom for the abandoned female bloody Vikings of Norway.

'It cheapens the doing your best for the nation thing' said Logan thinking himself hard done by but mostly seeing a way out of it all with at least some of his manhood still intact.

Once this fact had hit home to him Logan's resolve was clear. Frida just had to go, before she saw him off.

'It would not be easy' he confided to Chalkie 'the poor girl has got it bad but between you and me Chalkie.'

'Yes?' said Jock listening in.

Logan moved closer to Chalkie and lowered his voice to a whisper as Jock strained his ears.

'I don't think that moonshine stuff can be good for you...you know. Every time I go on a bender at Frida's with that stuff it gives me a sore thingy.'

The truth of it was that the poor girl had got it bad and was talking in terms of true love, matrimonial harmony and other such things. All of which would have sent a chill to Logan's spine long before if only he had understood a word of what the girl was saying, although it was clear Frida was to say the least keen. So it came as something of a shock to him when fresh from the sea and still wearing his yellow oilskins and heavy knit polo neck jumper arrived a catcher of big fish.

Bjorg passed Logan a note before quickly leaving as the café took on a strange atmosphere with everyone ignoring everyone like someone had just farted. Logan went to read the note but stopped when the fisherman began to make his way over to his table. The girl had clearly slipped him the black spot as the man approached the table with a clear look of evil intent. Frida began frantically shaking her head and biting her bottom lip as her man arrived at the table.

'À l'eau, c'est l'heure' said Compton as the café went suddenly quiet.

'Don't let him know you're scared Logan' said Geordie.

'It' said Compton.

Scared, thought Logan, the man was the very reincarnation of Bluto but if anything bigger and introduced himself by crashing a fist down to the table, which translated to Logan as something to do with a question about hospital food. With a quick exit not possible other than one on a stretcher Logan assumed his practised dumb innocent look and made pretence of reading the note before passing it to an Italian on the adjacent table. Thinking he needed a translation the Italian obligingly read the note out loud.

'Thisa man his a Frida man...ah bella signora Frida!' said the Italian clearly proud of his spaghetti English and pointing lovingly over towards the counter.

'Oops' said Compton as the Norwegian turned now to the Italian table with narrowing eyes and a thump of fist to palm that even the Italian now understood.

'Noa, no, no, ano...' protested the soldato getting the point at last and standing to profess his innocence with an expansive characteristic waving of arms.

He was carne morta.

All eyes now fell on the Italian as the café went deadly quiet but for the gasp from Frida at the counter. It was all suddenly serious and going goodnight Italy and likely not helping with him being Sicilian where in Palermo that sort of thing always ends up on a marble slab. His eyes eventually came up to rest on Bluto who moved quickly for such a big man as he heaved over the table and headed for the Italian.

Soldato was off through the door like a bolting rabbit, chicken feathers trailing behind and floating gently to ground as he went. Your man was outside and on his skis and heading for camp before Bluto had even ripped open the door.

'Train for that sort of thing do the Italians' said Chalkie 'you don't get many fights ending in draws in Sicily.'

'This place is becoming a dangerous place to hang around waiting to get your leg over' said Logan to Compton who felt someone must have sent Bluto a letter as they followed the Italian out into the night.

The big exercise couldn't come too soon for the Italian and for me too thought Logan as they walked back to camp. Amici.

26

Reports began to filter down through the grapevine that the Canadians had arrived and was confirmed when remnants of their forces were seen in the hills training with the Americans. They looked surprisingly alike although the Canadians had the definite collective look of someone used to being in snow. Not surprising for a nation living in five foot of the stuff from September through to early summer felt Logan but what was surprising was that both had arrived for the games with snow shoes.

'They live in igloos, fish through holes in the ice and they kit their army out with snow shoes not skis' said Logan 'every year in the UK we give odds of hundreds to one against for a white Christmas and we kit our army with skis.'

It was a mystery to many as to why the army had spent several weeks teaching men to ski who barely see two inches of slush a year, when walking over snow on a couple of tennis racquets can be learned in a matter of a few steps. It's as hard as putting on a pair of wellies felt Compton.

'It just doesn't make sense,' he said 'your Canucks native Indian the Inuit have three hundred words for snow and we have two but only if you count flake.'

'Fucking snow is two' said Chalkie agreeing with him.

The call to arms when it came was welcomed by all including the Russians who must have wondered when the damn thing was going to kick off. It was after all an exercise to test NATO's fast reaction to a theoretical sneaky attack into Norway from the top.

'Have the capitalist dogs kicked off yet Pushkin?' said the Russian general preening himself in the mirror held by his commissar. He always liked to look good in front of the men and had a new big hat to celebrate his appointment as commander of sneaky attacks.

'Our network of informers working for our esteemed KGB report no movement comrade general but it must be soon or their lightning quick reaction to our theoretical surprise attack six weeks ago will cock up our own theoretical winter defensive moving it into spring and the men look good in white camouflage comrade general.'

'Have the Barthshire's learned to ski yet Pushkin?'

'Not all of them yet comrade general the last report was some were still shitski.'

'Shit on the ski or just shitski Pushkin?' asked the general.

'Both comrade general' said Pushkin.

'Good' said the comrade general we can rest easy 'if you want me I will be at the ballet with my friend Boris and afterwards at big Igor's place.'

'Ah I hear that is good for the evenings on the tiles comrade general.'

'No, it is shitski Pushkin but they have happy hour for loyal party members on Fridays and girls drink free. Olga Sherbet is always there.'

'Is he?' noted the commissar for his little black book.

Deep inside the AMF's top most secret mobile battle command the generals sat before a huge wall map of Norway split east to west by a thick red line. The Red Army had been conveniently halted in straight horizontal line that split Norway in two and the Norwegians alone were holding bravely on while NATO readied the allied response. Don't hold your breath thought Logan as preparations to move out got underway with a heavy frost and a frozen generator.

'Conscripts, little more than kids fresh from a mother's teat are holding back the entire soviet army as we speak genlemen...it reminds me of the Alamo.'

Three star general Ludwig Wolfgang Swartz an all American boy down to his pearl pistols and chrome helmet stood before the map as commander in chief of operations. Before him sat an assortment of foreign brass imperialist dogs and lackeys with only one thing in common. Theoretically they were all on the same side. Ludo Swartz also liked to look good in front of the men and had his hair cut every morning to within a quarter inch of the wood. With his shades and medal banks including a new one for crossing over into Europe and his AMF badge he sure looked the part.

'What we got here you betcha' said the general turning from the map 'is a Montana stand off...am I right Krakowski?'

'Affirmatory general' said the general's aide and chosen flunky Captain Krakowski.

The war briefing over the overall battle plan was passed on down through the formations to arrive as a series of long walks through the snow for the BLI until the Red Army would capitulate and leave with tail between legs back into Russia.

'How unlikely is that?' said Logan 'for a nation that only twenty years ago had fought on through losses of nine or ten million soldiers'

Nobody was asking him. The only thing missing was a call for a cease in hostilities from the UN and a Father Christmas he was thinking. Battle plan in the actuality was officially to nuke the commie bastards as Swartz knew only too well from his days at the Pentagon. It was the only plan making sense to the general's eyes and with mutual destruction assuring a draw he could live with that.

Logan was never more happy to see an exercise start even if it did put him back in a tented igloo. Fresh and bouncy from the battle brief the Barthshire's commanding officer set to briefing his own command for their part in the overall folly of the strategic plan as he assembled his lot in a modest caravan trailer pulled by a Norwegian halftrack called a Snowcat. From the look of the colonel Logan could see he was old school.

Something to do with his half frame reading glasses and an attitude of stance and a pretence of over intensity to all that was said that translated him to Logan as a phoney bastard until he opened his mouth and Logan saw he was also a dope.

A dope from birth the colonel was something of an enigma wrapped up in a bumbling idiot and one of the school of dimwits that saw life as black and white due to missing grey matter thought Logan as the two exchanged body signals. Passing the message on to the RSO Logan left the briefing room as the colonel continued to harangue his junior officers. He didn't like Logan either as he was clearly not one of his lot but one of them...an attached alien. Something to do with an attitude of stance that said you are a phoney bastard felt Logan as he returned to the warmth of his land rover content to know the days of the colonel blowing a whistle twenty miles from the front were thankfully long since gone.

'Thanks be to the medium to short range missile' he said to Compton as he closed the rear flap and picked up his headset ready to receive the next message.

Battalion headquarters now formed a defensive circle in a clearing deep in some forest and had arrived by convoy only the day before. The location was a closely guarded NATO secret known only to the top brass, a few dozen loggers and anyone able to follow lines in the snow made by half a dozen halftrack heavy vehicles. At the colonel's earlier briefing to the troggs he announced that the Barthshire's along with Norway, the US and Canada were the blue army. At these temperatures why not felt Logan raising his hand much to the annoyance of the colonel.

'Yes person at the back' said the colonel taking the first of his not one of us stances.

'Can you speak up we can't hear you at the back...sir' said Logan.

Opposing the goodies were the red army baddies who were made up of three battalions of imported Germans and the Alpine chicken company of yodelling Italians. What man of imagination thought that one up whispered Logan? Assigned to brigade headquarters in a complex of vehicles that included the battalion commander and his entourage of hooray Henrys and something called Jonty, Logan waited for hostilities to break out. It was the long awaited lightning quick counter offensive that had been six weeks in the making and as many months in the planning. Rumour had it they were going north as Compton tuned to the shipping forecast listening out for the name Viking useless though this was sitting in a forest three hundred plus miles further north. Nonetheless it raised some interest as it sounded right.

'Fair Isle, Viking, North Utsire wind northerly variable, blizzards increasing, rough becoming fucking awful' shouted over Compton wearing his earphones and making like everyone in the vehicle was as deaf as he was.

'At least in the back here we will be under cover' shouted Logan back at the earphones.

'You what?' said Compton.

'North thirty miles then a right pincer movement after a feint attack' called over Chalkie arriving from the latest briefing and climbing in over the tailgate.

'Faint as in weak?' said Logan 'why am I not surprised?'

'Feint as false' said Chalkie tapping his nose with his finger.

Clearly someone must have spelt it out for him thought Logan as he dusted off the freshly blown snow and roped down the tailgate flap. Bugles of war were beginning to sound outside but the back of a land rover was all Logan wanted to see of it as the weather worsened by the hour.

They took two days getting into position ready to attack and then a day getting out of position and then another day getting back into position and they hadn't even kicked off yet. By the fourth day and the third move in as many hours Logan had lost all interest and enthusiasm for the freedom of the western world. So too had battalion HQ from what he could see from the state of the wall map whenever he delivered a message into the caravan. With the brigade headquarters little more than a shiny pin surrounded by a ring of numbered flags and a splashed coffee stain nobody in truth had a clue what was going on.

Come the fourth day there were that many holes in that many wall maps on that many walls the pins were dropping like confetti and nobody other than a private first class cleaner of the caravan at AMF battle HQ really knew what was going on, although even he was relying on a third grade memory. Likewise was the colonel attending one of his daily situation briefings. Spotting a pin on the floor the colonel promptly picked it up and put it back in.

'Well dang me ah do declare if we ain't got ourselves a wide receiver out there a lickity spit yes siree...we got a blue pin twenty miles inside enemy territory on the locationary positionals map and I only just went out momentarily for a convenience visit to the bathroom!'

Only the Americans understood a word of it as all other faces gave up a look of did anyone get that but somebody had to show willing. It was the colonel.

'Good show for the old blue pins up there lickity splits' said the colonel trying to appear enthusiastic still without having a clue what the man was saying.

'That's a lickity spit colonel, ah think you'll find lickity splits is a pair of them there lesbians doing un-American activity am I right Krakowski?'

'Affirmatory' said the general's aide.

On the fifth day they received yet another pin move requiring a break of tent and drive through the night to where they had been just the night before. Snow was falling heavily as they settled down to leaguer the night away with Geordie and Compton asleep in the cab and Chalkie in his bag on the floor in the back, when from the front came the sound of shouting followed by the slamming of vehicle doors. Hardly hearing through his earphones Logan felt the vibration of a door slamming and raising the rear flap peered out to the night. All was darkness but for the swirling of heavy snow as Logan dropped the flap with a sigh of resignation before deciding with a second deeper sigh that he really should go and take a look outside.

Pulling on his gloves and goggles, checking his fly was secure and zipping his Parka Logan left in search of the commotion and feeling his way down the vehicle in blinding snow he arrived at the cab door. It was open and Geordie and Compton were missing. Slamming the cab door Logan turned to retrace his steps when the lone figure of a man on skis appeared away to his side. Logan let out a loud gasp as others now appeared and were making straight for his vehicle. With a flash of red armband Logan knew instantly who they were. They were Germans.

Shouts and bangs, flashing torches and sounds of engines starting were at once all around. Headlights were turned on and beams of light crossed as vehicles drove off in all directions but up as through the trees came the sound of men in total disarray. Snowcats, engines revving wildly were driving anywhere to escape taking awnings, ropes and skiers with them as they fled to the trees. Everywhere was chaos made worse by both sides wearing the same NATO white camouflage. Friend and foe alike were chasing and calling and leaving in a frenzy of disordered panic until suddenly it was over and an eerie silence fell on the camp. The battle was o'er and all was deathly quiet but for the wind and sound of fresh skis arriving to group around the one remaining vehicle.

'Hello one, how do you read me over' asked an overloud voice coming from the radio inside the rover as the rear flap was opened wide.

'Hände hoch Englander' said a voice as his mate grabbed the sleeping Chalkie off the floor by his boots. 'For you zer war is over!'

They always say that said Logan to himself as inside the land rover Chalkie peered out from his sleeping bag to a semicircle of torches.

'Some of us are trying to get some fucking sleep here you know, noisy bastards...ah!' he said as with a pull of his legs Chalkie left the vehicle to land flat in the snow.

Now fully awake and very noisy Chalkie turned Yorkshire strop awkward threatening his captors from inside his bag and screaming utter filth as he was pulled from his cover and frog marched away to one of a number of German Sneykatz. The sound of the land rover engine startled Logan hiding directly underneath it as he was, until with a rattle of snow chain the land rover drove off into the trees taking with it what remained of the German ski patrol. Lying flat down in the snow Logan could only watch as lights from vehicles and torches began to disappear into the night until suddenly he was alone to the dark.

Abandoning Arctic sense and hardly thinking Logan was quick to his feet and chasing wildly after the disappearing lights. Running and scrambling through the deep snow he was losing ground as the lights grew ever smaller until, all at once, they were gone. He was alone in the Norwegian Arctic, in a blinding snow storm and without cover. Shit said Logan to himself suddenly taken by the danger of his plight. His legs aching from the run Logan paused to take stock of the situation. Shit bloody shit he said again and to make matters worse the snow storm looked to be turning into a blizzard. Oh shit bloody shit, oh shit and more shit said Logan again as, with visibility now down to a few yards, the situation had turned entirely iffy.

With visibility dropping with each minute Logan knew he could freeze to death within feet of rescue and not be seen. Stupidly he toyed with the thought of removing his white camouflage to be seen but by whom and he would need each and every possible layer of clothing to survive.

'Shit' said Logan 'I forgot to put my tights on.'

What an idiot he shouted, calling out to himself and knowing that in his panic he was thinking like one. Shelter he bellowed to the wind, he needed to find shelter and quickly as quickening his pace he chased in vain after the vehicles until strength drained from his legs and movement at speed seemed impossible. Logan knew he needed to find cover or rescue and quickly. Without either it was certain death, nice one or not as Sven would have it. His mind raced with every possible option but there was only one. He must keep moving or die.

Time and distance left him as minutes turned to hours and hours were lost to the night. Snow and now ice was forming thickly on goggles and around his mouth. Every turn was a tunnel of blinding snow and he was losing any sense of direction. Feeling started to leave his hands and had gone from his face as he began to tire. Strength drained from his body with each step and as the forest thinned and the wind grew stronger he knew he was nearing the end. A feeling of desperation engulfed him as an overwhelming desire to sleep overtook his body. Logan knew this would mean his death even without Sven and his ten daft things not to do in the Arctic.

'Zer heart slows as you sleep, the body cools and you are gone but it is a good way to die they tell me...no pain.'

'Shit' said Logan now scared as he was desperate as he fought the thoughts away banging his arms to his chest and clenching his fists to return feeling.

Stopping without cover in the open is only one above forgetting to zip back up he shouted to himself knowing he must not stop again without shelter. Staggering further into deeper snow his foot caught on an unseen branch at the top of an incline and he fell. Down he went, tumbling and cursing his luck until coming to an abrupt and undignified sudden stop. Feeling a drop in the wind Logan raised himself up on his knees and turned to look up at the bank above him as he wiped clean his goggles. By sheer chance and the luck of Odin he had stumbled over an overhang on the edge of the tree line. Open ground fell away into total darkness before him. At last free from the biting wind his mind cleared as he moved further into the bank. His spirits lifted at his luck. He had found shelter.

Clambering back up the incline Logan pulled and snapped at anything he could break from the trees before sliding back down and scraping a rough hole in the snow Logan crawled in. He was barely inside when the roof collapsed. Cursing he moved further along the bank to try again. This time he went deeper packing snow hard down about him as he went. Life began to return to his hands and feet but the effort sapped his strength until pausing to rest Logan could at last hear the sound of his own breathing.

Able to turn he pulled the branches inside making a bed of pine as snow was packed behind to seal the entrance. Everything was suddenly dark and silent as a tomb and the wind outside became little more than a distant rush of trees. Removing his goggles and gloves Logan rubbed life back to face and braving the cold placed icy hands to his armpits. Where the hell is that buddy Chalkie when he's needed he said to himself before his mind switched to Frida and then to Bjorg as having a bigger pair before moving to all three of the girls together. Why not he said it was his erotic fantasy.

Soon the sounds of the blizzard died away completely as snow fell like a blanket to cover his coffin in the snow. Logan fought to stay awake but was losing the battle and as exhaustion overwhelmed his body he surrendered the fight with thoughts of the lovely Roxanne.

Eyes opened to dawn. He was alive and the sun was shining through the thinner snow of the entrance. Light and the sun was never more welcome. Pushing a small hole to the outside Logan was amazed to see the dark shapes of army vehicles. The night had been spent in a snow hole not thirty feet from a sleeping bag and a cup of steaming cocoa. Moving to push himself out Logan paused as he heard someone speaking German.

'Achtung' said the voice 'we begin again...where are zer Barthshire's headquarters Englander unt what is zer plan of attack?'

Opening the hole bigger and straining now to see, Logan could make out the back of an open Snowcat. It was Chalkie and under heavy interrogation...the German swine.

'Wie hef zer veys of making you talk' said another voice.

'You can sod off' said Chalkie admirably showing true grit 'I ain't telling you owt!'

That really is appalling use of English thought Logan grimacing with the shame of it as the German sounded like he spoke it better than what our Chalkie did but they don't teach everything at German secondary schools.

'You can do what you like Fritz you can beat me up and pull out me finger nails but I ain't telling you nowt.'

'Owt and nowt' said the voice sounding puzzled 'was ist das in Deutsch, this nowt word?'

'Er sagt nichts Herr Oberst...nowt ist Englisch sprechen fur nichts or zer nothings.'

'Ah so and...owt?'

'Owt is anysinks I sink mein leader.'

'That's right, you heard it, owt and nowt' chirped in Chalkie.

The German officer was not a man to be trifled with, he had been well trained in the dark arts of military interrogation and knew that sooner or later Chalkie would crack vide open. They always do, but ven? He would use threats first then nice guy nasty guy and slowly he would break his man. It was only a matter of time and finding the key to Chalkie's inside hidden fears.

'Very well you vill not hef any cooked breakfast.'

'They're here and here thirty miles north then a right pincer movement after a feint attack' said Chalkie pointing away at some map.

He had only collaborated hadn't he. Only told them where the BLI were based and bubbled the plan of attack. The things men with do for a full German breakfast.

'Give him the Wurst!' barked the Oberst.

'No, no, don't hit me' shouted Chalkie pleading pathetically.

'Wurst is German for sausage you ignorant Yorkshire git' said the first voice 'Ven can vie let zer bastard go Oberst...bitte, please?'

The poor German having spent the best part of the night with Chalkie had obviously had enough of his moaning and appalling use of English. Chalkie had barely time to chomp on his sausage before the engines of the Sneykatz revved and they sped off in a cloud of blue exhaust fumes leaving Logan still in a hole. In no great rush to be captured as he hated German sausages as they always have too much meat in them he recalled remembering back to a school exchange trip and an unforgettable Bratwurst moment Logan remained doggo.

Staying in his snow hole for a good five minutes to allow them to get well away he was about to burst out when there came the sound of skiing above him followed by a turning halt. Thinking they had returned Logan stayed more doggo until his spy hole began to widen and other holes of a strange orange champagne hue began appearing. It was unmistakable. Some dirty bastard was taking a leak.

Bursting out with much snow and a loud cry of watch where you're peeing he suddenly appeared like a phantom from beneath the ground. Startled by the sudden appearance the man let go of his member and with a shriek followed by a cry of despair pissed well down his leg. It was a rule number five and the man was only one of Sven's lot. So much for his Arctic training thought Logan as he dusted himself free of snow and smiled up at the astonished face of the Viking.

'Take me anywhere warm serving a full English breakfast' demanded Logan shaking the Norwegian's left hand.

They arrived back at AMF headquarters just as the reports of his missing presumed frozen to death were coming in. These things are always exaggerated said Logan to the general's aide modestly admitting only to near death as his story grew with each telling. Reports of his heroic escape by fighting off a whole German ski patrol to evading capture and a night spent alone deep in a Norwegian forest surviving on pine nuts and a handful of lichen caused more than a little excitement within AMF headquarters. Not unnaturally it gave some sort of proof of training and the colonel hotfooted it with the RSO to pick up his man. The twenty something mile trek through the wilderness alone at night in a blizzard or so Logan had it, deserved him that felt Logan. That and his finding his way by feeling the moss growing on the north side of the trees...oh yes.

'Quite an Arctic survival story soldier' said the general's aide sounding and looking more than a little sceptical.

Taken with the story of his epic survival Logan was brought before the general himself and was into his third post breakfast coffee and was switching to decaffe by the time the colonel and the RSO arrived at battle headquarters. Hardly able to hide the disappointment that it was not one of his own lot the colonel nevertheless sat through another version of Logan's story but it was not just the survival that interested the top brass. Of interest was that the enemy had obtained 'by torture' the location of their respective HQ and moreover they knew of the battle plan.

This made for an even bigger stir than Logan's return to life, for with that information headquarters immediately moved and a trap was set in the full knowledge of where the red Army were likely to attack.

'Of course' said Logan speaking to the assembled brass in the caravan and milking it for all it was worth once the colonel arrived, 'it might also be worth an understanding that the word feint would be heard as faint by the Germans and so would translate as a weak attack would it not sir?'

'Your point being' said the general not having a clue and sparking his aide to life.

'Red army would not deploy troops and would therefore be weak at this section of the line general...as you were about to say' said Krakowski with an eye to his bright future career.

'Damn right Krakowski, as I was about to say.'

You don't get on in the army as an aide by not thinking things through for your general felt Logan as he and the bullshitting Krakowski walked away from the briefing.

'Tell me soldier' said Krakowski 'you really do all that fucking stuff?'

'Not all sir, between you and me...that lichen's fucking awful.'

'Affirmatory' said the captain 'but the moss is true right?'

'Affirmatory' said Logan blowing smoke from his stogie.

Even armed with a foolproof plan given by Logan it still needed an amazing overnight slog on skis for the BLI to outflank the Italians and wrap the whole thing up. It was the talk of the exercise that the BLI had seen off the Alpine troops. Not in the Italian camp of course as the rumour had it but the Italians stopped laughing at the BLI after that.

Seeing the war in a far grander scale than from the back of the land rover placed an entirely different slant on events for Logan.

'It was all a matter of where you place your coloured pins and strategies, plans of attack and pincer movements, lines of supply, superior weaponry, air power and speeds of advance...all fascinating stuff.'

'Fascinating' said Compton but not really listening with his head in a book.

'What it all seemed to come down to is how many pins had dropped on the floor and how many the general still had in his little box.'

'Fascinating' said Compton pausing to look up 'the caribou is the north American name for the reindeer.'

'I knew that' said Chalkie, the lying bastard.

27

Saying goodbye to Norway was bitter sweet and ended with a dance of sorts at the local school. On stage was one of Norway's top bands called something known only to the Norwegians but they looked good and they were good if you were into hand knit jumpers and syncopated rhythms from a length of string rising up from a tea chest.

'What you've got to remember is that even the Quarry Men and the Shadows were once skiffle groups' said Geordie.

'How far you going back? Einstein's ancestors were once cave men' said Compton.

Music or not everybody went to the dance as it was free and they were leaving the next day so it was a sort of farewell night for everyone but without anyone there to say farewell to Logan for one left early. It was either that or dance with himself as the Norwegians largely gave it a miss or more accurately gave it a no miss. Even in the Harewood there was always someone to refuse a dance with you he said complaining to Chalkie who was searching for his stolen Parka in a long line of them before taking the first one to hand and recycling the theft. They left the next morning in a convoy of buses heading south past raging rivers of snow melt water. Spring had arrived and all thoughts of Frida and the last months were melting like snow with each and every mile south.

Back in the UK they arrived to fog and drizzle and a hot bath to warm up in before Logan left for the nearest pub and then on to anywhere with a Kentish barmaid he could talk to or was it a barmaid of Kent? He arrived back in barracks to the news they were returning to Bulford the following day with the land rovers. That's not news that's awful news said Logan collapsing to his bed before hanging his bayonet on the wall as the stove burned red and stank the room with an acrid smell of wet coke.

'I miss Norway. I miss the grandeur of it and the open friendliness of the people. I miss the clean air and the snow and the aurora borealis and that lingering smell of burning Norwegian wood but most of all, what remains with me is the smell of Compton's singed socks' said Logan before turning over. 'And some of the other stuff as well like Elke's hairy arms and Bjorg's mammoth tits and that big Valgerd girl but not that bloody moonshine.'

'Oh shit' said Chalkie coming in from the washroom and moving over to Logan's bed to give it a shake.

'Piss off Chalkie...I know it's you.'

'Hey up Logan, there's a taxi asking for you at the guardroom.'

'Oh very droll, tell it to come back the day after tomorrow Chalkie' said Logan pulling a pillow down over his head as the light clicked off.

Arriving back at Bulford within days Logan fell to a deep depression.

'There's something about this place that saps enthusiasm. It's like living in a perpetual déjà vu' felt Logan.

'You can say that again' said Chalkie as Logan turned to Compton to get some sense.

'The whole bloody place is pointless' he said 'at least with Catterick there was some horizon to it all, some end point...an end to the futility of the existence. Here? Well there's just nothing...there's just nothing to do.'

'Nothing wrong with having fuck all to do' said Chalkie listening in. 'I don't want to do anything, well contented doing nothing I am, anyone can be a busy fool. Having nothing to do is what I like about the place, same as Geordie.'

'Futile Chalkie, that's what it is, a futile existence.'

'Contemplation of a futile existence...bit deep for a Tuesday, bit black dog don't you think Logan?' said Compton.

'Your trouble is you need to get out more, why don't we slope off for a Bovril.'

'Read a book?' said Compton.

Try as he might Logan was unable to shake off the feeling made hopelessly worse by the impossibility of escape, even Colditz had their glider he said but to deaf ears. He was alone in Bulford for the duration and alone in the army for eternity. There had to be something more than just waiting out the years in meaningless existence when an idea flashed to his head. What an idiot thought Logan...I can go AWOL!

'That's it!' said Logan.

'That's daft' said Chalkie but Logan was not to be deterred by an idiot from Yorkshire, he was off...already he had purpose.

Wednesday morning Logan rose early and skiving first works parade sneaked back into the barrack room. He was packing his bag when Chalkie arrived to look for him.

'First a bus to Salisbury then a train to...' Logan paused.

'To where?' said Chalkie.

'To...Paris, the Foreign Legion, they take everybody and anybody on the run do the French, no questions asked. They're daft like that are the French '

'So where are you really going?' asked Chalkie again as Logan left later that afternoon for the bus.

'Off' said Logan overdramatically shaking Chalkie by the hand before turning and heading off to catch the twelve minutes past six bus to Salisbury...the fast one.

Six hours later he returned to a sleeping barrack room well pissed and spent up. Only Chalkie was awake as Logan staggered in on a bendy line heading to his bed before collapsing down.

'Bastard taxi drivers' said Logan rolling over.

'Back already are we Pierre?' said Chalkie looking over.

'You won't believe how much a third class ticket to Paris is...bloody British Rail.'

'Don't tell me about Paris' said Chalkie 'I'm the poor bastard having to pay an arm and a leg to get to Leeds and you have to go via London from here, would you believe it? Adds fucking hours on to the journey unless you go by bus! That's a bus first to Salisbury then...'

Chalkie paused, he was talking to himself again 'it's not subsidised you know' he said throwing a blanket over Logan, shoes and all.

'Piss off Chalkie...I know it's you' said Logan.

'Why don't you two wake every fucker up then?' said Jock not anticipating an answer and getting out of bed 'I need a bastard piss now.'

'Keep it down' said Geordie thumping his pillow in annoyance.

'Shhh' said a voice somewhere further down the room.

Logan's head spun with the drink as his mind reeled in search of a cheaper plan. You need money to run away to anywhere worth running away to he was thinking. In a haze of booze sleep came instantly and he slept soundly through the intermittent opening and closing of the door and the whispered bastards as men headed off to the corridor for a better have one now than later.

'Logan of the fucking Legion' said Chalkie chuckling to himself 'whatever next?'

'British Legion. Courage mon ami' said Compton sleepily from the next bed.

'Shhh' said the voice from down the room.

Logan had given himself a mission but to what and where he would go eluded him. His ancestral estate for one, or more accurately his non ancestral-intestate was an option no longer. Returning to that which you no longer have was as nonsensical as it was impossible, and with the house languishing in the hands of some thieving non relative Logan ruled it out of his possibility list along with Paris, and Bernice. At least he did until he received a letter or more accurately an invitation card requesting his pleasure to attend the wedding of Miss Bernice Wellfitt to Mr William Wordsworth Drinkwater esquire.

'Wordsworth?   Fucking   Wordsworth?' exclaimed Logan stooping to retrieve an enclosed note from the floor that reminded him of a promise made and long forgotten.

'Dearly beloved we are gathered here in the sight of God' began the vicar smiling benignly down over his pinch nose spectacles at the couple about to not be put asunder.

It had been a busy week for the rev with three funerals and a wedding, plus another one in an hour and a post registry blessing at two o'clock for a couple of til death us do parts whose troths had died a death before their partners and were up for a second run as his mind strayed momentarily to the bastards who had pinched the lead from the chancery roof. Standing alone and feeling vulnerable with his back to the dearly beloveds and the inevitable crying baby Logan watched on as troth was plighted. Spliced, hitched, hooked and sealed with a kiss it was suddenly over bar the fighting. Bernice ever ready and Billy the Wimp were pronounced not to be put asunder. Amen.

One door closes another one shuts thought Logan turning to smile over at the three bridesmaids dressed in virginal blue and white with red shoes that denoted something esoteric was going on further up the leg. Everyone a virgin said Logan...once. Turning further round his eye caught the smile of Mrs Wellfitt sat invitingly alongside her ex and dressed daringly in a figure hugging powder blue coat with plain white cotton blouse open down to the naughty third button showing just a hint of purple lacy bra that took the vicar's mind from his lead nickers to others in a matching set. Naturally as he was in church, Logan didn't look too much but could see the rev was getting hot under his collar. It was a new youthful look for Angela Wellfitt that said come up and give me one sometime which in church was downright disgraceful thought Logan having another look and thinking about it.

'Penny for your thoughts' said Angela Wellfitt doing the fried bread after it was all over, 'the weather stayed nice for it don't you think?'

'I didn't get time to look up' said Logan.

'Naughty boy' said Angela cracking another egg to go with his bacon, sausage, beans, fried bread, mushrooms and tomato.

'You need to keep your strength up my lad.'

'Not only are you a bloody good shag Angela, you're a bloody good cook as well' said Logan getting a well deserved rap on his knuckles. He didn't get two eggs in Norway.

'Mrs Wellfitt to you' she said smiling over a wicked smile.

Missing his connection Logan arrived in Salisbury just as the pubs were opening and left the station heading for the Stable Bar at the Bernie Inn which was a favourite Sunday night squaddie hangout for drunks and drinks alike. The place was empty but for that stale smell hanging over from a heavy Sunday lunchtime mixed with the fresh smell of lemon washing up liquid and dropped chips. He was about to leave when the door at the end of the bar opened to a group of kilted highlanders fresh from a wedding and in good spirits for most of the evening and right up and until the fight.

By then an adopted Scot with name of Jimmy he ducked just in time to miss the first flying glass and saw the stool coming even before it left the floor. With empty glasses beginning to arrive like exploding grenades from every direction Logan was off through the door only to run foul of a marauding erstwhile friendly highlander.

'Do you want some, do you want some?' asked the Scot squaring up and ready for it but not the haymaker as Logan whacked him a good one.

Never ask a question if you are not ready for the answer thought Logan as the man went down in a sprawling heap of kilt and spread of leg that proved him a true Scot if a little stubby one. Behind in the bar the fight raged on bursting out through a second door and into the courtyard as police and fight fans arrived both and scuffles moved into the road to be met with yet more police.

'Carter Barracks' said Logan from the back seat of the taxi and being asked to pay up front as someone from the barracks had done a runner on the driver only the day before.

Bastard well wasn't me was it said Logan objecting to paying the man and leaving the cab for the bus station. Not the last bus of the night it was empty of squaddies but for two smokers who went upstairs as Logan settled himself at the front for the long ride to camp. His mind wandered back with thoughts of the evening and the fight without a reason other than to have one. He arrived at barracks annoyed at the Jocks, the taxi driver, the army and the world but mostly he was annoyed with himself and at the mess he believed his life was in.

Logan walked up the road to the spider and was back in despair. A light was on over the notice board as he passed the troop office veranda and he paused to read next day's orders. Double guard duty for Easter read Logan 'for crying out loud' he said finding his name on the list. Annoyed before, now he was really pissed off and more than annoyed by the time he arrived at the barrack room. It was empty other than for Compton who was on his bed reading.

'They are all watching some old war film on television' said Compton returning to his book 'it's crap but there's a lot of dead ruddy Germans in it if you like dead ruddy Germans and over the top ruddy acting dear boy.'

Hack war films were a favourite hate of Compton's and anyway he liked the peace of having the barrack room to himself.

'Oh' said Logan without really listening as he took out a writing pad and pen before sitting himself at the barrack room table to write a letter.

'Sir,' he began using the standard army format for official letters before scrumpling it up and starting again, this time placing his name rank and number to the top right. At length he finished and reading through the letter again signed beneath the 'your obedient servant' as was standard procedure.

'I don't think so' he said licking the envelope and sealing it with a thump before heading for the NAAFI to get totalled.

The unmistakeable sound of a Junkers Stuka dive bomber blasted out from the TV room as he entered the NAAFI heading for the main room. A double guard was the last straw and was as welcome as an empty NAAFI on Sunday night. Punitive and unjust is a double guard he said to himself as he downed a second Newcastle. That's because we were away in Norway he said out loud as the shutters slammed down over the counter.

'Last orders, you haven't called last orders yet' said Logan negotiating a bottle with the top off before sitting back down.

*

'Sir, On considered reflection I consider myself stagnating in this regiment if not in the entire British army and submit this my resignation...' read the major out loud before looking up. 'You do know you can't resign from the army don't you Logan? Is this an application to buy yourself out. Is that what you mean?'

The major was sympathetic to his subordinate's obvious distress and clearly looking for some answer but it was not the major's sympathy for Logan that got him to meet the colonel within the hour but the threat of a copy of the letter being sent to Logan's MP. Logan found the colonel was also sympathetic to his major's subordinate's obvious distress and he too looked for an explanation but it was not the colonel's sympathy that got Logan his posting out, it was the threat of a copy of the letter being sent to the Queen...God bless her.

'Look,' said the colonel fizzing a little more soda to ruin his single Islay malt before lowering his voice and moving closer to the major. 'Between you and I Timmy, what we need is to get rid of the bugger...any thoughts Timmy?'

Clearly he and the colonel were thinking on similar lines as the major's mind went to a recent communication from the War Box marked confidential.

'What we need is a volunteer posting somewhere perhaps Willie' was what the major said as the colonel's eyebrows lifted with the look of inspiration followed by one of positive intent.

'So where is this place then' asked Chalkie coming in from the showers and changing quickly to catch the early bus.

'It's all a bit hush, hush. A volunteer posting for a newly formed signals troop somewhere hot with a lot of sand where you will need a knotted hankie is what the SSM said giving me the wink and I am first on the list' said Logan. 'First come first served is this one sounds like. Likely somewhere exotic with a beach it seems to me but wherever, I am out of here heading for an all over sun tan.'

Compton returned from the cookhouse bearing the news of Logan's posting and confirmed the SSM's hot list was now on the troop notice board with Logan's name on the top.

'The clerk says they are short a few bods but names will go in the hat if they are short. One way or the other it's a quickie as the final list will be typed up and posted with this evening's orders.'

'The Radfan?' said Chalkie 'never fucking heard of it.'

'Sounds a bit Welsh don't you think if you count Wales as exotic' said Jock joining the group gathering around Logan's bed.

'The place is somewhere South Arabia and hot the SSM told the office clerk' repeated Compton.

'That's exotic and hot too Arabia, harems and all that' said Logan.

'The clerk said it's hot all right' said Compton before being interrupted by Chalkie.

'Yes well it would be wouldn't it with all that sun' he said checking his watch for the bus and combing his hair.

'There's a bastard war going on' said Compton shocking the room.

'A what?' said Logan.

'A tribal thing up in the hills with the Yemen, a communist led insurrection? A fucking uprising.'

'Tribal thing in the hills and an insurrection...how big?' said Logan suddenly concerned.

'You mean someone out there is shooting?' said Jock suddenly interested.

'Oh they don't fuck around in insurrections in the Yemen Jock' said Compton.

'Appen you can get shot, so what?' said Chalkie quite unexpectedly and suddenly becoming dead face serious as a profound hush descended on the barrack room. 'It's what we trained for isn't it...I seem to remember that's what it was about when we joined up. Queen and country and duty and all that...and if Logan's going?'

Chalkie took a deep breath and shrugged before walking slowly to the door as the room went gob smack quiet. Pausing only to look back over his shoulder Chalkie took another long deep fatalistic sounding breath before with a shake of his head, his hand grasped the handle. It was a Kitchener moment. The door opened and he silently left the room.

The exit was as sensational and dramatic as anything the English football team had done since the formation of the world cup and was as dramatic as they get. Eyes darted around the room from man to man. Suddenly it was make your mind up time. Who would be next? Minds raced as Compton now stood. It was another Kitchener moment, they would be queuing up next.

'That's me...I'm to the troop office' he said patting Logan on the shoulder and sucking air though his teeth as he also now left through the door.

Agonising seconds passed as Jock now stood. 'I'm going for a piss' he said breaking the tension...'aye, and then to the troop office.'

You little beauty thought Logan as the pressure grew to be almost unbearable as others now followed him out until there was only Logan.

Bastard he thought I will only have to go now. A tear came to his eye but it was not a tear of fear it was a tear of pride in himself and to each of them but mostly Chalkie. Even if it was a decision Logan never remembered making, the irony of it was not lost on him as he left for the NAAFI heading for the troop office first to see the list. His name was there proudly up at the top and below, reading like a roll of honour were all the others but for the one missing name.

'Where's that bastard Chalkie White?' said Logan to himself running a finger down the list, 'there's no Chalkie. The bastard's only done a runner!'

At seven o'clock the final list was typed to orders and officially posted outside the troop office. Beneath it was the full list for the Radfan signed sealed and fully committed down to the last man. Up at the NAAFI the evening turned into something of a jingoistic affair full of false patriotism that would never exit through sober mouths unless from empty heads. It went on until last orders when the NAAFI shuttered up and they staggered back down the hill to barracks. They were asleep to a man by twelve, drunk and tired from a mentally exhausting day and an overdose of self praise.

Chalkie arrived back in the early hours stoned out of his mind and making a hell of a din as he made for his pit via the waste paper bin and the end of Compton's bed.

'Some fucking bastards put my bastard fucking name on that bastard fucking list' he got out before collapsing onto the bed and falling dead asleep.

'What a bastard' said Logan before rolling over.

The End

About the Author

Christopher Harcourt was born in 1940s post war England. Having missed national service and finding life behind a desk boring he joined the army where he rose to the rank of target.

Serving in a variety of military theatres around the world, the last period of service being with what are now called special forces, Chris left the military on marrying for a career as a private of industry.

Widely travelled much of his writing is based on his own military observations mixed with a sense of irony and humorous experiences.

Earlier writing successes for the BBC just after he left the army left him near starvation until the search for a publisher moved him to eBooks.

Christopher J Harcourt is the author's pseudonym and he writes non-military based books under another name.

Married with two children he now lives in Worcester.